PATCHWORK FAMILY

BOOK IV

CELIA'S CURE

M.H.P. Rosenbaum

BLACK BEAR PRODUCTIONS

Published by Black Bear Productions
815 Simon Greenwell Ln., Boston, KY 40107
mhpros@hughes.net

Cover art by Rivkah Walton/studio-rw.com
Book Layout and Cover Design
by Maggie Pagratis/Custom-book-tique.com

For my grandchildren, who keep me hoping for the future.

CHAPTER 1.

TUESDAY, MAY 25, 1954

Cecilia McAlister was not disturbed by the blood. She'd been expecting it, for a couple of years now.

In sixth grade last year, when their Health teacher had shown them the list of danger signs for cancer, one of the boys had questioned "Unusual Bleeding." When was bleeding ever "usual," he'd wondered. Celia had been among the few students in the room, girl or boy, who'd known.

Trouble with having a psychologist for a mother, she thought now. *You know more, but you're always a little weird.*

She sighed, looking at the brown spot in her underwear. *This would have to happen on my thirteenth birthday, when I'm supposed to sit in front of everybody and open my presents. At least it didn't happen at school. Did it?*

Anxiously, she checked the back of the skirt she'd worn today, which she'd flung over the side of the tub with her petticoat slip. Luckily, both the blue dotted-swiss skirt and the white starched crinoline were still pristine.

But it was more than self-consciousness that made her heart sink, more than the small curl of cramping that made her stomach twist. She had been hoping that her birthday would mark a shift, or at least a break, in the gloom that had been clouding the family for the past few weeks. *Ever since David left.*

4

David had been a contestant to be a new member of the family. That's how Celia thought of him: as though he were one of those people on TV, on *I've Got a Secret*. As though they were trying to figure him out and he was trying to give them clues; if he won, he would stay, but if they asked the wrong questions they'd never know who he really was, and he'd lose.

He had been coming to visit on weekends from the Rolling Meadow Juvenile Remedial Institution, where Mom worked, for several months. They hadn't been easy months—he'd been moody and mercurial, going from bright good humor to snarling hostility in a flash, for reasons that often weren't clear.

He'd mocked Celia's brother Jamie for his bookishness and his Jewish religious practices; treated her blind sister, Beth, as though she were an exhibit in the zoo; condescended to Joy, the youngest. With Laurie, the brother who was colored, like David, he'd alternated between a kind of hero worship that Laurie didn't seem to notice and a rivalry that Laurie noticed all too well.

Celia he had mostly ignored, though she'd tried to befriend him. She'd been six years old when Beth and her biological brother, Rob, had been adopted. They had been five and four then, scared and skittish from having been abandoned and living on the streets of Harrisburg. It seemed to Celia that it had been easy to bring them into the family—easier than it had been to absorb five-year-old Jamie, a year earlier, when he was still frozen in fear from having survived a Nazi concentration camp.

But Celia, as one of the two—along with little Joy—born into the family, had felt possessive and protective of the newcomers. "Little mother," Mom called her approvingly.

She'd tried to be that way with David, too, giving him advice and trying to help him get his reading up to speed. Sometimes he seemed to crave the attention, other times he'd snapped at her for bossiness.

Not that he was the only one, she'd thought. *Now that we're growing up, the other kids seem to resent it when I tell them what to do. They don't seem to get that I'm only trying to help.* So David's resentment seemed of a piece with her growing feeling that what she'd thought of as a strength in herself seemed to make her the object of criticism by her younger siblings as well as David. *I can't win,* she'd thought. *What's wrong with me?*

Then one day in March, right after Mom's birthday, actually, there'd been a kerfuffle. The adults in the household—Mom, Dad, and Ruby Jones—and Celia's older brothers, Laurie and Jamie, seemed to know what it was all about, but they'd annoyingly kept the details from the younger ones. Something to do with a knife, Celia knew. She remembered hearing earlier that David had seen his father stab his mother to death when he was only three, so she supposed they were worried that whatever had happened meant he was having some bad reaction to that memory.

Dad was afraid David was a danger to the rest of the family; Mom didn't agree. They'd been quarrelling behind closed doors and edgy with each other in a way Celia couldn't remember their ever being. She'd asked Ruby about it once and Ruby's worried face had immediately smoothed to a brown mask as she assured Celia everything was fine: "All couples have rough patches once in a while; your mother and father will get over this one." Since it hadn't occurred to Celia until that minute that there was any chance they wouldn't, this was less than comforting.

She sighed again, sprinkling Woolite on the gusset of her white cotton panties. Then she scrubbed the folded cloth halves of the crotch together under running water, cold so as not to set the blood, as Ruby'd taught her long ago after a nosebleed. When she had the spot down to a faint stain that she thought would wash out the rest of the way in the regular laundry, she wrung the panties out and hung them on the bathtub faucet to get dry enough to put in the hamper later.

Then she poked into the cabinet under the sink for the supplies Mom had shown her when she put them there months ago. First came the elastic waistband with its garter-belt-like dangling clips at front and back. It took her a minute to get it placed right, then she realized it would be too hard to manage the back one the way it was, so she shifted the whole thing till the longer back tab was hanging in front.

She opened the box of Kotex pads and extracted one. Fumbling a little, she got one of the long gauze ends threaded through the belt tab. She let it hang free as she shifted the waistband around again so the long tab was behind her where it belonged, then reached down to pull the pad up between her legs and secured the other gauze end to the shorter tab in front of her. She looked at the effect in the mirror over the sink for a minute, holding the bottom hem of her white blouse up out of the way, backing up against the tub and standing on tiptoe to get her lower body in view.

Not very attractive. Good thing no one will ever see me like this. The thought of some future husband flitted briefly into her mind, but the idea was too theoretical to worry about now.

She unlocked both bathroom doors—first the one into Beth's room, so that Beth could get in when she needed to, then the one into the room she and Joy shared. She peeked out, but Joy wasn't there, so she grabbed a towel and held it around her waist as she hopped to the bedroom door and closed it.

Then she went to her dresser, got out clean underwear and a pair of bright red knee-length pedal pushers, and pulled them on. She put the towel back in the bathroom, hung up her skirt and petticoat, and collapsed onto her bed. *Finally, I can relax.*

Not for long, though. Through the wall between this room and theirs, she could hear the rise and fall of Mom and Dad's voices. They weren't shouting, exactly, but they didn't sound happy.

It's my birthday, she thought rebelliously. *They shouldn't fight on my birthday.* Embarrassed at her own childishness, she added to herself, *And I became a woman today. That's the way Ruby always puts it: "When you become a woman." So Mom at least should pay some attention to that.*

Mom had told her there were cultures where a girl's first menstrual period was greeted with celebration and special rituals. God knows she didn't want that; the very thought of the looks on her brothers' faces at such an event made her toes curl. But she did feel like getting some sort of recognition: a fond, proud smile from Mom; even a sentimental mistiness from Dad. *And it would take their minds off David.*

Celia got up, went into the hall, and knocked on their bedroom door.

CHAPTER 2.

THURSDAY, JUNE 4, 1954

Dad was crying, really crying, in great gasping sobs. Celia had seen her brothers cry any number of times, but she'd never even imagined Dad—cool, composed, commanding Dad—breaking down. She shifted in her bed, feeling guilty that she'd pretended to be asleep just now when he came in to kiss her and Joy goodnight. Guilty and... was that other sensation shame? *Yes,* she thought. *As though I'd walked in on him naked. No: that would just be embarrassment. This is more like I'd* spied *on him naked.*

Yet she certainly hadn't intended to eavesdrop; she wished she wasn't hearing this now. *Should I do something? No, Mom's out there in the hall with him.* He'd called her "Lassie," she'd called him "Carino." Their special pet names, that she'd only overheard them use a handful of times over the years. *So maybe things will be ok with them now.*

Her intervention a couple of weeks ago had seemed to help. They'd been distracted by her "becoming a woman" news, as she'd hoped, and afterwards they'd closeted themselves in the study for a long discussion that left Mom red-eyed and Dad pale, but they'd come to dinner holding hands.

There had been more conversations in the next few days, but peaceful ones, and tonight Mom had told them all that David wouldn't be coming back: she and Dad, she said, had decided he needed more therapy before he was ready to be part of a family. Mom had been optimistic, but Dad less so, which made Mom cry in a sad, resigned way. The children had gathered around to comfort her; Celia had knelt to put her arms around Mom's waist where she sat on the ottoman.

So she had been in earshot when their world shattered, though she still didn't quite understand what had happened. Her brother Laurie—the oldest and the first adopted, the one who'd been part of the family even longer than Celia—had leaned over and murmured, "Don't worry, Mom, I'm still here. You've still got a colored kid in your collection."

Celia was still trying to figure out what he'd meant by that when the unthinkable happened: Dad had slapped Laurie across the face, twice, forehand and back, hard enough to knock him to the floor. They were all stunned. Dad had spanked Joy once, under great provocation, but that had been a judicious, almost solemn thing, and had never been repeated. This, this spontaneous violent lashing out, was unheard of and deeply frightening.

Laurie had picked himself up and run out of the house. Dad had fled to the study. Joy had started to cry, and Celia found herself comforting her while fighting her own tears. The others had talked and worried until Ruby chivvied everyone upstairs. Celia looked back as she left, to see Ruby pulling Mom to her feet and into her arms.

Jamie had sloped off to his own room, solitary as usual, but the rest of them had felt the need for support and gathered up in the third floor music room. Robbie was worried about where Laurie had gone. Celia was worried about Laurie for a different reason: they were all used to his being the older brother, the one in charge when the adults weren't around. If the adults were occupied and he was gone, who was going to take care of things? Jamie certainly wasn't going to fill that gap.

Me, Celia had thought. *It's up to me. That won't be bossy, it won't be wrong for me to try to help.*

So she had calmed them down as best she could, saying more confidently than she felt, "Mom and Dad agreed about David, finally. They'll fix things with Laurie, too. Everything will be all right."

An idea had come to her, looking at Beth's pensive face and remembering what she'd told them she was learning about Quaker meditation. "Here, everybody hold hands," she'd said. For once, nobody objected to Celia's taking charge. Then, as they obediently linked in a circle, she said, "We're going to pray. But we're not going to say anything, we're just going to think about them: about Dad and Laurie and Mom… and David. Just—what was that thing you told me, Beth?—just hold them in the Light."

It had helped, it really had. When they were finished, when Celia had felt somehow that the time had wound up, they'd all gone quietly to bed, even though it wasn't even ten o'clock yet.

Now, hours later, Celia lay in the dark, listening to Joy's soft snuffling in her sleep, thinking about Dad crying, and knew she'd never sleep. Mom and Dad had gone into their room. She slipped out of bed, out of the room, and tiptoed past their door. She crept down the back stairs into the kitchen, hesitated a moment, then tapped softly on the door to Ruby's apartment.

Somehow she wasn't surprised when it opened almost immediately. Ruby pulled her through the door and across her shadowy sitting room into her bedroom. The dim yellow glow of her bedside lamp shone on the photograph of Ruby's long-dead husband, then Ruby snapped it off and her dark face blended into the darkness of the room. "What on earth are you doing wandering around without your robe and slippers, child?" she scolded, folding Celia into the bed and wrapping her arms around her.

"It's not cold," Celia said, but let herself be cuddled. That's what she'd come for, she realized. That, and—

"Why did Laurie say that, about Mom still having a colored kid?" she asked. "I mean, does he really think Mom and Dad adopted him because they're, I don't know, putting on some kind of an act, sort of showing off how broadminded they are or something? You don't think that, do you?"

Ruby exhaled a long breath. "No, I don't think that," she said. "Remember, I've known your daddy since he was a little tiny boy, and your mother since right after he met her. Your mother brought Laurie home when he'd been abandoned at Rolling Meadow and they weren't set up to take care of a baby there. But the reason she kept him on and she and Sean adopted him was because they just flat-out fell in love with him."

"But why did he say that, then?"

"Laurie's starting to grow up, to realize he's going to have to cope with being black in a world that's full of pitfalls for him, even though he's been sheltered by being in a white family. Having David around confused him a little about what his place is in the family."

"But you're part of our family."

Ruby chuckled a little. "Well, bless you, Celia; I am and I'm not. Lord knows I couldn't love you all more if I'd given birth to your dad myself. I've given up a lot to be with this family. Sometimes I think maybe too much. Still, it goes beyond white and black…no matter what my sister thinks." She muttered the last phrase half under her breath and sat silent for a minute, cradling Celia in the bed, then she seemed to come back to herself. "In any case, Laurie and your dad are going to be fine. I saw them going up the front stairs a while ago, with their arms around each other."

"Dad was crying just now," Celia whispered.

"That's good," Ruby said.

"That's good?"

"He's not shutting himself off from it."

"Mom was with him."

"Oh, Seanie. Then that's very good."

After that they were quiet for so long Celia thought Ruby might have fallen asleep—her own eyelids were getting heavy. But she roused herself enough to whisper, "How come you know so much about people?"

"I just listen, child. I watch and I listen. Now, just you rest. In the morning it will all be much better, you'll see."

Celia sank into slumber.

CHAPTER 3.

FRIDAY, JUNE 5, 1954

The boat was rocking. Were they sinking? It had been so nice, sailing along in the sunshine with the breeze in her hair, free of all responsibility and trouble, watching the white foam of the wake trailing behind her. And what was that jabbing her shoulder?

"Cissy, wake up," came an insistent voice that Celia realized had been mingling with the sound of the gulls in her head for some time. *Joy. I was asleep, dreaming.* Her eyes opened and she fixed her bleary gaze on an unfamiliar ceiling.

Fretfully, she pushed Joy's hand away and sat up. "What is it? Where am I?" *Ruby's room,* she saw even as she asked. Last night came back to her, coming here for comfort, snuggling into Ruby's flannel-covered back. "Where's the fire?" she asked Joy, who was now yanking her sleeve impatiently.

"Some girl," Joy said. "She says you invited her over. She's in the living room."

That girl who talked to me in the library last Saturday... what was her name? Rita? No, Rima. Celia pulled away from Joy with a huff. "I didn't invite her for the crack of dawn," she growled.

"It's twenty to ten!"

"What? That's not possible." But Celia thought of the way that ordinarily, the sounds of the others getting up would wake her; here in Ruby's room, she was insulated from the usual morning uproar. "Why didn't somebody wake me up?"

"Ruby said leave you alone, you had a rough night." The ten-year-old twisted a sheet corner, looking away from Celia. "I didn't know where you were, this morning. I thought... I thought something happened."

"Sorry," Celia said. "I was—upset. I couldn't sleep, so I came down to Ruby."

Joy nodded, brown eyes huge in her narrow face. "That was awful, last night," she whispered. "What Dad did, then Laurie running out like that."

Celia pressed her little sister's hand. "It's ok now," she said. "Ruby saw them together on the stairs last night." She didn't think it would be right to tell any of the others about Dad crying. Ruby was different; she was almost like Dad's mother. But the other kids didn't have to know. *Probably wouldn't want to know. Part of me wishes I didn't.*

She pushed Joy aside a little. "I'd better nip up the back stairs and throw some clothes on before Rima thinks I vanished in a puff of smoke. Let her know I'm coming, will you?"

Ten minutes later, Celia skidded down the front stairs and into the living room. Rima was on one of the settees, looking at a *New Yorker* cover of two little girls staring through a shop window at a bride mannequin. As Celia looked, Rima tossed it back onto the coffee table with a scornful twist to her mouth. She looked even older than Celia remembered from the library.

What am I going to talk to her about? What does she want with me, anyway? She's at least two years older than me—a freshman in high school, for Pete's sake. Even as she thought this, she moved forward into the room. "Hi," she said. "Sorry I overslept. There was a little fuss last night with my brother that threw us all off, but—"

"Your brother Jamie?" Rima said interestedly.

"No, Laurie. He—wait, how do you know Jamie?"

"I don't, really. I've just seen him in my Advanced Algebra class and noticed him because he's younger than the rest of us. I guess he's pretty smart, huh?"

"I guess. Listen, I haven't had breakfast yet. Mind coming into the kitchen while I eat?"

"Copacetic," Rima said, getting up.

"'Cope-a-set-ick'? What's that mean?"

"'Everything's ok,'" Rima answered as Celia led her through the dining room into the kitchen. "It's a Jewish thing, according to my mom."

"Oh, are you Jewish? So's Jamie, actually."

"I know. I've seen him at services. We don't trek all the way down to Lancaster every week, but I guess he does?"

"Yeah, he goes down with the Epsteins, these people Mom knows from work. Hi, Ruby, this is Rima—um, sorry, I forgot your last name. This is Ruby Jones."

"Shapiro. Nice to meet you, Mrs. Jones. Is it Mrs.?"

"Yes, it is." Ruby smiled at them. "Celia, I made French toast and left it in the oven on warm. Everybody's had theirs except Laurie. It's probably shoe leather by now, if you'd rather have cereal. Rima, would you like something?"

"No, thanks, I've had breakfast already," Rima said, sliding into the breakfast nook at Celia's nod.

Celia pulled the toast out of the oven and viewed it with a critical eye. "Nothing wrong with this that a lot of maple syrup won't cure," she said. "Like a lot of things in life."

"That's the truth." Ruby patted her on the arm as she crossed the room, then disappeared into her apartment.

Celia forked some French toast onto a plate, drenched it with syrup, poured herself some orange juice, and sat down across from Rima. Rima was gazing around the kitchen as if she'd never been in one before. Celia tried to see the familiar room through a stranger's eyes: clean, shabby, old fashioned... comfortable. She took advantage of Rima's abstraction to say a silent grace and sketch a quick sign of the cross, then dug into her breakfast.

"Sure you don't want anything to eat?" she asked the older girl.

"I'm sure." Rima swiveled to face Celia again. "So Jamie's Jewish but you're not, right?" She waved her hand in a vague cross shape; evidently she'd noticed.

"Right," Celia said. "Most of us are adopted, you know. Jamie's the only Jewish one."

Rima's eyes flickered, but then she seemed to snap her attention back and asked, "And your one brother is a Negro, right? What's that like?"

"'What's that like?'" Celia repeated. *What does this girl want with me, anyway?* "What do you mean, what's it like? He's my brother. He's been my brother since before I was born. I mean... oh, you know what I mean. He's always been here. It's just like however it is for you with your brothers and sisters."

"I don't have any brothers or sisters."

"Oh. Sorry."

"Don't be. I literally don't know what I'm missing."

"Just like I don't know what it would be like to have a family where everybody was alike, instead of a patchwork like ours." Celia finished her breakfast and brought her dish and glass to the sink, adding them to the unwashed breakfast pile already there.

Just as she was thinking guiltily that she ought to wash them, Ruby came out holding her own bed sheets in a bundle. "Leave those, child," she said kindly. "Run along and play with your friend."

A hot flush of mortification rose up Celia's cheeks, but Rima winked roguishly at her and Celia calmed down. "Thanks, Ruby," she said. Then, to Rima, "Want to go up to my room and listen to records? I've got the new Debbie Reynolds."

"Ok," Rima said, following her up the narrow back stairs. "But don't you have something jazzier? How about 'Shake, Rattle and Roll'?"

"Mm, my brother Rob might. I'll ask."

For the next two hours, they lounged around in Celia and Joy's room, listening to music—they'd compromised on Louis Armstrong and the Mills Brothers—and chatting desultorily. Celia still couldn't figure out quite what this older girl was doing with her.

Finally Rima stretched, sat up from where she'd been sprawled on Joy's bed, and said, "Guess I'd better get going. Poor Princie's been waiting for me long enough."

"Who's Princie?"

"My dog, my German Shepherd. I left him tied up in front, but he—"

"You brought your *dog* here?"

"Well, yeah. I didn't try to bring him into the house or anything, what's the big deal? He's perfectly harmless."

"I told you when I saw him outside the library the day we met not to bring him along. My brother Jamie's afraid of dogs, you have to get him out of here."

"Oh, come on. He's a big boy. It's about time he got over that, anyway, don't you think?"

Celia ran out of the room and down the front stairs, Rima hot on her heels. "You don't understand," she growled over her shoulder. "He was... they... oh, hell, just get that dog out of here before he gets home."

She grabbed Rima's raincoat from the telephone chair in the front hall and thrust it at her, not caring that she was being rude. She flung open the front door and gestured angrily at the big dog, who was just getting to his feet, lead chain clanking against the boot scraper Rima had tied it to.

"I don't get it, what's wrong?" Rima protested.

Celia was frantic; she could see Jamie approaching the house. "I said, 'Take him away!'" she yelled.

Rima still wouldn't do it. "But he's gentle, he wouldn't hurt a fly," she insisted. "You can't be afraid of him, look, just hold your hand out—"

"Get him *out* of here!" Celia screamed.

Ruby came to see what the commotion was about and took in the situation immediately. "Young lady, take that animal away this instant," she commanded.

At the street end of the walkway, Jamie had crumpled to the pavement, crouched with his hands over the back of his neck. That sight seemed to get through to Rima. Without another word, she unhitched her dog and walked away, circling Jamie. Shoulders hunched and head ducked, she disappeared down the road.

Celia and Ruby both started down the walk to Jamie, but before they could get to him he jumped up and ran past them into the house. He would head to his secret hiding place, Celia knew; there'd be no point trying to say anything to him until he'd had a chance to pull himself together.

"Come help me with lunch," Ruby sighed.

Happy for some occupation, Celia set to making sardine sandwiches while Ruby heated up a pot of onion soup. Laurie and Mom showed up when it was ready; they'd evidently been talking and had come to a resolution of last night's upset. They kept sending each other little smiles across the table.

Ruby gave them a thumbnail account of what had happened with Rima's dog while she wrapped a sandwich to save for when Jamie felt up to rejoining the world. Mom and Laurie were both concerned but nothing could really dent their good mood.

Celia was happy for them, but she was still upset herself. So she was just as glad when Laurie's friend Linda showed up and they both went for a walk out back. As soon as lunch was cleared up, she hurried after Mom into the living room.

"Mom, can I talk to you?"

"Sure, baby, what is it?"

Mom sat on the armchair in the corner and raised her arms invitingly. Celia plopped down on her lap and suddenly, to her own surprise, burst into tears. Mom put her arms around her and cuddled her the way she used to do when Celia was small.

After a few minutes Mom said, "Can you tell me about it?"

"I don't know, it's just everything. Mom, last night was so awful, and I tried to get the others to feel better but I couldn't get to sleep and then I—I heard Dad in the hall, and I just couldn't go out there and do anything, and so I went to Ruby because you were with Dad and he needed you, and then today there's this girl I don't even know and I had to be polite to her and she brought her stupid dog and now Jamie's all upset with memories from the concentration camp coming back on him and I just don't know what to do!" She dissolved into sobs, wishing she could get back on that boat in her dream and sail away.

Mom held her, rubbing her back in comforting circles for a while. Then she said, "You know, Celia, it's not your job to make everybody happy."

Celia sat up, sniffling. "It's not?"

CHAPTER 4.

MONDAY, AUGUST 2, 1954

Laurie's mother was here. *Laurie's mother,* Celia repeated to herself, the phrase strange on her tongue, hard and wrong in her mind, like a grain of grit in an oyster. *But this won't turn into a pearl. This is just… wrong.* Mom *is Laurie's mother.*

She tried to imagine what it must be like for Laurie. For one thing, searching for his birth mother was a way of helping him get his balance back after the ruction with Mom and Dad. In an odd way, it seemed to cement his place in the family even more firmly—showing that they cared enough about him to be willing to help him get in touch with his roots, his origins, the identity of his blood and bone.

For another thing, it would satisfy his need to understand what had happened on that December night almost fifteen years ago, when he'd been found in a basket at the gates of Rolling Meadow. Laurie was always so strong and capable, in charge when the adults weren't around. He was the one they all relied on, especially before Dad retired from sea duty last year and started working at the Navy Depot. Laurie was Celia's rock, a solid fixed point to hold onto when storms buffeted her. He'd been shaken at the turmoil over David's leaving, but had come back stronger than ever.

For the first four years of her life, it had just been Celia and Laurie; the advent of baby Joy caused little more than a ripple in their lives. And though Jamie was older than Celia, he hadn't come into the family until she was five. So she knew Laurie well enough to sense there was a flaw in the seemingly solid surface of Laurie's unflappable manner. She'd glimpsed an occasional sense of hurt, of insecurity. *He needs to know why she gave him up, whether she found something missing in him.*

And now she's dying, Celia thought, watching the men from the ambulance carry the stretcher with the little black woman, hardly bigger than a child, up the stairs to the larger spare room. Mom and Dad and Laurie had visited her yesterday at the private hospital where she had been taken in as a charity case, and Laurie had had a fit over the way the staff condescended to her and bossed her around, so the folks had agreed to bring her home here. Last night there'd been a family meeting where they'd talked about the new responsibilities they'd all have, caring for her where they could and taking up the slack left by the adults focusing their energies on her. *Lung cancer. Not much they can do but make her comfortable, Ruby said. It's going to be awful.*

The ambulance men were rattling the empty stretcher back down the stairs now, and disappearing out the front door into the torrid heat outside. It was cooler indoors, but not by much after so many days in a row in the nineties.

Celia had a thought. She dashed up the stairs and into her and Joy's room, where she unplugged the old rotary fan swiveling slowly on their desk. She carried it back down the hall to the spare room at the head of the stairs and stood in the doorway. Ruby and Mom had just finished settling the patient into the rented hospital bed they'd shoved the room's regular furniture aside for.

Mrs. Laurence, she reminded herself. *Funny that turns out it was supposed to be Laurie's last name. Wonder what his first one was?* It gave her a little shiver to think her brother'd had another name once, almost as though he had a secret identity.

"You can't be cold," Laurie's voice came from behind her.

She half turned in the doorway, gesturing with the fan. "No, cat on my grave or something. I was just bringing this."

"They have one," Laurie said, nodding his head toward the window. Celia saw that they'd put the window fan from Mom and Dad's room in there; it fit the frame from side to side and halfway up, and was set to suck warm air out of the room.

Her shoulders sagged a little, but Laurie squeezed one. "It was nice of you to think of it," he said.

Mom turned from the bedside. "More than that," she said. "It will be useful. The window fan alone won't be enough, I think. Mrs. Laurence is going to need lots of air circulating in here. Put it on the dresser, please, Cissy—just shove that radio aside. Pull the pin so it stops rotating, and turn it so it blows past, not directly on her. That's it, good."

Ruby finished adjusting the oxygen mask over Mrs. Laurence's face and straightened up. "I'm going to get a dish of that tapioca pudding I made for Jamie yesterday," she said. "Maybe she'll feel up to eating some when she wakes up. Think you can handle that?" She looked at Laurie.

Laurie took a deep breath, gazing at the unconscious figure with uneasy longing. "I don't know; can I?"

"Sure you can, Warrie," Celia said, using the babyhood nickname she'd recently revived. She gave his upper arm a double tap with her fist, their childhood gesture of affection.

Laurie smiled at her and moved toward the bed as Ruby left the room and Mom followed. As she passed Celia, she said softly, "I'm going to sort through some old snapshots of Laurie growing up to show her when she wakes up. Want to help me, sweetie?"

"You bet," Celia said as she turned away. At the door again, she looked back. Laurie had settled onto a chair by the hospital bed. He was staring at his mother, face rapt.

Maybe there'll be a pearl after all, Celia thought. Then she mentally shook herself. *A little treasure for Laurie, maybe, to have that resolution. But a lot of grit to cover, too.*

She softly closed the door and turned to follow Mom, but almost bumped into Jamie; he'd been looking over her shoulder at Laurie and his mother. His face looked bleak.

"Did you want to go in?" she asked him.

He shook his head as they started down the hall. "I'm happy for Laurie, but it's hard to watch. To see him getting his mother back and to know that can never happen for me. Dad told me last night that he was happy they could give this to Laurie, on general principles and because it would help heal the rift between them from Dad hitting him that time. And they're glad to be able to help this lady—you know them, always saving the world." His words had a wry twist, but lacked the usual savagery of his sarcasm, Celia noted.

They stopped outside his bedroom door and he went on, "But it's too late, really. Dad said the minister from the AME church she used to go to is going to stop by every day if he can, and Dr. Caldwell from the hospital. That's great, but I couldn't help thinking that's more attention than she's ever gotten before; too bad some rich white people didn't get interested in her when there was still a chance for her."

Jamie went into his room and closed the door. Celia stood there for a moment, chewing over what he'd said.

The door to Mom and Dad's room was open. As she stepped in, she realized Mom had heard, as well. "It's so sad," Celia said to her. "That lady's life is ending, and she's never had anything: no family, no happiness, no ordinary success."

"Oh, I don't know," Mom said, setting aside the baby book she'd been leafing through; Celia stretched out on the bed beside her. "She made a great sacrifice to save the baby she loved, and now she can know it was successful. That's not a small thing."

"Is that what happened?"

"I don't know for certain, but I suspect so."

"But what about somebody like David? He can't seem to get started on life, he's just a kid, and he messed up the chance to be with us, to be happier."

Mom nodded; she dipped her head, but not before Celia saw her eyes welling.

"You did the best you could for him," Celia said, reaching for Mom's hand.

Mom took it. "And I'm still trying, but it doesn't seem to be enough. Sometimes nothing is enough. But I have helped other people, young people especially. And that keeps me going. That, and all of you, of course."

Celia had never made the connection before. "So you help people find meaningful lives, and that makes your life meaningful."

Mom patted Celia's hand with her free one. "My brilliant girl," she said. "Now, you start going through the snapshots in that shoebox while I finish looking at Laurie's baby book. Mrs. Laurence missed his babyhood; we can give her a glimpse of that, at least."

Celia picked up the box, trying to feel happier, but the doubts kept swirling around Laurie's mother and her tragic life. *Will my life be ok? That feeling I have that something's wrong with me; maybe I won't be able to make things ok for myself or anyone else. Not every life has a happy ending, maybe mine won't. Will David's? And even lives that are good have failures in them—look at Mom, trying to help David. Even she doesn't always have the answer.*

"Aren't there any good pictures in there?" Mom asked.

Celia started, realizing she'd been leafing through the shoebox without really paying attention. "Sorry, I was wool-gathering," she said, flushing. "I didn't mean to, I'm trying to help."

Mom tilted her head to one side, forehead wrinkling. "It's all right, sweetheart. No harm done. Don't be so hard on yourself. Goofing up is part of life, not the final verdict."

Easy for her to say, Celia thought.

Chapter 5.

Thursday, September 9, 1954

"Anybody?" Mr. Rocher said. "Anybody but Celia, that is?"

Cheeks burning, Celia lowered her hand. Mr. Rocher wasn't trying to be mean, she knew. He said it almost flirtatiously, as a good-natured tease. But the snickers around the classroom weren't good-natured.

Celia sighed. Only the third day of eighth grade, and already she felt she didn't fit in. Pine Springs had started a new system of moving from teacher to teacher instead of staying with one all day. This was a combined class, not just her homeroom; there were kids in it she only knew vaguely. They seemed to know her by reputation, though—the downside of having two brilliant older brothers.

She had been looking forward to the start of school. Laurie's mother had died almost a month ago, peacefully in his arms, but the sense of lost opportunities, of lives that didn't work out happily, had left Celia sad and uncertain. In a classroom setting, she knew who she was and what she could do, and she felt good about it—or had, until now.

After a minute in which no other hands were raised, the teacher shook his head and flapped a hand at Celia. She took a breath and answered the question: *"Brown versus Board of Education.* The Supreme Court decided it last spring."

"And what did the court say in *Brown?*"

"That 'separate but equal' education for different races is unconstitutional."

"Because?"

"Because it's not really equal; schools for Negroes are substandard."

"'Substandard'," Randy Jorkins snorted quietly from the desk across the aisle. "Can't just say 'lousy' like a normal person."

"Randy, did you have something to share with the class?" Mr. Rocher said.

"No," Randy growled, slouching in his seat.

"Well then, why don't you tell us how this decision relates to the Separation of Powers doctrine we discussed yesterday?"

Randy shot Celia a poisonous look as though she was somehow responsible for his being singled out and started to stammer through an answer.

Civics was the last class of the day. When it was finally over, Celia tried to escape to her locker without making eye contact with anyone. Still, she could sense her friend Barbara Leaper looking at her worriedly from the next locker over.

Randy Jorkins's voice sneered from behind them, "Oh, look, it's the Leper and the Brain."

"She's not a brain," Barbara protested before Celia could respond, "it's just that her brother's colored. That's how she knew about the case."

"Her brother's *what?"* Thick brows drew together, then flew apart as Jorkins exclaimed, "Laurence McAlister is her brother? The runner? I saw him win the eighth grade hundred yard dash a couple

29

years ago." He stared at Celia. "How come you're so pale?" he demanded. "You get leprosy cooties from Leper here?"

"That's Leaper, genius," Celia retorted. "And if I catch anything, it's liable to be stupidity cooties from you. Come on, Barb, I'm going to be late for my piano lesson."

The two girls hurried out of the elementary school into the September sunshine. "What a jerk," Celia said.

"Totally vacant," Barbara agreed. "Nobody home." They walked along in silence for a couple of blocks, then Barbara said hesitantly, "You know, though, Cissy, maybe you don't have to answer *every* question."

"I don't answer *every* question!"

"No, I know, I know, it's just…"

"Just?"

"Boys don't like girls who seem like they're showing off how much they know."

Celia was stung. Barb had been her best friend since first grade. She always stopped at Barb's little pink stucco house on the way to school in the mornings—Mrs. Leaper usually had sweet rolls or doughnuts, which Mom and Ruby didn't approve of for breakfast—and the two girls would munch them as they walked the rest of the way together, chatting companionably.

Lately, though, Celia found herself having to search for topics that would interest the other girl. Barb hadn't seemed to understand why Celia was so upset over Laurie's birth mother dying, for instance—the aching sadness of that last scene had only made Barb shudder and say, "Creepy," which Celia had chalked up to Barb needing to trivialize it to keep it from affecting her the way it had Celia. Now she wondered whether they'd grown even farther apart than she'd realized.

"You think I'm a show-off?"

"No, 'course you're not, just that… maybe it might seem that way to somebody who didn't know you as well as I do."

Celia was saved from responding by their arrival at her piano teacher's house. She thought of it as "the gingerbread house"; it was tall and narrow, with timber and plaster walls and a slate roof that hung low over the eaves like a hat pulled down over a forehead.

Barb picked nervously at the lettering on the mailbox at the curb. "How come her name is pronounced 'Say-shass' when it's spelled like it should be 'Sex-us'?"

You think I'm showing off when I have the answers, but you still expect me to know them, Celia thought sourly. So she snapped a little when she explained, "It's Spanish."

"Spanish? But I thought she was a J—you know, I mean a Jewish person." Barb half whispered the last two words as though they were an insult.

Celia managed to refrain from rolling her eyes. "Yes, she and Mr. Seixas are Jews," she said deliberately, inwardly smirking at her friend's slight flinch. "There are Spanish Jews, you know."

Barb raised an uncertain hand to one of her dark auburn pigtails and twisted the end. "There are?"

"Yes, though the Seixases were living in Germany before they came here, during the war." Barb looked at her blankly. "Hitler?" Celia prompted.

"Oh, Hitler, yeah."

"Listen I have to go in. I'll see you tomorrow."

"Ok, bye."

Celia couldn't help it. As her fingers picked out *Humoresque* on the keyboard, her mind automatically supplied the joke lyrics everyone seemed to know whether they'd ever heard of Dvořak or knew how to pronounce his name: *"Passengers will please refrain/ From flushing toilets while the train/ is standing in the station..."*

"Tcha, pay attention, child," Mrs. Seixas scolded gently.

Celia's hands fell to her lap. She didn't have Jamie's driven precision or Rob's natural instinct for music, but she usually did better than this. *What's wrong with me today?* led naturally to a general, *What's wrong with me?* which led to, "Mrs. Seixas, do you think I'm a 'brain'?"

Mrs. Seixas looked at her keenly. "I think you are a very intelligent, good-hearted girl," she said, pronouncing it "gehl"—she'd learned English in school in Germany, Celia knew, from a British teacher.

Celia's shoulders slumped. "My friend Barbara says boys don't like girls who know too much."

"You're much too young to be worrying about what boys think," Mrs. Seixas said firmly. "Now, mind on the keyboard, please."

Celia tried to stop thinking.

Chapter 6.

Tuesday, September 23, 1954

Celia couldn't stop crying. She knew she ought to try, at least; she was worrying Mom and Dad, who sat on either side of her bed, and Joy, bobbing anxiously beside it. But it was actually helping—each deep, gut-wrenching sob seemed to carry off another bit of tension and melancholy.

"Should I get the others?" Joy asked Mom and Dad.

Celia answered her. "No. It's not a nightmare or a flashback like Jamie has. I'm just sad. I don't need everybody's he...he...hel..." She collapsed into sobs again.

"Sweetie, why don't you go on down and help Ruby with breakfast," Mom suggested. As Joy disappeared from the dawn-dim room, Mom said to Celia, "Is this about David?"

"How can he be dead?" Celia wailed. "He was only Joy's age!" Standing at the open gravesite yesterday, next to the place where they'd buried Laurie's mother only last month, Celia had shed a few tears, but the whole scene had seemed unreal, as though it were happening on TV or in a movie. But this morning she'd awakened with a sense of doom pressing on her chest and the cold realization that she would never see that bright, mischievous, troubled face again. "He can't be dead," she whispered.

"I know," Mom said sadly. "It's always hard to accept that the people we know are gone, but the death of a child seems like a crime against nature."

Celia felt a twinge of guilt. She was making Mom unhappy, and Mom was struggling over David, too—Celia knew that she felt she had failed him. And now Mom was worrying over her.

"It's not just David," she tried to explain. "It's Laurie's mother, too—oh, I know she was old—" She huffed at the wry look Mom and Dad shot each other across her. "Ok, you know what I mean. Maybe not old, but a grownup. And she was sick; the cancer killed her. But David killed himself! How could somebody do that, just a kid?"

She let go of Dad's hand to take the tissue he offered her. He moved up to lean against her headboard and gathered her into his arms while Mom took both her hands and looked her keenly in the eyes.

"David was sick, too," she said. "With an illness just as dire as cancer, though it wouldn't show up under a microscope or a scalpel. I tried to help him get better, but it just wasn't enough." Her eyes filled. Dad removed one of his arms from around Celia and reached out to press Mom's shoulder. She tilted her head to one side so that her cheek rested on the back of his hand.

"I'm sorry, Mom," Celia said. "I shouldn't be making this fuss. You have enough on your mind. And you're going to need all your energy to take care of Laurie and Jamie; they're the ones the most upset by this."

Mom clicked her tongue and straightened up. "Laurie and Jamie had particular issues with David, it's true," she said. "But don't ever think your concerns are less important to us."

"That's right," Dad rumbled behind her. "You're our child, too, you know, even if you're not adopted."

Celia cracked a smile at the joke, though her chest was still heaving with the aftermath of the emotional storm she'd just gone through.

Mom patted her hand. "We can talk some more tonight," she said, "but if you're feeling better for now, we'd better get going or you'll be late for school."

At the word "school," Celia felt her face crumple and she started to cry again. Mom shot Dad an alarmed look and gripped Celia's arms. "What is it, darling? What's the matter? Did something happen at school?"

"Everybody hates me," Celia sniveled. *No, they don't,* she inwardly contradicted herself. *Don't exaggerate.* But it felt true on some level, and besides, it felt so good to have Mom and Dad's total attention for a change.

Still, she tried to pull herself together a little as she said, "Some kid called me a brain, because I knew the answer to something Mr. Rocher asked—it was about that Supreme Court case, you know, the one we all talked about at dinner? And then later, Barb said boys don't like girls who know all the answers. And then Mrs. Seixas said I'm too young to worry about what boys think, but that isn't the point. It's not like I want that jerk Randy Jorkins to like me, not that way. But I don't want people to hate me, either. But what can I do? I can't pretend I don't know things if I do know them, can I?"

"Absolutely not," Dad answered firmly from behind her. "You have to be true to yourself, and your intelligence is one of the essentials that make you who you are. And it's also, by the way, one of your most attractive traits; someday you'll meet people— boys and girls—who think that, too."

"I wish I could meet them now," Celia said sulkily. "The kids I know never used to care. Is this what it's going to be like from now on? What's changed, all of a sudden?"

"It's called puberty," Dad said. "I hate to say this to my little girl, but boys are going to be looking at you differently from here on out. And some of them are going to be threatened by your brain, when they're thinking with an entirely different part of their anatomy."

"Dad!" Celia protested, laughing in spite of herself. She sobered quickly. "So I'm right, it is going to be like this from now on? There's nothing I can do about it?"

Mom's brow creased in thought. "Maybe we should look into having you put forward a year, like Jamie," she said. "Or at least get you into some high school classes this year."

Celia sighed. "No, I don't think so," she said. "Thanks, but... I've seen what it's like for Jamie, in amongst older kids. He's not really one of them. He doesn't care, I guess, but I think I would. I don't want to leave my friends."

Mom raised an eyebrow.

Celia laughed wryly again. "Ok, ok," she admitted. "Not everyone hates me."

"And next year you'll be at County High," Mom said, "with a bigger pool of potential friends. I'm sure you'll find some other bright girls with a little more intellectual range than Barbara Leaper, nice as she is."

"But will their mothers give me sweet rolls every day?"

"Oh, now the truth comes out. *That's* why you always make time to walk with Barb in the mornings!"

"Mmm," Celia agreed. "And so Barb and I can gossip, though I'm enjoying that less these days. And I'd probably better cut back on the sweet rolls, too, actually—I've gained two pounds this month."

Mom shook her head sympathetically. "Too bad you evidently inherited my metabolism instead of your father's," she said. "Well, you'd better get dressed and get downstairs for your morning gruel."

She and Dad kissed her and went out. Celia found herself smiling as she went to the bathroom to splash cold water on her eyes. Nothing had been resolved, but somehow she felt better anyway.

Chapter 7.

Thursday, December 23, 1954

C elia threw her pen down, blotching the page before her. *Who cares, this essay is no good anyway. Jane Eyre, stupid whiner. But I know I'm supposed to admire her, so I'll have to think of something positive to write.* She glared at the paper, but no inspiration came.

Obviously, she had a couple of weeks to write it—until after the Christmas break. But she'd been hoping to have all her homework done before the holiday, so she could relax and enjoy it.

Giving up for now, she sighed and pushed away from the desk. She left the bedroom and wandered down the hall, noticing light seeping out under the door in the smaller spare room. She opened the door an inch. "Knock, knock," she said through the crack.

"Celia?" Laurie answered. "Hang on a minute." There was some rustling of paper and a scraping sound as of something being shoved across the floor—*under the bed*, Celia thought, *wonder what he got me.* Then he said, "Ok, come on in."

As she expected, he was wrapping Christmas presents. The box of giftwrap and ribbon that lived in the closet of this room was on the bed, and various books and other articles were scattered across the white coverlet.

Celia picked up the nearest book. It had a varicolored cover with a drawing of a boy in the center, surrounded by fanciful objects that reminded Celia of pictures she had seen of the work of Marc Chagall. "*Adventures of Mottel, the Cantor's Son,* by Sholom Aleichem," she read, stumbling over the unfamiliar name. "Is this for Jamie?"

Laurie nodded. "It's just been translated," he said. "It was the last thing he ever wrote, but he died before it was finished. It's about this Jewish kid coming to America, though. I thought Jamie would be interested."

Celia nodded. "Guess he will. He's really taking this thing about getting in touch with his Jewishness again seriously, isn't he?"

"More and more, since he turned thirteen last year," Laurie agreed. "That shindig he went to this week was a Hanukkah party, you know."

"I know. With *Rima Shapiro,*" Celia said poisonously.

Laurie looked up in surprise from the Christmas album of Irving Berlin songs he was wrapping. "You don't like her? I thought she was your friend."

"I don't trust her. She only cozied up to me because she wanted to get to Jamie. And she brought that dog here and scared the liver out of him. Then I guess she sweet-talked him after services on Yom Kippur and suddenly they're buddies."

Laurie finished taping a gift tag addressed to Mom onto his package, then cocked his head to one side. "But that's good, right?" he said. "Jamie likes her, too, and he's never really had a friend outside of the family before. And from what he told me the other night about the party, she might be getting to be not just a friend but a girlfriend."

Celia slumped down to sit on the floor next to Laurie, turning herself to lean against the bed. He was tall enough to do his wrapping from a kneeling position, but her head barely cleared the top. She turned her face, finding some ease in the soft chenille against her cheek. "I know," she sighed. "Maybe I'm jealous, that she likes him and she really was just using me. But those kids, Rima and her friends, they're all older than he is. What if they... I don't know, turn against him or something? That could really hurt him."

Laurie sank down on his haunches and gazed at her, puzzled. "Why would they? Some of them at least know him from that Advanced Algebra class Rima met him in. What would make them turn on him?"

"I guess you're right," she conceded. "They already know he's smart." She swiveled her neck to press her eyes against the coverlet.

Laurie shoved her knee to get her attention back. "What's the matter, Cissy? Has someone been mean to you?"

She lifted her head and shrugged dismissively. "Nothing important," she said. "It's just that this year, things seem to be changing. It used to be ok that I did well in school, people admired me for it." She flushed, wondering if he would think she was bragging, but he only nodded encouragingly, so she went on, "All of a sudden, this year, it's like everybody's turned into someone else, and I'm supposed to, too. Puberty, Dad says." Laurie snorted and she gave a reluctant grin, then went on, "So now I'm supposed to be all worried about hair and makeup—and I am interested in those things, but I'm not supposed to be interested in anything else, and it just makes no sense to me. Suddenly it's a crime to be smart."

Laurie shifted back to bend his knees up and wrap his arms around them. "Linda said something like that to me once, about people expecting different things from girls than from boys. But she's got a new friend, this beatnik type girl called Sydney, who doesn't even wear makeup and who talks about deep subjects and cracks snide jokes all the time. I think she's pseudo, myself, but Linda calls her 'refreshing'."

Celia twisted her ankles back and forth, watching her house slippers dangle off her toes. "Think I should become a beatnik? Somehow I think that's not my style. I look lousy in black, anyway."

Laurie laughed, which illogically irritated her. She shot him a glare but he was unimpressed. "Just be thankful you're still doing well in school," he said. "It's been better for me this year, but I had a horrible freshman year."

"Because you're a Negro?"

"No, most kids there are actually better about that than the ones at Pine Springs, and for a change I'm not the only one."

"Your new friend Roscoe."

"There was a senior, too, who was popular because he was in all the shows; he's graduated now. But no, I got screwed up because Pine Springs didn't prepare me well enough for County High."

"I remember," she said, thinking of the fuss last year when Laurie's grades had come in lower than they'd ever been. She had a pang of foreboding. "Do you think that will happen to me? God, if I don't even have doing well in school to feel good about —"

Laurie grabbed her knee again, but comfortingly this time, scrunching up the jeans material as he squeezed it. "I'll help you," he said.

"Will you?"

"Sure, and Jamie, too, the way he helped me, I'm sure he would. We can make a regular thing of it this summer, taking you through stuff like how to use a microscope."

"Oh, Laurie, that would be great."

"Can't have our little sister falling off the top of the heap," he said. "Speaking of heaps, I better get back to this wrapping."

"And I have an essay on Charlotte Bronte to write." Celia hauled herself to her feet as Laurie knelt up again. "I have presents to wrap, too. Let me know when you're through in here, ok?"

"Yeah, yeah," Laurie said with a grin. "I can tell you everything you need to know."

Chapter 8.

Celia pulled her raincoat out of her locker. It was damp from this morning. *No help for it,* she thought distastefully as she shrugged it on. As she took out her still-dripping umbrella, she became aware that Barb was fidgeting beside her instead of getting dressed to go. She'd stopped putting her hair in pigtails a while ago, and had it cut shorter; now she reached to where it used to hang as though she'd twist it if she could.

As Celia kept looking at her, the other girl muttered, "Um, Celia?"

"That's my name, don't wear it out." But neither smiled at the feeble witticism.

"It's just, uh, I'm not going home right now."

"You're not?"

"No, I, uh, and Carol and a couple of the other girls are going to that Domestic Arts club Miss Millerton is running after school."

"You're going to the Sewing Circle?" Celia asked disbelievingly, using the slighting name they'd both giggled over in the past.

"It's more than sewing," Barb said defensively. "It's cooking and stuff like how to iron a man's shirt so you don't make more creases and how to look for bargains that are really worth it and... all kinds of stuff a woman needs to know. I mean, we knew you wouldn't be interested, that's why I didn't say anything before, but—"

"You mean, I'm not really a woman?" Celia snarled to cover her hurt feelings.

That seemed to put some iron in Barb's spine. "No, of course not," she snapped. "You're just better than the rest of us. In your own mind, anyway." She slammed her locker door shut and stormed away down the hall.

Celia stood stunned for a minute, then slowly turned in the other direction, making for the doors. Someone was standing in front of her—Roger Gleeson. *Now what,* she thought exasperatedly. But she curbed her mood and forced her face into as pleasant an expression as she could manage. The kid was in her math class, the only one who got called on more than Celia. His intellect was obviously miles beyond any of theirs: Celia was smart and studious; Roger was probably a genius.

He also had thick, heavily pocked skin and Coke-bottle glasses over eyes that pointed in opposite directions. His hair was an unwashed mat on top of his head and shaved almost to the scalp on the sides and back. His clothes were ill-fitting and clearly secondhand. As far as Celia knew, he had no friends. Even the school bullies didn't bother with Roger—he was too easy a target.

So she schooled her tone and said, "Did you want something, Roger?"

He turned as red as if she'd slapped him. *Or kissed him,* Celia thought uneasily, noting how the flush left his pockmarks white.

He licked his lips and said hesitantly, "I saw the Leaper girl going back to a classroom, so I guess she's not walking home with you today. I just, ah, wondered… maybe I could walk with you instead?"

Oh, God. But Celia couldn't think of a way to put him off, so she just nodded. That seemed to make him even more nervous, but he fell into step beside her.

Neither of them said anything for the first block or so, crowded awkwardly under Celia's umbrella. Then Celia, cudgeling her brain for a topic of conversation, said, "What do you think about that polio vaccine that Dr. Salk discovered?"

The school had been buzzing with the news for two days; a childhood scourge might be eradicated. Now Roger's homely face lit up with enthusiasm.

"He announced it a couple years ago, but they just decided it was safe to distribute. Almost fifty-eight thousand people contracted it in 1952," he said. "Over three thousand died from it, mostly kids. This is going to change the world."

"Did you hear he refused to patent it?" Celia said. "The paper said he said, 'Could you patent the sun?' I don't think that's the same thing, though. The sun is just there; his vaccine took years to develop."

Roger nodded. "If we could figure out some way to harness the sun's power, the way they did with the atom for the Bomb, people could patent that. But the guy doesn't even seem to get what a huge thing he's done, he's so brilliant. Did you know he went to college when he was only fifteen?"

Celia heard a wistful tone in that last sentence. "Is that what you'd like to do, go to college early?" she asked. "My brother Jamie's been talking about doing that."

Roger shrugged. "Doesn't matter what I'd like. My parents want me to be 'normal.'" He crooked his fingers into quotation marks. "Instead, I'm…" He extended one of his index fingers and twirled it next to his head.

"You're not crazy," Celia laughed. "You're just smart."

"Around here, it's the same thing."

"Ain't that the truth?"

They were almost at the corner where they'd turn in separate directions, but Roger suddenly stopped walking. Celia went on a few steps before she realized it, then turned back and raised an eyebrow at him.

He was looking at the ground, hunched under the fine spring drizzle. "You're smart, too," he said.

"Not in your league," she answered.

He flapped a dismissive hand. "Smarter than anybody else I know."

"You should meet my brother Jamie."

He shrugged. "I know, all your family's pretty bright, I guess. But you're the one who's my age. I just thought—maybe we could, like, go out together some time? To a movie or something?"

The naked hope in his eyes robbed Celia of speech for a second. Then, as it started to turn to disappointment and humiliation, she quickly said, "Sure, Roger. Sounds like fun. Listen, I have to run. My, uh, mother is expecting me."

Lame excuse, she groaned to herself. But Roger grasped at it with relief.

"Sure," he said, backing away. "Mine, too. I mean, um, ok, I'll, uh, call you or something. Bye." He jogged off down his street while Celia turned for hers.

When she got to the house, she parked her open umbrella next to the others on the sheet of oilcloth Ruby had laid down in the front hall for that purpose, draped her damp coat over the newel post since the hall tree was already full with the boys' jackets, and made her way back to the kitchen.

As she'd hoped, Mom and Ruby were sitting there having a cup of coffee together and looking over the newspaper's weekly grocery bargain insert from the A&P. A plate of peanut butter cookies that Ruby had evidently made for after school snack sat on the table between them.

Celia plopped down on the breakfast nook bench opposite Ruby and wailed, "Roger Gleeson is going to call and ask me to go to a movie with him!"

Mom and Ruby looked at each other, then Mom said carefully, "And that's a bad thing?"

"Oh, Mom, he's the biggest nerd in school!"

"'Nerd'?" Ruby asked.

"It means 'misfit,'" Mom explained. "Especially a brainy one."

"I'm a horrible person," Celia said, putting her head down on her arms. She turned it to one side so she could speak and went on, "I shouldn't care. He seems like a nice enough guy. But he's... he's homely as sin, and he's just so *weird*... Well, not weird, exactly, but... like you said, Mom, a misfit. And if I start going out with him, it's going to make me even more of one. It's bad enough already without me dating the only person in school less popular than I am."

"Well, I have a simple fix for that," Mom said. "You're too young to date, and you can tell him your father and I said so."

Celia sat up straight, outraged. "Too young? But lots of kids I know have started dating!"

"We're not their parents," Mom said, both her words and her tone all too familiar to Celia. She opened her mouth to argue but Mom cut her off. "Think a minute, Cissy. Do you really want to override me here and go out with this boy after all?"

Celia snapped her mouth shut. *No, I don't. This is a good way out, but...* "But you'll let me date next year, right? When I start high school?" At Mom's nod she went on, "So what's the big deal? That's only, um, five months from now."

"That's five months you don't have to worry," Ruby said, getting up and collecting her and Mom's coffee mugs. "Take advantage of them and be young while you can. Do you want a glass of milk to go with your cookies?"

Celia blew her breath out, puffing her cheeks. "Yes, please," she said. She slumped back in her seat.

After pouring the milk, Ruby took out the old wallet she kept in the drawer by the back door. She pulled out a couple of dollar bills and brought them along with the glass.

As she handed her the milk and the money, Ruby reached over and patted her hand. "Get yourself a little treat next time you're out with your friends. It'll all work out, child," she said. "You'll see."

Celia's heart sank. *Nobody understands, they all just think I'm a silly little girl.* Then she caught Mom rolling her eyes at Ruby's back, giving Celia a sympathetic smirk, and felt a tiny bit better.

CHAPTER 9.

WEDNESDAY, MAY 25,1955

The once-familiar voice pulled Celia out of her absorption in the newest Heinlein novel. "Happy birthday, Cissy."

She looked up and smiled at the half-turned figure, shifting her feet as the library checkout line moved up a slot. "Thanks, Linda. How've you been?"

"I'm ok. I missed dyeing eggs with you guys at Easter."

"We missed you, too. And *somebody* missed you especially."

Laurie's ex-girlfriend's eyelids flickered, then her face set, warning Celia off the subject.

Celia ignored the warning. "He knows he screwed up," she said.

"Does he." Linda's tone was cool.

"Listen, I know how annoying he can be when he goes all protective, but he was just worried about you."

Linda sighed. "No, Celia. If it had been only that, we could have talked about it, about why Sydney makes him so nervous. But he actually told me he wanted me to stop seeing her."

"I know, I was eavesdropping," Celia admitted. "But he gets it now, that he can't boss you around that way. He really cares about you, Linda."

Linda sighed as she handed her books over to be stamped out. "I care about him, too. But it wasn't only about that. I needed time to think, to be on my own for a while, not part of a couple."

"And now?"

Linda shrugged and stepped aside as Celia took her turn at the counter. "We're about to go to the Adirondacks for the summer. It's a good place to think, our little island. I'll lie out on the star rock and stare at the sky, see if I get any inspiration."

Celia's old friend Carol Prosky came up to them then, brown curls bobbing. She'd dropped out of the "Sewing Circle" club after only a couple of meetings, to Celia's relief. *At least I still have one friend who doesn't buy into the Little Woman crap. On the other hand, in Carol's case it's probably more that she's used to having a maid do everything; she thinks she's above learning "domestic arts."*

"You finished?" Carol asked Celia in her piping voice.

"Yes," Celia said. "Aren't you checking out anything? You know Linda Marks, don't you?"

Carol shrugged and twitched her shoulders, smiling uncertainly at Linda. "No, I was just reading magazines, waiting for you. Hi, Linda."

"Hi, Carol," Linda said. "Do you two need a ride back to Pine Springs? We could walk over to my house, see if Mom is home with the car."

"No, thanks," Celia said. "Dad's picking us up and taking us both to my house for my birthday dinner. Want to come, too?"

"Nice try, kiddo," Linda laughed. "No, I'm going to need the summer to let my brains gel a little more. Have a nice one."

"What was that about?" Carol whispered as they followed Linda out the front doors and sat down on the library steps.

"Oh, she thinks I was trying to get her back together with Laurie," Celia said; Linda was now out of earshot. "And I guess she was right, a little. It doesn't seem fair, that they've split apart over something so stupid, when they still like each other."

"Do you think they were... doing it?"

For a second, Celia wasn't sure she'd heard the little voice correctly, but when she saw Carol's red-splotched half-averted face, she knew she had. "Carol!" she exclaimed. "What a thing to say! Of course they're not."

"Why 'of course'? Kids their age do it."

"Not people like them."

"Because they're so goody-goody?"

Celia gazed at her friend thoughtfully. They'd known each other since infancy. Carol lived down the road from the McAlisters', in a house almost as big as Celia's, but she was an only child. She was always the first to get whatever fad came on the market and her clothes were always a little bit fancier than anyone else's. But her family life was tense; for one thing, her mother had some condition that kept her in bed most of the time, and when she did get up she needed crutches and a leg brace. Carol almost never invited anyone there, and she liked to spend time at Celia's. Over the years, they'd confided in each other, played together with Barb, complained about teachers and shared fantasies about their futures. But they'd never talked about anything even vaguely touching on sex, and suddenly Celia wondered why.

"Not that," she answered now. "But because they're both too... serious, I guess is the word. Neither one of them would do that unless they were really sure the other person was the one for them, and obviously they aren't." She wondered how much she could share with Carol about Linda and Laurie's disagreement without betraying their private business, but Carol didn't seem to be interested in those details.

"What do you think it's like?" Carol was still whispering, clasped hands plunged between her raised knees as she sat on the step, shoulders hunched up around her ears.

"Sex?" Celia asked. "Gosh, I don't know. Nice, I guess, since everybody seems to want to do it."

Carol shuddered down her whole body. "Why would you? I mean, letting a boy put—you know. Like, would you do that with that Roger Gleeson?"

"Good gravy, Carol, I'm fourteen years old today! I'm not thinking about having sex with anybody, least of all Roger Gleeson." She'd told Roger about her parents' strictures on dating, and she thought he'd believed her, but she also thought he'd sensed her relief at having the excuse; he'd avoided meeting her eyes ever since. She was sorry to have hurt his feelings, but didn't really know how to do anything about it without encouraging him again. Sex, though, had never remotely entered into the equation.

"Listen, Carrie," she ventured. "Maybe you should talk to your mom about this. She's always home, after all." *Not like mine.* Then she was ashamed of the thought. *I know she'd do anything for me, job or not.*

Carol's head came up. Her eyes were shrewd. "Just because she's home doesn't mean she's paying attention to me, you know. Besides, I hate my mother," she went on fiercely. "And Dad—Dad gets so mad. Sometimes he, he hits…" She choked to a stop.

For the first time in the conversation, Celia was genuinely shocked. She'd known there was tension in the family, but not that it was this bad. "Oh, Carrie, honey, I'm so sorry," she said.

"Sorry? Why should you be sorry?"

That you don't have what I have, Celia thought but obviously couldn't say. "That you're so upset," she said instead. "Listen, you want to talk to my mom? She's a professional, you know, she could maybe help—"

"NO!" Carol grabbed Celia's arm and shook it. "You can't tell her, you can't tell anybody I was talking about this, ever as long as we live, promise me!"

Seeing she was near hysterics, Celia said soothingly, "Of course I won't: cross my heart and hope to die. Calm down, Carrie." She thought about saying something on the lines of it not being such a terrible thing to want to talk about, but decided Carol was in no mood to hear that.

Carol dropped Celia's arm and went back to that clenched hands position. They sat in silence for the few minutes until Celia could exclaim with relief, "Here's my dad."

Chapter 10.

Celia came in from deadheading the roses to find Ruby ironing.

"Would you show me how to do that?" she asked, edging around the ironing board to get to the sink and wash the glasses from the Kool-Aid Ruby had brought out to her and Laurie a few minutes ago. "Barb's taking some kind of lessons in an after-school club that include ironing, and I thought it was stupid, but I tried to iron my own blouse last night and it came out with worse wrinkles than I started with."

"There's a trick to it, like with everything else," Ruby said. "Especially blouses and shirts. You have to do the parts in the right order. Here, look, start with the collar, laid out against the board..."

Celia watched the demonstration till Dad's dress shirt, smooth and pristine, dangled from the hanger Ruby looped over the back of the chair at the end of the breakfast nook. Then she gazed at Ruby speculatively as she started in on a pair of Laurie's chino slacks and said, "Didn't you used to be a nurse?"

"I am a nurse," Ruby answered. "That's how I came to be in this house; I came to nurse your Grandma McAlister. Your grandfather promised to pay the rest of my nursing school tuition if I stayed."

Celia circled the ironing board again and slid onto one of the breakfast nook benches. "Didn't he keep his promise?"

"He would have, if I'd gone back. He left me a nice little sum when he died, you know. Your parents pay me, of course, but if I wanted to leave here and go back to nursing or do something else, I could."

"Why don't you? I mean, I'm glad you didn't, but if you could have had a career—"

Ruby kept ironing as she talked. "I did for a while," she said. "When I was married."

"That was before the war, right?" Celia remembered the picture that sat on Ruby's nightstand of her husband in his sailor's uniform.

"That's right. Your grandma died, and then after a few years your grandpa did, too, and… well, the house was empty with your dad in the navy. That's how I met Lester, actually—I was staying in Philadelphia with my sister Pearl and her family. Sean had just gotten into Annapolis, which was pretty unusual for a non-commissioned seaman, but Lester had been a cook in the Enlisted Men's Mess at the navy docks and Sean had met him and introduced us."

Ruby hung up the slacks and started in on a cotton dress of Mom's. "We got married and I used some of my bequest from old Mr. Mac to finish my LPN—Licensed Practical Nurse—training. I never got a chance to go on to the next level, to be a Registered Nurse, before Lester was transferred and we moved west, to San Diego. He shipped out on the *Arizona* just in time to get killed at Pearl Harbor."

Celia already knew about that. She made a sympathetic face, then said, "Wait, though, go back a little. Why did you stay here in the first place, after Grandma died? Why didn't you go and finish your training then?"

Ruby pursed her lips for a minute as if debating what to say. Then she hung up Mom's dress, turned off the iron—though there was still a pile of wrinkled clothes in the basket by her feet—and slid onto the bench opposite Celia.

She didn't speak for a minute, looking down and rubbing a work-roughened finger over an old scratch on the table, her nail shining like pearl against her dark bronze skin. Finally she said, "Your grandfather was not an easy man. He could be kind; he adored his wife, and he was very generous to me, but he had a terrible temper. I know now that some of that was the brain tumor that finally killed him, but I think he was never a soft or gentle sort."

She clenched her fist on the table and looked up at Celia. "Even before she died, he was awfully hard on... on Sean and..." She licked her lips and glanced away, then drew a breath and seemed to start again. "And after she went, it got worse. He could be violent. He, he beat your dad something awful, sometimes for no good reason—not that there's ever a reason to treat a child the way he did, but sometimes he took after him for no reason at all. And sometimes I could help."

"Was he... was he violent to you?" Celia whispered.

Ruby thumped her fist softly on the table. "He wouldn't have dared," she gritted out. "He needed me to take care of Mrs. Mac, and he knew I wouldn't put up with it. Right from the beginning, I tried to stand between him and... and Seanie. But we none of us thought I would be here so long, Mrs. McAlister's heart was so bad. It took the influenza epidemic to finally carry her off. I was nineteen when I came here and twenty-seven when she died, and by then I just couldn't leave. I couldn't. I loved—that little boy, and he needed me to shield him as best I could, and comfort him when I couldn't." Ruby pulled a rumpled handkerchief out of her apron pocket and mopped her eyes with it.

Celia didn't know where to look; she'd never seen Ruby cry before. She got up and fixed a glass of ice water and set it at Ruby's elbow, then sat down again.

Ruby nodded in thanks and sipped at the water. "By the time Sean ran off to join the navy and... and Mr. McAlister died, I—I was at a loss."

Wasn't there another child? Celia thought, remembering something Mom had said once, about an estranged brother. *That's what she's not mentioning. I wonder why?*

But she let the question go as Ruby resumed, "Lester was a cheerful, easygoing man. He was happy enough for me to go on and get my LPN license after we were married, but of course he expected me to follow where he went, so that's how I ended up in California. Only after he was killed, well, Sean had married Martha by then, and she'd brought Laurie home when his mother had to abandon him, so I came back here to help out, and then you came along, and—well, I just never left again. I got to love your mother, and you kids weren't so bad, either."

Celia chuckled dutifully, but said, "Wait a minute. Why 'of course'? I mean, about following your husband? I can see where you'd want to be with him, you'd miss him if he went without you, and being in the navy he didn't have any choice where he went, but what if he hadn't been? What if he'd been... oh, I don't know, a factory worker, and just decided he wanted to go out West? Does the man automatically get to make decisions like that?"

Ruby seemed glad of the shift in subject. She got up briskly and turned the iron on again. While she waited for it to heat, she said, "In a good marriage, people listen to each other."

"But if he decides against her, the wife has no choice?"

Mom came into the kitchen from the back stairs, changed out of the summer suit she'd worn to work into cotton slacks and a sleeveless blouse. "What's this about a wife having no choice?"

"A smart woman knows how to get around a man," Ruby said. Celia thought she sounded a little defensive.

Mom cocked her head to one side. "'What every woman knows'? Really, Ruby, aren't we past games like that?" She turned to Celia. "A marriage is a partnership. As in any partnership, sometimes a couple will pull against each other, and one will be strong in one area and the other strong in another. There's no formula for how to make decisions, you have to look at each situation separately."

Celia thought about her conversation with Carol on the library steps and was tempted to bring that into the conversation, but remembering Carol's frantic insistence, decided to keep her promise of silence.

Mom went to the fridge and pulled it open. "Isn't it your turn to help with dinner tonight?"

"Me and Joy."

"Joy's not home from swimming yet. How about you help me get the salad started while Ruby finishes up there?"

"Ok." Celia took the bell peppers Mom handed her and started to wash and seed them. "But, see, I've been thinking about this split between Laurie and Linda. You know how it started?"

Mom nodded as she scraped some carrots. "Laurie wanted her to stop seeing that girl Sydney."

"That's what I mean. Why does he get to decide who she sees?"

"He doesn't, that's why she got mad."

"I know that. I mean, why did he think he did? Today he said she must not care about him if she didn't do what he wanted. How can you show someone you care about them and still do what you feel is right for you? Especially if you're a woman?"

"That, my dear, is a question for the ages," Mom said. "If I ever figure it out, I'll let you know."

"Martha," Ruby put in, "you're scraping those carrots to splinters. They're not men; give them a break."

Mom laughed and eased up on the peeler. "Pretty sharp remark, there, Ruby," she said. "We'll make a New Woman of you yet."

But this is nice, Celia reflected, *the three of us working here in the kitchen.* She sighed, slicing the peppers on the cutting board.

CHAPTER 11.

MONDAY, JULY 11, 1955

I've got a job! Celia exulted. *A real job, that's not babysitting!* She spun on her stool behind the narrow counter, glancing around the cramped storefront reception area of the China Box, a new carryout restaurant in Carlisle. One of her babysitting clients, Mr. Huff, had opened it and his wife had suggested he offer her the job.

She shivered a little, partly because of the air conditioning and partly from excitement and partly from nervousness. Marie Andretti, the manager, had walked her through the procedures several times and watched her take a few phone orders on her own before giving her an encouraging pat and leaving. "You'll do fine," she'd said, and Celia had confidently agreed.

But now she wasn't so sure. What if she forgot something? What if she screwed up an order? What if she messed up with the cash? *I'm only fourteen,* she thought defensively.

Then the phone rang at the same time as the first customer walked in to pick up his 5:00 order and for the next three hours she had no time to be nervous. Marie came back in at 8:00 to tally the cash register and pack up the overnight deposit bag for the bank. "You'll do this after tonight," she said.

Celia gulped, forgetting about her aching back for a minute. "I will? All by myself?"

Marie pushed her jet-black wavy hair back off her face and smiled at her. "You're a smart girl, I know. Mrs. Huff was bragging about how you figured out what was wrong with her little Josie when she wouldn't wake up that time."

Celia blushed with pleasure. "It was just that Mrs. Huff had told me they'd given her nose drops for her cold, and when I looked in their medicine cabinet I saw the bottle was the same size and color as the one for the eye drops, so I figured..."

"But you were smart enough to call a doctor right away, too."

"Actually, I called Ruby. Ruby Jones, the lady who takes care of us? She's a nurse, and she told me to call the doctor because she knew that eye drops usually have belladonna in them, and that's poison, so... But anyway, that's not the same thing as knowing how to figure out the cash box if there's any problem." *Still, it's always nice to have someone think my being smart is actually good for something. And for something useful, not just wool-gathering, or being a brain at school.*

"Maybe not, but it shows you have a cool head and good judgment and you know when to ask for help. You'll catch on in no time. Oh, look, is that your mom?"

Celia peered through the front window to see Mom's blue Dodge pulling up. "Yeah, it is. Thanks, Marie, see you tomorrow!"

It had been drizzling on and off all day, and the temperature must have been ninety at least. The inside of the car felt like a steam bath, even with all the windows open. Besides Celia's aching back, her feet throbbed and her head felt as though someone were tightening a scarf around it and the smell of old grease in her hair and clothes was nauseating. Still...

"How was your first day at work?" Mom asked.

"Wonderful," Celia sighed happily.

"Have you had supper?"

"No, there was no time to eat. From the minute the evening orders started coming in, it never let up."

"Well, Ruby saved some chicken salad and biscuits for you, and she made cherry crumble for dessert."

"Mmm." Celia luxuriated in that prospect as Mom got onto the Pine Springs Road toward home. Then she said, "Mom, that manager, Marie, she wanted Mr. Huff to hire someone so she could go home over the dinner hour and feed her husband. But she works the lunch hour and all afternoon, then all day on the weekends. Her kids are grown up, she says. I didn't want to say anything, but wouldn't you think her husband could feed himself once in a while? Or at least help her? She works as many hours as he does driving his cab, I bet."

Mom gave a humorless laugh. "You'd think so, wouldn't you? I'm sure, in a similar situation, your father would pitch in, but he's a rare man."

"You mean he knows how to cook something besides pancakes and hamburgers on the grill?"

"Oh, yes, Ruby taught him the basics. He can put together a tuna casserole with the best of them. Of course, like any man I've ever heard of, he can stare into a refrigerator stuffed with excellent leftovers and then go make himself a peanut butter sandwich because he doesn't see anything to eat."

"But he doesn't have to, and neither do you, because we have Ruby."

"That's right, we have Ruby. She's our 'wife'."

"Do you think I'll have somebody like Ruby when I grow up?"

"I doubt it. Times are changing and people are less interested in doing domestic work. In any case, it's a rare thing to have someone as smart and well educated as Ruby willing to do it. We're very lucky." Mom pulled into the driveway.

"Maybe I'll marry a rich guy," Celia said.

"Maybe you will. Then all you'll have to worry about is how not to die of boredom."

"I could still have a career."

"Indeed you could," Mom said as they rolled into the open garage. "I hope you will, not least because a rich husband can die and leave you with nothing, like your friend Susie's mother."

"Susie Hannigan? I haven't thought about her in a long time. Where did they go, anyway?"

"They moved to Camp Hill, where they wouldn't keep running into people who 'knew them when.' Elsie Hannigan had to scrub floors to support herself and her kids when Chuck died so unexpectedly, and so young. She couldn't stand the pitying looks and the snotty comments disguised as concern."

The two of them had gotten out of the car and Mom activated the new automatic garage door. Celia rather missed the old folding double doors. "He was in the navy, wasn't he?"

"The reserves. They booted a lot of young officers after the war ended. Chuck had that thriving stock brokerage from his father, so he thought it didn't matter, and they spent everything he made to keep up appearances."

Celia hadn't heard Mom sound so bitter before. As they walked up under the front door portico light, Mom looked at her expression and shook her head dismissively. "I'm a little sensitive, I suppose, when I think about those women."

"Navy women?"

"They always looked down their noses at me, you know."

"Because you were a foster child?"

"No, they didn't know that, I don't think. No, it was because your father was a noncommissioned seaman before he went to Annapolis, and then he went there on a scholarship. Nothing else mattered: not how good an officer he was, or how hard it had been for him to make good without a conventional background—he was just considered second class. His first commander had said to him, 'My worst Academy man will always get a better rating than my best non-Academy man.' Idiots," she huffed as they went in the front door. "And even though he did make it to the academy, he wasn't the right 'kind' of academy man. That's why we don't socialize at the Officers' Club any more than we can help."

"You guys don't socialize much anyway, do you?"

"No time," Mom said, waving as she went into the study.

Celia made her way back to the kitchen. "Ruby, I'm starving," she said.

Chapter 12.

Saturday, August 20, 1955

The grass in the shade of the old barn was still soggy from yesterday's rain, but today the sun was beating down and the temperature was in the nineties, so the girls were glad of the damp and the cool. They were sitting on a bench up against the rough wood, kicking their heels after racing each other down from the house. Celia wondered whether maybe they should have stayed there.

Barb was here, and Carol, and Patty Lebo, another girl from Pine Springs. "What do you think high school is going to be like?" Carol asked the others in her little high voice.

"Different, my brothers say," Celia answered. "A big jump harder academically, and socially of course there'll be a lot more people."

"Boy people, especially," Patty said, wriggling her shoulders and giggling. Barb nudged her in the side and the two of them and Carol laughed. *What was funny about that?* Celia wondered, thinking about the fraught conversation she'd had with Carol on the steps of Bosler Library.

"The trouble with you guys is," she said, "none of you have brothers. You act like boys are some different species. They're just people, you know."

For some reason, that made them laugh even harder. Then Barb said slyly, "Like Roger Gleeson, you mean? He keeps following you around, and giving you cow eyes. I hope your brothers don't do that."

"You're behind the times," Celia said. "Roger's parents finally got the message that he's got a brain bigger than they can cope with at County High. They're sending him to boarding school this fall."

"Aw, poor Celia," Patty said. "What will you do now?"

"Not sit around waiting for some guy to notice me," Celia snapped. "Listen, let's do something."

"Like what?" Carol asked.

"Uh, oh," Barb said. "I know that look. She's going to come up with something weird."

"Not weird," Celia said. "I was just thinking, here we are at the barn, with all that space and different kinds of neat junk inside. Why don't we act something out?"

Carol rolled her eyes. "You mean like when we were little and used to run around pretending to be ponies? God, Celia, we are about to be freshman in high school, you know."

"No," Barb said. "She means more like in an Andy Hardy movie, you know, 'Come on, kids, let's put on a show!'"

Patty, whose family had only moved to the area a couple of years ago so hadn't known Celia since first grade the way the other two did, hooted derisively. "You're kidding!"

"Of course she is," Celia said, irritated at Barb. "We're not putting on a show for anybody. I just meant something for ourselves, acting out a story that we like."

"What for?" Patty was incredulous.

"Just for fun. Don't you like to think about favorite stories, and how they might be to be inside of, and even how you might make them come out a little different?"

Patty mimed deep thought, fist to her chin, wispy blonde hair limp around her face, then said, "Ummmm…no?"

Then Carol piped, "We might as well try it. There's nothing else to do, unless we go back and watch TV or something, and there's nothing but kid shows on Saturdays."

So they got up and went around to the small side door. Inside, the barn was dim and hotter than the shade in back had been, with motes of dust and old straw floating in the shafts of light from the opening on the upper level.

"Why do you have this barn, anyway?" Patty asked. "You don't have horses or anything."

"No, but there used to be," Celia explained. "This was a farm in my great-grandparents' time. My grandfather sold off a lot when my grandmother was sick for so long, but we held onto this part, and the woods behind."

"So what story are we going to do?" Barb asked.

"How about *The Sword in the Stone?*" Celia suggested. The others looked blank. "About young King Arthur?" she prompted.

They shook their heads and Patty said, "How can we do a story about a king? We're all girls."

Celia said, "That doesn't matter. He's just a little boy in it, anyway. Nobody knows who he really is. He grows up with a foster father, Sir Ector, and his son Kay. They have to hide him, see, because his mother and the old king had him secretly and they're dead now, so Merlin hid him. But they call him Wart and everybody looks down on him. And then Merlin comes to tutor him and turns him into all kinds of animals, and finally at the end they go to a tournament and there's the sword stuck in a stone and only the rightful king of England can pull it out."

"Ooh, can I be the boy?" Barb said. "My hair's the shortest."

"Sure," Celia said, pulling an old horse blanket off the wall and slinging it over her shoulders. "And I'll be Merlin. Carol and Pat, you can be Sir Ector and Kay."

"How do we do that?" Carol said doubtfully, tugging at her own brown ringlets.

"Well, if you're Ector, you mostly sort of stomp around and say sort of stuffy British things, you know, like, 'Dash it all,' and 'What mischief are you boys up to now, what?' And Pat, Kay should be sort of bratty and jealous because Merlin's giving the Wart all the attention and Kay thinks he's the important one. But he's not a bad kid, really, and he likes Arthur underneath it all."

"I don't know how to act," Patty said.

"It's not acting, exactly, it's just sort of putting yourself in the story."

"It sounds like a stupid story. Who ever heard of a boy named Kay? And what do you mean, this Merlin turns the kid into animals? I get that he's magic or something, but why do something dumb like that?"

"So he can learn," Celia said. "Strength and power from the pike—you know, that's a kind of fish—and courage from the hawks, and community from the ants, and freedom from the swans…"

"Geez, how many animals does he turn into? And what will we be doing while you and Barb are doing that?"

"Well, you can be the animals, too. And we can switch off being Merlin and Arthur, if you want." But Celia could see she was losing them.

"I've got a better idea," Carol said. "Let's go back to my house and listen to records. I've got that new Four Lads album."

"Ooh, yeah, let's do that," Patty said. "You never ask us there, and I heard your bedroom is neat-o."

"But I thought we were going to…" Barb started feebly.

Celia could see she was only doing it to stand by Celia, so she shrugged at her and shook her head. *Even with that new adjustable turntable Laurie got me for Christmas, they'd rather go to Carol's,* she realized. The other three girls raced out of the barn, chattering about music. Celia hung the horse blanket back up and closed the door behind her as she followed them out.

CHAPTER 13.

WEDNESDAY, SEPTEMBER 28, 1955

Celia was having a hard time concentrating in Freshman Biology. Usually she did fine, to Dr. Barrett's evident surprise; he probably remembered how Laurie had floundered in this class, since Pine Springs Elementary hadn't given him the science background kids from the other grammar schools had. But Celia'd had the advantage of Laurie's help over the summer. Jamie, who was good at science and math in any case, had helped, too. This wasn't her best class, but she was doing all right and keeping abreast of the others.

Today, though, she couldn't stop thinking about Emmett Till. The idea that a boy her own age could have been brutally murdered just because he was black and had supposedly been fresh to a white woman horrified her.

Then, too, it seemed worse somehow because he had been from up North. The South had always seemed to Celia to be an alien, frightening place. She'd heard of lynchings—murders by mobs—and Jim Crow laws that kept Negroes separated and relegated to inferior schools and poor neighborhoods and even substandard public bathrooms and drinking fountains. But on some level she had assumed that those hatreds could never have an impact on a Northerner, even if he was down there temporarily.

Yesterday, spending the day in Yom Kippur services with Jamie, she'd kept running the details over in her mind. She'd seen the picture of the boy's mutilated face in Laurie's *Jet* magazine, in the coffin the mother had insisted be left open so everyone could see what had been done to her son. She couldn't get the image out of her mind. Then, afterwards, some people had tried to talk to Laurie about it.

Yom Kippur was the Day of Atonement. Jamie had been going around the family ever since Rosh Hashanah, the Jewish New Year, ten days ago, apologizing to everyone for wrongs he'd committed over the year—specific things in some cases. This year, all he'd had to say to Celia was, "I'm sorry for anything I've done to make you unhappy or give you a hard time."

Celia had answered with what she'd prepared to say: "Well, I'm sorry I was so snotty to you about your birthday present to Ruby. She liked that perfume fine, and anyway, I knew she would be happy that you thought of her, even if it wasn't her usual sort of thing. I was worried that Joy and I weren't going to get our scrapbook for her finished in time, and I took it out on you. I apologize."

Jamie had given her a wry grin. "Oh, Cissy," he'd said. "You're an amateur when it comes to snotty remarks. I'm sure I've said much more cutting things to you, and I don't even remember them. Apology accepted."

"Yours, too."

If it had been Laurie, or any of the others, really, that exchange would have ended with a hug. Since it was Jamie, she'd just smiled back and gone on her way, feeling surprisingly lighthearted. *Like confession, only faster.*

Then, on Yom Kippur, which Mom jokingly referred to as "Instant Lent," total strangers started coming up to Laurie and apologizing to him about Emmett Till's murder, as though the mere

70

fact that Laurie also had black skin made him some kind of substitute they could use to alleviate their own feelings of shame and guilt over what had happened. Laurie had been puzzled and uncomfortable at it; Celia was terrified. *What if people who don't have such benign intentions decide he's a good scapegoat for something some other Negro was involved in?*

The biology class was finally over. Leaving, Celia gave a rueful glance at Dr. Barrett; she knew he'd noticed her distraction. But he only nodded understandingly, then gave an admonitory look under his eyebrows. *Message received: Ok this time, but don't do it again,* she thought.

But by the time she'd settled at a cafeteria table with her lunch, she was back to thinking about Till. She didn't notice she'd shredded the corned beef sandwich Ruby had made till Barb said, "What did that sandwich do to make you so mad?"

Celia looked down at the crumbs on the piece of waxed paper the sandwich had been wrapped in, then at the strings of mutilated pink flesh. She shuddered, pushing the mess away from her as she tried to push the image from *Jet* away from her mind.

Barb looked at her shrewdly. "You're thinking about that colored kid, aren't you?"

That's why we're still friends. She does understand some things about me better than anyone else. Celia nodded. "It's bad enough that it happened at all," she said slowly, reflecting on it as she spoke. "But it's worse now that that jury has acquitted the murderers."

Carol, across the table next to Barb, spoke up. "You can't call them murderers," she protested. "You just said it yourself: the jury acquitted them. There was no proof."

"No proof? His great uncle saw them take the boy away that night; that other guy heard them beating him in the shed. There was..."

"But why would a jury let them off, then? They were there, you weren't. They're the ones who heard all the evidence."

"They spent less than an hour on it! And later they said they were sitting around in there drinking soda!"

"That's down South, anyway," Carol said. "Nothing to do with us."

"You think Negroes don't have problems in the North? My brother can't even get served at the Hamilton Restaurant unless he's with one of us. The only reason we still go there is my mom says it's a way to get them used to the idea that sitting next to a Negro isn't going to contaminate anyone. Maybe we don't have lynchings, thank God, but being a Northerner didn't help Emmett Till."

"But what about that kid's mother?" Patty said from beside her. "She hardly even cried, they said." Her freckles stood out on her face, which had paled in the heat of the discussion.

Celia blew her hair up off her forehead in frustration. "Grief affects people different ways, my mother says. And some people don't like showing their emotions in front of strangers; my brother Jamie's like that. And anyway, what are you saying? You think she secretly murdered him herself, snuck down there and beat him to a pulp and shot him and tied a heavy fan to him and dumped him in the river?"

"Well, there was that life insurance policy she had on him. She could have fixed it so somebody else did it for her."

"For four hundred dollars? Would you listen to yourself? Would your mother murder you for four hundred dollars? Or any amount of money?"

"Well, of course not," Patty said in offended tones. "But my mother's not..."

"Not what? Not black?"

Patty shrugged uncomfortably, but Carol said, "Still, he shouldn't have whistled at that woman."

"That's a capital crime now? Whistling?"

"It's just that, you know, with *them...*"

"'With them' what?"

"My father says you have to be careful with n-Negroes, especially the boys. They can get—carried away easier than whites."

Celia gaped at her. "Carol, you've known my brother Laurie since we were all little, how can you say something like that?"

Carol ducked her head and mumbled, "He's not like the rest of them."

Celia was too stunned to speak, but Barb rolled her eyes and shoved Carol in the ribs. "Geez, that's just ignorant," she said.

Carol bridled at that, and Celia felt the conversation slipping out of control. "Wait, wait," she said. *Carol's father is a bigot, and he hits Carol and maybe her mom, too,* she remembered. She licked her lips and said carefully, "*My* father says that a lot of people who are angry and scared about things they can't control put their feelings on people who are different because that's safe. He says we all have to try to keep our emotions out of conversations about touchy things like racism."

"You haven't been keeping your emotions out of this conversation," Patty sniped.

"No, I haven't," Celia admitted. "But I'm going to start trying. Could we just step back a little and go over the facts of the case, this one case, without making sweeping generalizations, and see where that gets us?"

The other three girls looked at each other.

"Sounds like a good idea to me," Barb said.

Carol's tense shoulders suddenly relaxed a notch. "Ok, I'm game," she said. "Those brains of yours must be good for *something*, Celia."

Yeah, thought Celia, *they must, mustn't they? Maybe I can make a difference here. Maybe I can give them a new angle on this without coming off as some kind of weirdo. Maybe I can tell this story in a way they can hear.* Drawing a deep breath, she marshaled her facts and started to lay them out.

Chapter 14.

Thursday, November 17, 1955

Finally, they were going to play basketball in gym. Celia was excited. So far this year, they'd been doing calisthenics, which was boring, and gymnastics, which Celia wasn't good at; she was fast and strong, but she wasn't particularly limber, and she didn't like even the modest height of the parallel bars. Basketball, though, she'd played in the driveway with her brothers practically since she could walk.

But not lately. Rob and Laurie had been fighting, really fighting, even getting physical with it. That seemed to be over now; they'd made up and had a long talk with Dad, during which, according to Laurie, he'd told them about that estranged brother Mom had once told Celia existed. *The one Ruby avoided mentioning, that time we talked about why she stayed with us,* Celia realized. *But the boys had evidently never heard of him.* Dad had also told the boys he'd had an abusive father, which Celia already knew from Ruby. Finding out all that had somehow worked to solve the tension between Rob and Laurie, but no one had felt much like playing since then, and it was too cold outside for basketball, anyway.

So now she waited patiently while Coach Vaughn divided the class into teams, and nervously while he assigned positions. *I'm pretty tall, so maybe...yes!*

"McAlister, you'll play forward," he'd just said.

Stomach fluttering with anticipation, she trotted onto the court, sneakers squeaking on the polished floor. She aligned herself in the forward area next to a new student, Judy Hartzell, who was even taller than Celia and who had the sort of physical confidence that made even their baggy navy blue gym bloomers look like a quirky style choice rather than a clownish joke, the way they looked on most girls.

When she'd arrived at the school and had her first gym class with Celia, Judy's eyes had widened during roll call when Carol had said, "Regular," and been dismissed from gymnastics practice for the day.

"Excuse me," she'd called, raising her hand. "What does 'regular' mean? They didn't have that at my last school."

The girls Celia thought of as "the Domestic Arts Club crowd" had all giggled and Coach had turned red. "It means you have your 'friend'," he'd mumbled, turning away to bark instructions for setting out the practice mats.

"My friend?" Judy had repeated blankly. "What friend? Somebody is visiting her from out of town, you mean?"

"No, silly," Patty had hissed. "You know, getting the painters in."

"'Painters'?"

"It means she's menstruating," Celia had said clearly from where she stood halfway across the room.

The other girls had squealed and blushed and poked each other; one of them jammed a thumb toward Coach's back and goggled at Celia as though the man somehow wouldn't know what the word meant or at any rate shouldn't hear it.

But Judy had just nodded thanks at Celia with a slight roll of the eyes. *So now I've finally got a chance to speak to her.*

"Hi," Celia said to her in an undertone. Coach Vaughn was explaining the rules, which Celia already knew.

The other girl evidently also felt she didn't need to listen. "Hi—Celia, right? I'm Judy."

"I know. I heard you came here from Japan, is that right?"

"Yeah, our last posting. My dad's in the navy."

"Mine, too! At the Depot in Mechanicsburg."

"Jinx!" Judy said, and they grinned at each other.

Then Coach Vaughn blew the whistle and play began. Celia quickly began to feel she ought to have listened to what he was saying before. The other girls acted as though the lines demarcating the play areas were invisible shields, like the Gardol in that toothpaste ad on TV; they stopped at the zone margins as if they were cliff edges. Celia hopped from one foot to the other, waiting for someone to pass her the ball.

Finally, it happened. The basket was in front of her, a little too far to try for, but the way was clear thanks to Judy on her right, guarding her. Celia gave her a grateful nod and started dribbling toward shooting range, jinking a bit to dodge someone trying to block her from the left, but keeping a steady rhythm with the ball, relishing the light tapping as it hit the floor and the slaps against her palm as she drove forward.

The whistle stopping the play came like an unwelcome stab of light in a dark room, jolting her out of her semi-trance, making her stumble and almost overbalance. Before she'd had a chance to regain her equilibrium, the coach was shouting at her.

"What did I say about dribbling, McAlister?"

"Um, I, uh, couldn't hear you too well, Coach."

"You weren't listening, you mean. Leaper, fill her in."

With an apologetic look at Celia from her place in the center position, Barb said, "Only dribble three times."

Celia didn't understand. "Three times before what?" she asked.

"Three times, period," Coach said. "For three seconds. Then you pass."

Sure she was misunderstanding, Celia said, "But, I mean, how do I get the ball to the basket, then?"

"It's called teamwork, McAlister. A concept you're evidently lacking."

"Don't argue," Carol stage-whispered as Celia opened her mouth again, but she couldn't stop herself.

"I know how to play on a team," she protested. "I play with my brothers all the time."

Coach Vaughn rolled his eyes. "These are girls' rules, McAlister. You are a girl, aren't you?"

Some of the other girls giggled, but Barb looked mortified on Celia's behalf and Judy, she noticed, looked just as astonished as Celia felt. Cheeks burning, Celia pressed on. "But that doesn't make any sense," she said, trying to keep her tone reasonable. *There must be some mistake here.* "Why should my being a girl mean I can't dribble a ball more than three times? It's not like that requires some super strength or something. I mean, it's just a ball…"

She trailed to a stop as the coach's eyes narrowed and his face purpled. "Bench, McAlister," he roared. "Now! Prosky, come in for her."

Carol gave Celia a sympathetic look as they passed each other, but it was a solidarity-against-the-teacher sort of sympathy; she didn't really understand Celia's fury and frustration. Celia slumped down onto the bench and quietly steamed to herself for the rest of the period.

In the showers afterwards, Judy looked over the low tile divider between them. "I don't get it, either," she said, soaping her arms. "I used to play pick-up games on the base in Tokyo all the time, girls and boys together. I never heard of this three-dribble crap."

Celia sighed as she finished rinsing off. "No point trying to fight City Hall, I guess," she said, thinking of how little effect her reasoned arguments about Emmett Till had had on Patty. She hadn't made much of a difference with Carol and Barb's attitudes, either. Dad had told her, after that conversation, "You can't reason people out of a position they didn't reason themselves into." Turned out his advice to keep emotion out of conversations about race were more to save wear and tear on her own feelings than any expectation of changing people. *I bet this girl would listen to reason, though.* "Hey, do you have lunch next period, too?"

Chapter 15.

Monday, December 19, 1955

C elia looked at her fingernails in dismay. After working on them all morning, she'd gone outside for a snowball fight with the other kids and Dad and their newly reunited Uncle Kevin. She'd thought the polish had dried, but when she got back inside and pulled off her mittens, she realized she hadn't waited long enough.

And I wanted them to look nice for Christmas, she mourned, surveying the ruin of her morning's work. She thought she might be developing a bit of a crush on Uncle Kevin. He was good looking and talented and funny, and his being here had made Dad so happy. She found herself hoping he noticed her particularly in the mob of nieces and nephews he'd been introduced to today.

She mentally shook herself. *Don't turn into a ninny like those other girls.* Not only had they carried over their silly club into high school and found a teacher to sponsor them in "domestic arts," Patty had gradually withdrawn from Celia since the Emmett Till conversation, and Carol and Barb couldn't understand Celia's frustration over the girls' basketball rules.

But thinking of her familiar friends reminded her of the new prospect. She draped her damp mittens on the side of the sink in the bathroom she shared with her sisters and went back through the bedroom to the hall phone. She picked it up and dialed 411.

"Information," came the expected voice.

"Oh, hi, Jeanie," Celia said. "It's Celia McAlister."

"Hello, honey, does your mommy know you're on the phone?"

It was an old joke, from when Celia was six and had tried to get the number for the North Pole so she could call Santa. Celia dutifully chuckled, then said, "I want to call a girl named Judy Hartzell. Her family just moved into the area, here in Pine Springs, I think. They're not in the book yet. Her dad's in the navy?"

"I know who you mean. No, I think they live in Newville, actually. Let me take a look." There was a clicking sound and some rustling, then the operator came back on the line. "Here it is," she said. "I was right, it's Newville, so not too far from you."

Once she had the number, Celia pressed her finger down on the telephone's disconnect button and dialed again. Judy answered on the third ring with a prim, "Hartzell residence, Judy speaking, I hope you're calling for me."

Celia laughed out loud. "I am," she said. "This is your lucky day."

"Celia? Oh, thank God. I'm alternating between dying of boredom here and hiding in closets so my mother won't make me hang tinsel on anything else. I think my toothbrush holder is next. What do you want to do?"

Celia was delighted at the warm reception, but immediately a wave of uncertainty washed over her. What if Judy thought what she had to offer was boring or weird? *One way to find out.*

Taking a breath, Celia started, "Well, actually..." Then she chickened out a little and decided to come at it obliquely. "I don't know if you feel like doing anything outside, but I just had a marathon snowball fight with my family and then we built a snowman, so I'm thinking of something indoors."

"Me, too," Judy said. "I've been shoveling the walks, just to get away from the Great Tinsel Marathon of 1955. I've had enough of the winter wonderland. They don't get snow like this in Tokyo."

"They don't usually get it here, either," Celia said. "At least not this much, not before Christmas."

"So anyway, what were you thinking? Playing some records?"

"No—it's not that I don't like music, I do, and I even like listening to it sometimes, but—"

"I know. Sometimes it's Dullsville. So what else?"

Celia licked her lips and cleared her throat. "Uh, sometimes my family likes to, you know, read aloud. So I was thinking maybe you and I could do a story or a play or…"

"*Cyrano de Bergerac!*" Judy exclaimed immediately.

"Oh, perfect!"

"You have it?"

"Sure."

"Ok, I'll bring mine. Listen, I've gotta boogie. I can catch a ride with my brother Rick. He's going into Carlisle but he's about to leave so I'll just have time to get the book and find my shoes."

"Oh, we don't live in Carlisle, but we're on the way." Celia gave her directions to the house.

"Great," Judy said. "See you in a few."

An hour later, they were happily tucked up on the couch in the otherwise empty TV room with their copies of the play, half-finished mugs of cocoa on the coffee table in front of them.

Judy, reading the part of Cyrano, declaimed to Celia's Roxane, "'Your name is like a golden bell hung in my heart, and when I think of you I tremble, and the bell swings, and rings—'"

The door had opened behind them as she read, and suddenly Uncle Kevin was there, leaning over the back of the couch and reciting from memory, "'Roxane! Roxane! Along my veins, Roxane!'" He swung around in front of them and knelt extravagantly at Celia's feet, arms wide.

His blond hair and blue eyes were like Dad's, and the shape of his mouth, but his cheekbones and chin were different, and the glint of mischief in his face was one she'd never seen on her father's.

Then Celia registered that he was mouthing the word "Line," at her.

Flustered, she went to Roxane's response: "'Ay, this is love.'" Then she realized he'd meant for her to cue him his line. She could feel a self-conscious flush rise in her cheeks, but he went into the next passage without a hitch.

> "'Ay, true, the feeling
> Which fills me, terrible and jealous, truly
> Love—which is ever sad amid its transports!
> Love—and yet, strangely, not a selfish passion!
> I for your joy would gladly lay mine own down,
> —E'en though you never were to know it—never!
> —If but at times I might—far off and lonely—
> Hear some gay echo of the joy I bought you!'"

Then he leapt lightly to his feet, pulled off an imaginary hat and swept it before him in a low bow. "Fair desmoiselles, farewell," he said. "I must away. My lord my brother wishes speech with me. Ruby says to tell you there's fresh gingerbread in the kitchen for you and your 'little friend.'"

"'Little friend'!" said Judy. "What am I, Trumpkin the Dwarf?"

Uncle Kevin chortled as he left the room. Judy sank back into the corner of the couch and fanned herself with her book. "Mercy," she said.

"I know," Celia agreed. "Isn't he cute? We've all just met him; he and my dad were estranged for years. He only arrived for the first time this morning, but I think I've already got a crush on him."

"Much good may it do you," Judy said sardonically.

"Well, I realize he's my uncle and all, I just meant—"

"No, I meant he's, you know, tripping the light fantastic."

Celia could see that was supposed to mean something to her other than that Uncle Kevin was a good dancer, but she couldn't imagine what it was.

Judy twisted uncomfortably and said, "I'm not trying to be mean or anything. It doesn't matter to me either way."

"What doesn't? I don't get it."

The other girl took a deep breath. "I mean that your uncle, unless I'm way off base, is queer as a three-dollar bill."

"'Queer as a…'" Celia tried to think where she'd heard that phrase. Once when the boys were talking, and one of Laurie's friends said— "You mean he's homosexual? How could you possibly know that?"

"No, you're right, I couldn't. Forget about it, just forget I said anything. Listen, it's getting late. Should we go grab some of that gingerbread and then finish Act III before my brother gets here?"

"Ok. I'll introduce you to Ruby."

They got up and headed for the kitchen. *Maybe Uncle Kevin will be there,* Celia thought.

Chapter 16.

Barb and Judy had been metaphorically circling each other all afternoon, warily sizing each other up like a couple of squirrels suspecting each other of wanting to encroach on each other's acorn hoards.

Celia snorted to herself at the image, painting colorless nail polish on the small run in the stocking she'd worn last night. "Does that work?" Judy asked interestedly, looking over from the copy of *Playboy* the girls had purloined from under Laurie's bed.

"Sometimes," Celia said. "Better than just throwing them away after one wearing, anyway. At least the run was high up on the thigh, so it won't show."

"And what were you doing to get a run 'high on the thigh,' Celia, huh?" Barb smirked. She was peering into a hand mirror, poking at her auburn hair, which had grown to her shoulders again. Lately she'd been trying to coax it into a Veronica Lake curl over one eye.

Celia huffed in disgust. "That idiot Randy Jorkins made a grab for me behind a potted palm at the Navy Depot New Year's Eve party last night."

"After how nasty he's been to you in school?" Barb exclaimed. "The nerve of him!"

"So it would be ok if he'd been nice to me in school?"

"Well, not if you didn't lead him on or anything, you know," Barb said.

"I was actually back there in the first place because I was trying to get away from him."

"So maybe he thought you were playing hard to get."

"Barb!"

Judy sat upright on Joy's bed, across from Celia's, where she'd been lounging with the magazine. "So either Celia was leading him on or she was playing hard to get, but either way he gets to paw at her?"

"No, of course not," Barb said. "I just meant, you know, it's just natural for boys to take the lead."

"Yeah," Judy said. "Like it's natural for dogs to like to roll in shit. Doesn't mean I have to like it." She went back to the magazine.

The thick silence that settled over the room made her look up again. "What?" she said. "Don't like my language? Sorry. But the fact remains that there's a lot that's 'natural' that we decide not to do. And people—guys, especially, it seems to me—pick and choose what 'natural' behavior they think will let them do what they want in the first place. Take this character Jay Smith. He's got an article here called, 'A Vote for Polygamy,' all about how 'natural' it is for men to want to play the field. But he doesn't mention 'natural' things like wolves, for instance, who mate for life."

"They do?" Celia asked. "Wolves?"

"Yeah. Not only that, greylag geese do too, but sometimes they mate with their own sex."

"Oh, come on."

"It's true. There's a scientist called Konrad Lorenz who's done a bunch of studies. According to him, sometimes a male pair will add a female and the three of them will form a bond. Hey, Celia, think that cute uncle of yours will get busy with your mom and dad?"

"Eww." Celia threw her pillow at Judy, who fielded it one-handed and tossed it back.

"Your uncle's a homo?" Barb whispered.

"That's what Judy thinks," Celia said. "I haven't had a chance to ask Mom about it since he went back to Chicago a few days ago."

"You talk to your mom about stuff like that?" Judy said in surprise.

"She talks to her mom about everything," Barb said darkly.

"Who else am I going to talk to about stuff like that?" Celia said, thinking of Carol and Patty and feeling just as glad they'd declined to come over today. "Girls our age who are just as ignorant as I am?"

"Hey," both other girls said in unison. For once, Judy's voice sounded as squeaky as Carol's.

"Well, sorry, but I trust my mother, who's a psychologist on top of being a very smart lady, to know more than anybody else around about stuff like this."

Barb and Judy looked at each other with more camaraderie than they'd shown so far. Before Celia had a chance to get too irritated by that, Barb gave up on her hair, got up from the desk chair she'd been perched on and threw herself across the foot of Joy's bed, reaching for the *Playboy*.

"Enough of the egghead talk," she said. "I want to see the centerfold."

"Speaking of homos," Judy said, opening the magazine in the middle and passing it to Barb. "You want to ogle pictures of naked women?"

"Don't be silly," Barb said absently, drinking in the photo. "Girls can't be homos. Ooh, gosh, look at the jugs on her!"

Now it was Celia and Judy's turn to roll their eyes at each other.

Celia capped the nail polish bottle and set it on her nightstand, then draped the nylon stocking over the end of her bed to dry and joined the girls on the other bed. She craned her neck to see the magazine over their shoulders.

"Think we'll ever look like that?" Barb asked. Celia thought she sounded almost nervous at the prospect.

"C'mon," Judy answered. "Nobody looks like that."

The model was seated at a vanity table, facing the camera as though the readers were her mirror. Her bare breasts rested on her folded arm; there were diamonds at her neck and ears, and a fluffy white powder puff in her hand.

"Who's that man in the doorway supposed to be?" Celia asked.

"I dunno. Her date?" Barb ventured.

"Then why's he facing away from her?"

"Maybe it's Hugh Hefner," Judy said.

"Still doesn't explain why he's not looking at her." Something about that aspect of the photo made Celia uneasy. "It's creepy," she said.

She pushed herself up off the bed. "Hey, you guys want to read something, or act out a story?"

"Oh, Celia," Barb said. "Sometimes you're so immature."

Chapter 17.

"Unbelievable," Celia sighed happily as Mom got off the narrow couch and twisted the knob to turn the television off.

"Too true," Rob agreed, jumping up from where he'd been sitting on the floor leaning against Laurie's legs by the wicker chair in the corner of the TV room. "Those fireworks were the nuts."

"Never mind the fireworks, I meant the skaters. I wish we could have seen the whole Winter Olympics, the way people in Europe could."

"I think they've been talking about that for next time, in 1960," Mom said. "You're right, Cissy, that little clip they just showed only whetted my appetite for more. I would have loved to see Tensley Albright take the gold."

Laurie snagged a couple of empty Coke bottles, nodding his head. "Especially since she was hurt so badly only a couple of weeks before, cutting her ankle like that. And now she's the first American woman to be Olympic skating champion."

"C'mon, Laur," Rob said impatiently from the door. "I want to show you what I figured out to do on Mom's old guitar."

"Ok, ok, keep your hair on," Laurie said as they left the room.

Celia kept sitting on the couch, staring at the blank TV screen.

"Something on your mind, sweetie?" Mom asked. She came back to the couch and sat down again as Celia shrugged.

"It's just, I don't know, looking at Albright I kept thinking how strong you'd have to be to skate like that." She sighed, then added poisonously, "I bet Coach Vaughn couldn't do half those moves."

Mom huffed a laugh. "I'd hate to see him try, actually. Can you imagine Coach Vaughn in tights and a little skirt, twirling with one foot in the air?"

"Ugh." Celia shuddered. Then she grinned. "I think I'll imagine him that way next time he starts lecturing me about girls' rules and how we're just too delicate to dribble a ball down the court."

"I don't think the rule's only about that," Mom said mildly. "It's supposed to encourage teamwork, so no one person hogs the ball."

Celia shrugged. "Maybe. But that's not the feeling I get when he starts scolding. You know, last week he said it was a waste of time teaching girls sports anyway, since we'll just get married and have kids and never use it."

"Among the many things that are wrong with that remark," Mom growled, "does he think having kids doesn't require a strong, healthy body?"

"Do you think Tensley Albright thinks about that? How skating's going to help her be a mother?"

"I have no idea. I would think she's got enough on her plate at the moment—she's a pre-med student at Radcliffe, you know."

"She is? Where does she get the time?"

"I suppose she's taken leave or something to do the Olympics, but I wouldn't be surprised, with her drive, if she doesn't go on to Harvard Medical and make a whole other career for herself."

"Wow." Celia mulled that over for a minute, then snickered, "Carol says all female athletes are 'queer,' but Barb says it's not possible for a woman to be a homosexual. I don't know which remark is stupider."

"There's a lot of ignorance out there on the subject, for sure," Mom agreed ruefully. "Part of the problem is that a lot of people, even professionals who should know better, don't take female sexuality seriously."

"Why not?"

"Well, my theory is that it's because lesbianism doesn't involve the *sacred sperm,*" Mom said, pronouncing the last two words in a comically exaggerated whisper.

"Oh, horrors," Celia said, clutching her forehead dramatically. Then she went on more seriously, "Um, speaking of sacred sperm..."

"Yes?"

"Judy thinks Uncle Kevin is one."

"A sperm?"

"Mom! A homosexual."

"Yes, he is," Mom said calmly.

"Why? I mean, why would he do something like that? He's so handsome and—you know, got a great personality and everything, he could get a woman to like him easily."

"Honey, there are a number of theories on the causes of homosexuality but the one that I'm sure is not true is the idea that homosexuals just decide to be that way because they want to do evil criminal acts."

"Of course not," Celia said indignantly, thinking of her clever, charming, kind uncle. "But what, then?"

"The most popular theory these days is that they have a psychological illness, caused by traumas in childhood—often blaming the mother, as usual." Mom grimaced.

"But if that's true," Celia objected, "then why isn't Dad one? He had the same mother, and anyway, from what Laurie and Rob say Dad told them, it was their father who was mean to them."

"Yes, that's the biggest flaw in that reasoning," Mom said. "But meeting your uncle and getting to know him has made me surer of something I'd started to think because of some of the kids I treat at Rolling Meadow. I'm coming to the conclusion that some people are attracted to their own sex because they were just born that way."

"Really? Wow, I don't know anybody who thinks that. I wish you could tell me about some of those cases, but I know you can't talk about patients. It must be amazing to be able to get into people's heads that way."

"That may not be the whole story. Sex is a complicated subject, and human sexuality has a lot more variation and subtlety than you'll find looking at pictures of Janet Pilgrim."

Celia nodded, then the full import of what Mom had just said hit her and she felt herself flush red. "You know about that *Playboy?*"

"I spotted it in Laurie's duffel when he got back from Chicago, then I saw it in your room."

"He keeps it under the bed now." Celia bit her lip and said, "Are you mad?"

"No, I'm not. I'm a little concerned, though. It's natural for you, especially at your age, to be interested in sex and looking for information. The trouble is, there's very little available that's realistic, and certainly not *Playboy.* Those photos have been retouched and airbrushed to remove any flaws and imperfections; nobody is as perfect as those women. And that's another problem; the magazine is designed to appeal to men, and treats women only as objects of their desire."

"So you mean I don't have to look like Janet Pilgrim?"

"I mean Janet Pilgrim, whatever her name really is, doesn't look like those photos in real life."

"But I want boys to be interested in me."

Mom stood up. "Look at me," she commanded. "Do I look anything like Janet Pilgrim?"

Celia looked at the familiar, beloved figure and tried to see her as though she didn't know her. Mom was rather heavy in the hips and legs, and kind of flat-chested, she realized. Celia thought her face was beautiful, but she could see how other people might think her Italian features were a little strong. Suddenly she realized the silence had stretched on a little too long. "Oh, Mom," she started apologetically. "You have beautiful eyes, and your hair—"

Mom raised a hand to stop her. "I know what I look like, honey," she said. "I'm not ugly, but I'm no raving beauty, either. Yet I managed to snag the handsomest man I know."

They grinned at each other, then Celia said, "And you have a career, too."

"I do, God help me. And let's not forget my six gorgeous, brilliant, wonderful children."

"No, let's not forget them. However do you manage it all?" Celia laughed.

Mom smiled, but then said seriously, "It isn't easy, Cissy. As I've told you before, I don't know if I'd be able to manage it all without Ruby. As it is, I sometimes feel—"

The door to the TV room opened and Joy looked in. "Mom, phone for you. Someone from Rolling Meadow—some kind of emergency."

Mom rolled her eyes at Celia. "As I was saying…" She hurried out of the room and Celia went back to staring at the empty TV screen.

CHAPTER 18.

SATURDAY, MARCH 31, 1956

Is this a date? Celia wondered.

She supposed it was, since it involved a boy asking her to do something with him. But it was the middle of the day, for one thing; she'd always thought of dates as happening in the evening. For another, they were just having lunch at the diner in Pine Springs—not eating at a real restaurant for dinner, or seeing a movie, or going to a party. That's the sort of thing Jamie did with Rima, or Laurie with Linda now that they were back together.

She shrugged off the thought as the waitress plunked down their burgers and fries. Celia moaned a little as she bit into the soft seeded bun surrounding the beef patty.

The boy sitting across from her—Bobby Jumper, his name was—widened his eyes. "Were you that hungry?" he asked with some distaste.

"Mmm, no, sorry," Celia said, putting down the hamburger and taking a gulp of her chocolate phosphate. "No, it's just that it's Passover; I haven't had any bread with yeast in it for almost a week."

"What's 'Passover'?"

"It's a Jewish holiday. About when Moses led the Israelites out of Egypt?" Bobby looked blank. "Anyway, they didn't have time to make regular bread, so every year for a week Jews eat unleavened bread to commemorate it."

"Sounds stupid."

He didn't seem to think he'd said anything offensive; he was calmly munching away and dipping his fries in ketchup, tilting his head back to get each one into his mouth without dripping on his shirt.

Celia kept her voice even as she said, "Jesus didn't think so. The Last Supper was a Passover meal."

Now he gaped at her. "Why would he do something like that?"

"Because, like I said, it's a Jewish holiday, and Jesus was a Jew."

"No, he wasn't!"

"Of course he was. What do you think he was?"

"A Christian, of course. Everybody knows that."

She opened her mouth to argue, then thought, *Nice first date, Celia. Get into a religious squabble.* So she only said, "You're a Catholic. Ask Father Shea about it some time."

He shook his head at her. They ate in silence for a few minutes, then he said, "Anyway, what's it to you what some Jews did thousands of years ago? You're Catholic too, I see you at Mass."

"My brother Jamie's Jewish."

"Yeah, I heard that. That other brother of yours is colored; that mean you have to eat watermelon?"

What am I doing with this creep? "Bobby, I've known you since we were in fifth grade. How come I never realized you were a prejudiced jerk before?"

She shoved away her half-eaten meal and got up.

"Wait a minute," he said. "What'd I say?"

She hurried out of the diner but he was on her heels, jamming the last of his burger into his mouth and slapping a couple of bills down by the cash register as he followed her out. "Hey, wait up, will you? What are you so mad about?"

"I don't know how to explain it to you," she said.

"Ok, don't explain it. Just don't go nutso on me." He came up beside her and insinuated his hand around her upper arm. "C'mon, baby," he said, lowering his voice to what he probably thought was a sultry tone.

Celia looked at him in disbelief. "'C'mon *baby*'?" she repeated. "Come on where?"

"I thought we could go over to that shed behind the softball field at school, make out a little."

"Jesus Christ!" she exclaimed in disbelief.

"Now, don't be like that. It'll be fun."

"Fun for you, maybe."

"Aw, give me a break," he said. "That Patty Lebo says you're loose."

"I'm *what?*" She didn't know whether the betrayal of her one-time friend hurt worse than the particular accusation.

Bobby, looking at her with narrowed eyes, went on, "Ok, I can see maybe that's not true. But you don't want to get a reputation for being frigid, do you? Besides, I bought you lunch."

Without another word, she jerked her arm out of his hand and started for home, ignoring his plaintive, "Hey, where you going?" and then, huffily, "See if I ever ask you out again, weirdo!"

That afternoon, she went along with Mom and Joy and Laurie to Confession at St. Pat's in Carlisle. It always made her self-conscious to go with them; she felt as if the heavy velvet curtains that closed the confessionals wouldn't keep her words private, though she knew from experience that those in the nearby pews couldn't hear anything but a low murmur of sound from the booths.

She pushed the thought out of her mind. *It's not like you're going to say anything so terrible. Anyway, you want to have Communion on Easter tomorrow.*

So when the panel slid open and Father Shea's familiar silhouette appeared, she began her usual litany of fibs and minor disobedience and fits of temper. Then she said, "I ate meat today, too."

"Did you forget about the Lenten fast?" the priest asked.

"No, I just really wanted it. It was the bread more than the meat; I haven't had any this week, because of Passover. But I wanted the meat, too. I know Lent will be over tomorrow, but I just kept thinking about how good it would taste and I couldn't wait."

"I see. Well—Celia, is it?"

"Yes, Father." She did love Father Shea; he was nothing like the pastor, Monsignor Bucholtz, who was rigid and sour and never gave her the feeling he was even listening in Confession.

"Well, Celia, if the strictures of the Lenten abstinence bother you that much, don't do them."

"I don't understand."

"The Lenten sacrifice is supposed to be joyous. If it's causing you pain, find another way to focus on Our Lord."

Celia was stunned. "I thought it was like iodine, if it doesn't hurt it's not working."

Through the dim screen, she could see his hand go to his mouth; he seemed to suppress a cough, but he only said, "No, child. Pleasing God should be your greatest pleasure."

"Oh. Well, I'm not sure I'm ready for that, but I'll try."

"Good. Was there anything else?"

"Mmm, oh, yeah, I took the Lord's name in vain."

"Were you angry?"

"Not exactly angry, more surprised than anything. This boy I was with wanted to, uh, make out with me."

"And did you?"

"No, sir."

"Then when you say your penance, which will be five Our Fathers and ten Hail Marys, you should also thank God for preserving you from temptation."

"Believe me, Father, it was no temptation at all. Um, Father, maybe you should have a cough drop or something?"

But he simply told her to begin reciting the Act of Contrition while he said the words of absolution.

Chapter 19.

Sunday, May 6, 1956

"**B**ut be ye doers of the word and not hearers only, deceiving your own selves," Father Shea read. Celia's mind had been wandering, but something about that line snapped her attention back. "For if a man be a hearer of the word and not a doer, he shall be compared to a man beholding his own countenance in a glass." *I don't do enough,* she thought. *I just think about my own problems all the time.*

Father Shea was still reading: "And if any man think himself to be religious, not bridling his tongue but deceiving his own heart, this man's religion is vain."

As the meaning of the words sank in, Celia felt a wave of hot embarrassment flow across her face, as though the reading had been directed at her personally. Her blood buzzing in her ears, she lost track of the rest of the readings, numbly standing for the Gospel, then sitting again and losing herself in her thoughts during Father Shea's homily, which she usually listened closely to.

Laurie's friend Roscoe was staying with them for the last month of school. His father had recently been paroled, and his mother had gone along with him to their new home in Chester, but Mom and Dad had offered to let Roscoe stay with them to finish out the year at County High. The past week had been a choppy one.

99

Roscoe was edgy and combative, seeming uneasy living in a house more luxurious than he was used to, and one filled with mostly white people, at that. He'd done some verbal sparring with Celia on Friday night, then disappeared before dinner and not come back until the wee hours, which had triggered a confrontation with Dad the next day.

Celia and the others had sat at the lunch table in the screened porch and listened to the raised voices in the kitchen—Roscoe, Dad, and Laurie. Mom had handed Celia the platter of tuna sandwiches and exchanged a speaking look with Ruby, then the two of them had hurried to the kitchen.

Celia had gone into mother mode, passing the sandwiches and apportioning the Jello mold, starting up a thin line of bright chatter that Rob and Beth joined her in, but Jamie had sat rigid and nervous while Joy slumped dejectedly at the other end of the table, swirling the ice cubes in her glass of punch.

The voices in the kitchen sank to a low murmur, then Dad, Mom, and Ruby had come back into the porch. Dad had rubbed his hands together and said, "I could eat a horse, but I guess I'll settle for tuna sandwiches." Celia wasn't fooled. He'd looked shaken and tender, as though he'd been wounded in some way.

When Laurie and Roscoe joined them, everyone was carefully polite, but Celia knew she wasn't the only one who'd been relieved when the meal was over and everyone could escape to their afternoon activities. She didn't know what, if anything, Laurie and Roscoe had originally planned for the afternoon, but Laurie's girlfriend Linda called—they'd been together again since the Emmett Till murder, but Laurie was still extra careful to be attentive to her. So Celia had found herself stranded alone on the porch with Roscoe and feeling resentful about it.

"So," he'd said to her over the rattle and hum of Joy and Jamie helping Ruby clear up the kitchen, "guess your old man knows how to beat people up without using his fists."

His sly allusion to Dad's having been abused by his violent father, a fact most of his own children hadn't known until recently, had infuriated Celia. "I guess you'd know all about that," she'd snapped. "At least as long as you're here, you know you won't get beaten up by anybody's fists. How's your 'old man,' by the way?"

Roscoe had flinched and snarled and flung himself out of the porch and into the house through the door at the back of the front hall, not to be seen again till dinner, while Celia had wandered out to the hammock to brood.

At the time, she'd felt justified in her ire. Dad had looked so hurt, and Roscoe had been causing minor and major ructions all week. But now, hearing the words of the Epistle, it seemed to her that she'd been enjoying feeling superior, using sharp words to tease and cut this troubling interloper, not "bridling her tongue," but "deceiving her own heart."

Except the words in the passage were "his" and "man," of course, she thought. Then she dismissed the thought—*not the point here.*

After they'd gotten home from Mass and Celia had changed out of her church clothes, she ran into Roscoe in the upstairs hall coming out of the guest room; he'd stayed home with Jamie.

Celia gathered her courage and stopped him with a hand to his elbow. He turned, suspicious and wary.

"Roscoe, I just wanted to apologize," she said. "I shouldn't have spoken to you the way I did yesterday. I was upset because Dad was unhappy, but whatever happened was between the two of you, and what I said hurt you without helping him in any way. And it was way out of line for me to make remarks about your father—I don't know anything about him. I really am sorry."

Roscoe stared into her face for a minute, then down at her hand where it still rested on his arm. "That's two," he said.

"Two?"

"Apologies. In two days. First your dad, now you. I don't know as anybody ever apologized to me for anything before."

She squeezed his forearm. "I bet that's not because nobody ever hurt you before," she said softly.

He pulled his arm away and turned his shoulder to her. "I don't need to be the star of anybody's pity party," he grumbled, but she thought the words lacked conviction.

"Don't worry," she said lightly. "It's too hard to pity a porcupine." The upstairs hall was dim and silent; the others were all downstairs already, waiting for brunch. With sudden resolve, thinking about Mass that morning, Celia said, "Roscoe, God can help, you know." *Oh, God, that sounded preachy and awful. He's going to sneer at me, I know it.*

He was motionless, still looking away from her. Then, almost too low for her to hear, he said, "You think?"

Celia swallowed. "I do. That's how Dad got through his hard times, you know. God, and Ruby. They'll both be there for you if you just ask."

"Just ask."

"I know it sounds hard, but once you start, it's easy. Like me talking to you just now. You just have to trust a little." He twitched his head, a minute nod. *That's enough,* she told herself. Then she said aloud, "Come on, pancakes will be ready soon."

She went down the back stairs into the kitchen with Roscoe trailing behind her. Dad was standing at the stove; the cast iron pancake griddle was just starting to smoke slightly. Celia wrapped her arms around him from behind as he poured the sizzling circles of batter, and rested her head on his back for a second.

"Everything ok, Cissy?" he asked.

"Mmhm," she said. "Just love you."

Dad half turned to wrap an arm around her shoulders and kiss the top of her head. "Love you too, honey," he said.

Celia saw Roscoe push through the swinging door into the dining room, head down and shoulders up.

With an internal sigh, she disentangled from Dad and followed him. At the table, Mom was saying, "That's Methodists, sweetheart. They've had women preachers since their religion started, this is just going back to their roots. But I don't think the Catholic Church is going to let women become priests, not in our lifetime."

Ruby snorted. "In the AME church, women didn't wait for permission from the men to preach. Maybe I should have stayed with them."

Mom nodded at her. "The Catholic world is a man's world, that's for sure."

"It's not fair," Joy sulked.

"No, it's not, but it's the way things are."

"That's one of the things I like about the Society of Friends," Beth put in. "Their women could always preach." Beth had gone from talking about Friends or Quakers as something she'd learned about from a friend to actually making a commitment to them; Celia wasn't sure how she felt about her sister really leaving the Church, and wondered why it made her uneasy when the fact that Jamie wasn't even a Christian didn't bother her at all.

Roscoe drove that thought right out of her head. "Celia would make a good preacher," he said.

Celia bridled for a moment, thinking he was being sarcastic. Then she re-evaluated his tone. *He's looking away from me,* she realized, *not staring the way he does when he's poking at me. He really means it.* She sat back, stunned. *I got through, that soppy little embarrassing exchange meant something to him.*

She wondered why it seemed so important, beyond just making a guest feel better. *Because it means I can help people. I can't be a priest, obviously, but—maybe I could be a psychologist, like Mom? But even Mom couldn't save David… I'll just have to think about it some more.*

Chapter 20.

Thursday, July 19, 1956

Celia tried not to panic when she heard the back door out of the restaurant kitchen slam. She'd known that the Chinese cook, whom everyone called George—she had no idea what his real name was—had been angry about something. The shouted Cantonese had made that obvious enough. His wife, known as Mrs. George, had put in a few soft sentences, among the few Celia had ever heard from her, sounding somehow stubborn and sulky rather than pacifying; whatever she'd said, it had obviously made no difference.

After a couple of minutes of silence from the back, Celia made her way into the kitchen from the front counter. Mrs. George was stolidly chopping bok choy. The GIs who worked as packers and deliverymen, moonlighting from the War College, were perched on their stools in front of the big, deep sinks. Fred was smoking unconcernedly, Jack looked amused, Pablo was deep in thought.

"What happened?" Celia asked the room in general. "Sergeant Ohara?" she said formally. She spoke to Pablo because he was the least likely to condescend to her, and because he shared her amusement that people who saw his name assumed he was Irish, then were taken aback to discover he was Japanese-American. When she'd come to know him well enough to ask, "Um, 'Pablo'?" he'd answered, "Because my real name is Francis Xavier," and been pleased when she'd seen the humor in his having a nickname even farther removed from his Japanese heritage than his real name.

Now, though, he said with some bitterness, "I don't speak Chinese. We're not all alike, you know."

"That's not fair," she said, stung. "You know I don't think like that."

"You think too much," Jack put in. "Pretty little gal like you, gonna hurt your head."

The lines of the unseen alliances in the room shifted; Pablo somehow was suddenly not "one of the guys" but "one of the civilized people." Giving Celia an apologetic grimace he said, "He was mad about the new soy sauce."

"The soy sauce? He doesn't like the quality or something? Does Mr. Huff know?"

"The boss only cares that it's cheaper than what they were using before," Pablo said. "No, it's the brand that's the problem."

Celia picked up one of the packets they included in all the orders. There was a line drawing of a fat, jolly, seated figure grinning on it. "'Laughing Buddha'?" she read. "What's wrong with that?"

"The laughing Buddha is a god," Pablo said. "He brings luck and prosperity." Seeing Celia's face still blank, he went on impatiently, "How would you feel if you went to China and they served you, oh, say, ketchup that said 'Jolly Jesus' on it, with a picture of Jesus cavorting around?"

"Oh," she said, understanding. The conversation was cut off by the sound of the phone in front. The current situation crashed back in on her. "Pablo, what am I going to do?" She checked the watch Mom and Dad had given her for her fifteenth birthday a couple of months ago. "It's after five o'clock. There are already dozens of

106

orders waiting out there, and here's somebody calling with another one. Is George coming back?"

"Probably," he said.

"But what should I do?"

"Keep on keeping on," he said unhelpfully. "Better catch that phone."

An hour later, the little front room of the China Box was filled with angry people. George had come back after half an hour and set to cooking with his usual ferocious skill, but they were still running forty-five minutes behind on the orders. Celia had been telling people on the phone that they couldn't get a slot sooner than 7:15, but the orders she'd taken earlier were still fluttering on their spikes on the wall, disturbed by the milling of the dissatisfied customers in front of her.

Fred brought a big brown paper sack out. Celia read the name off the order slip stapled to the top of it and took the grumbling customer's money, bruising her hip as she caught the cash register drawer against it. Another man was in front of her, complaining loudly.

"What was the name, sir?" she asked patiently.

When he told her, she checked the order board. Her patience suddenly snapped. "Sir," she said firmly, "your order is for 6:15. It's not going to be ready at 6:15, but it's only 6:00 now, so you can't yell at me until then."

Before he could respond, a woman shoved the man aside. "I placed this order yesterday," she exclaimed. "I have a dozen ten-year-olds at home, waiting for their birthday party dinner. How much longer is it going to take?"

"I'm terribly sorry, ma'am, but I can't make it come any sooner. The cook is working as fast as he can."

"You shouldn't have taken so many orders if he can't fulfill them on time. How old are you, anyway?"

"Usually he can do this many," she said, avoiding the question about her age. "There was a—a bit of a holdup today."

"What about my order?" another woman asked.

She gave her name and Celia turned to check. Then the man who'd shouted at her was in front of her again. She prepared to defend herself. "I apologize," he said. "You're absolutely right about it not being time for my order yet. And in any case, whatever's gone wrong, it's obviously not your fault. I shouldn't have berated you about it."

For the first time since this catastrophe began, Celia felt tears forming in her eyes. The man evidently realized his kind tone had gotten behind her defenses. He flapped his hands at her, backing away. She choked back the tears, nodding at him, and firmed her resolve to deal with the next order, which had just come out of the kitchen. *I can do this.*

By 8:30, they were all caught up: the orders filled, the board empty, the phone blessedly silent. In the kitchen, the guys were hosing out the woks and stacking up the piles of folded boxes, ready for tomorrow's orders. Celia was just finishing totting up the day's receipts and tucking the cash into the night deposit bag when Marie, the manager, came in.

She looked around the quiet, empty room that had so recently been a roiling mass of angry, complaining people. "One of your customers tonight was a friend of mine," she explained at Celia's surprised look. "He called me and said you were in trouble and might need help."

"It's ok," Celia said. "Thanks anyway."

"I know this job isn't very satisfying," Marie said. "You're going to college someday and all, you have better things in front of you. But you can learn from dealing with things like this."

Celia thought about the crisis there'd been with Linda's friend Sydney last month. Linda had called at midnight, frantic that the other girl had taken an overdose of pills. Mom and Ruby had gone over with Laurie immediately and dealt with the situation; Celia, hearing the commotion from her room, had felt almost resentful that no one was asking for her help, then foolish: what could she have done? She was awed at Mom and Ruby's cool competence. Sydney was in a mental hospital in Philadelphia now. Closer to home, Celia was beginning to worry about Carol, who seemed increasingly erratic and temperamental.

Marie's right, she realized. *I can use what I learn here to deal with other upsets.*

"It's all right," Celia repeated. "I handled it."

CHAPTER 21.

WEDNESDAY, SEPTEMBER 12, 1956

The day had been warm, but it was cool now—perfect sleeping weather. Still, Celia couldn't sleep. *Should have said something when Mom and Dad came in to kiss us goodnight,* she told herself. *It would be making too much of it to say something now.*

So if that would be making too much of it, why couldn't she relax? She tried saying the rosary in her head, the way Mom and Ruby sometimes did when they were troubled; even by herself, the repetitions of the prayers and the meditative focus often calmed her. She chose the Joyful Mysteries to put herself in a better frame of mind, but stalled on the first one. The Annunciation: the angel telling Mary that, though she was a virgin, she would give birth to Jesus, sired by the Holy Ghost.

Wonder if the Holy Ghost likes sweaters? she couldn't help but think. Then she gave a silent snort. *Ok, that's it.*

She got out of bed, put on her robe and slippers, and padded out into the hall and around the abutment to the right, to the door of Mom and Dad's room. Their light was still on; she rapped softly and pushed the door open to Mom's "Come in."

Mom was just turning from braiding her long, dark hair for the night. Celia could see in the mirror behind her where she'd missed a few wispy strands. Dad was ready for bed, too, standing near the foot of it. "I was just about to hit the head," he said. "I'll be right back— don't start without me. Unless you need to talk to your mother alone?"

The offer was tempting, but Celia told herself sternly not to go all missish. "No, I'll wait for you," she said. "Take your time, nothing's on fire or anything."

She shucked her robe and slippers and crawled into their bed and Mom slid in beside her, pulling the big patchwork quilt over them both. It had been a long time since Celia had looked at it closely. She fingered one of the squares that had the symbol signifying her on it— a child's block sporting the letter "C." Laurie's was like it, only with an "L"; there were the Hebrew letters meaning "life" for Jamie; Beth's was an angel, Rob's a pair of sneakers; Joy's squares had appliqued flowers on them. There were gemstones for Ruby, an anchor for Dad, and the Greek letter "Psi" for Mom, because she was a psychologist. The whole quilt was bordered with the McAlister tartan.

"Why are there still some blank squares?" she asked.

"In case more children come along," Mom said.

"'Come along'?" Celia squeaked in alarm. "You and Dad aren't trying to…"

"No," Mom said. "That's not what I meant. I mean children who might happen into our lives, that fate or God or the vagaries of the juvenile justice system bring our way. I had thought David was one of those, but it wasn't to be." She brooded for a minute, then said more briskly, "Not that it's any of your business what your father and I do in our—personal lives."

Celia could hear Dad brushing his teeth; he'd be out with them soon. "Well, it's a little my business," she said. "It would affect all of us to have a new baby in the house, and it would be kind of embarrassing for all my friends to know—"

Mom raised an eyebrow. "'To know'? Do you, or they, suppose their parents have stopped being intimate now that they've achieved the lot of you as the pinnacle of their lives' goals?"

"Ok, ok," Celia said, laughing a little as she covered her ears with her hands. Then she dropped them and said seriously, "But this all does have something to do with what I wanted to talk to you about."

Dad got into bed on the other side, smelling of Dial soap and mint. Celia snuggled down, bracketed by her parents.

Mom said, "Sex? Did you have some questions? I know that last time we talked, you seemed to have a pretty good grasp of—"

"No," Celia interrupted. "I get the whole birds and bees thing. It's just that Coach Vaughn said something in Health class today that really bothered me, and I'm not sure why. Maybe I'm making a mountain out of a molehill, but I just can't stop thinking about it."

"What was it?" Dad asked.

"He was talking about sex, in that mushy, roundabout way they always do in school, you know, and my mind was sort of drifting, and then I heard him say, 'Girls, would you wear a sweater someone else had already worn? Well, boys feel the same way.'"

Repeating the remark, Celia felt a little silly; it seemed trivial and stupid here and now. But her parents' reactions told her it didn't seem so to them; they obviously thought what Coach had said was offensive and inappropriate.

Mom breathed in sharply and Dad swore under his breath. Then he said, "I'll break his neck."

"You'll do nothing of the kind," Mom said, but Dad's threat—though she knew it wasn't literal—caused a little warm glow under Celia's breastbone.

A few years ago, back when Jamie was in eighth grade, a teacher had been mean and unfair to him, and according to Jamie Dad had marched over to the school in full Navy Commander mode and verbally crushed the teacher like a bug while the principal hovered ineffectually. At the time, she'd been awed that her own father could wield such power, and pleased that he'd come to Jamie's rescue, but a small part of her had been jealous, as well: Jamie got a lot of attention because his years as a small child in a Nazi concentration camp had left him with flashbacks and nightmares and other problems, and it sometimes seemed to Celia that nobody ever noticed her.

Then she was ashamed of feeling that way; of course Jamie needed for the family to rally around him and comfort him when he woke screaming, and to keep dogs and even pictures of rats away from him—that's what families were for. And of course she didn't wish she'd had those horrible experiences herself. And finally, of course it wasn't true that no one noticed her; it was more that they didn't worry about her. She just didn't usually need the same kind of emergency attention some of the others did. Still, it was nice to have evidence that when something did happen she needed help with, Dad would be just as quick to rally to her aid.

And Mom, of course, who was now saying that, as a woman and a psychologist, she should be the one to confront "Mr. Vaughn."

"He likes to be called 'Coach,'" Celia said.

"I'm sure he does," Mom said darkly. "And I'm sure he likes to strut in front of a classroom of adolescents and say disgusting things, but he's not going to get away with it. I don't know why they let gym teachers teach Health class, anyway. They're usually not at all trained. Just because they know how to use their bodies effectively doesn't mean they actually understand anything about them." She flounced on her side, turning toward Celia, and punched her pillow.

"So what he said," Celia ventured, "I don't quite get why it made me feel so... icky."

"Good word for it," Mom said. "It's because he was implying that girls are nothing more than a garment or some sort of object that can be spoiled or tainted by her actions, and that her worth is nothing more than her bodily functions."

"And," Dad put in, "that the only reason for deciding whether or not to engage in sexual activity is what boys might think about it. It's an attitude that's insulting to boys, too, by the way, implying that they would be that superficial and think about girls as objects."

Celia nodded as the reasons for her unease crystallized. She pursed her lips and blew out in relief. "Ok," she said. "I see. He seemed so sure, though, and he's always talking about how he's certified in sports medicine."

"Must have gotten his certificate out of a Wheaties box," Mom scoffed. "I'll have a thing or two to say about that tomorrow, as well."

By the time she got back into her own bed, Celia was feeling much better. Still, her sheets were cold and she was a little shaky from reaction.

"Cissy, do you want me to come in with you?" Joy's voice came from the other bed.

"That'd be nice," Celia admitted. She lifted the covers to let Joy slip in. As she curled around the warm body of her little sister, she felt herself relax at last. Mom would take care of everything tomorrow. Celia could picture her striding in, briefcase in hand, in full psychologist mode with an overlay of Angry Mother. She almost felt sorry for Mr. Vaughn.

Chapter 22.

Thursday, November 22, 1956

Beth handed the turkey platter up to Celia where she perched on top of the kitchen stepstool and Celia stretched to slot it into place in the cupboard over the refrigerator. "That's that till Christmas," she said as she stepped back down.

"And that's the kitchen for now, isn't it?" Beth asked, skimming her hands over the empty drain board.

"Looks like it," Celia agreed. "Finally. Seems like there should be more than two of us on kitchen duty for Thanksgiving, doesn't it?"

Beth made the little body twitch that she did where sighted people would shrug. "Ruby's exhausted after all that cooking, of course. She's in her room, listening to her Gilbert and Sullivan records. Dad and the boys are watching the football game, but they all have other things occupying their minds," she said. "Then Laurie's going to be calling Roscoe to talk about the end of the bus boycott in Alabama. Jamie's not interested in the game, but he had a hard time getting through the meal in the first place; he needs to be away from the kitchen right now. Joy's upstairs writing a poem." She stopped and bit her lip, then went on, "And Rob—Robbie still hasn't gotten over that quarrel he had with Laurie last year, you know. Things are all right between them, but he's struggling to figure out some things

115

about himself and where he belongs, in the family and in the world. I gave him a book I thought might help; he's reading it now."

How did I not know all that? Celia wondered. She smiled at her sister. "Everybody comes to you with their troubles, don't they, Beth?"

Beth smiled back. "I'm just a sounding board. They bounce their worries off me and that makes it clearer what they need to do, without me doing anything."

"I don't think it's that simple. You're just really good at listening."

"Did you want me to listen to something? I thought you'd rush off to the game as soon as we finished here, but I noticed you were pretty quiet at dinner, and while we were washing the dishes. Is Coach Vaughn still giving you a hard time?"

Celia let the mask she felt she'd been wearing for days fall away; Beth couldn't see her face, in any case. *Maybe that's why it's easy to talk to her.*

"You're right," she said, reaching forward to tweak Beth's bent collar into place over the silk scarf she had knotted around her neck. "I have been upset lately. But not about Coach Vaughn: whatever Mom said to him that day, she got him treating me—and the other girls, too—like we're made of cut glass. Kind of annoying, really, especially since he seems to have missed the point. But kind of funny, too, to see him dancing around us." She sighed and rubbed a finger across her lip. "No, it's something else, maybe nothing, but I don't really think so. I'm worried about Carol. You're away at school a lot, but you must remember my friend Carol Prosky?"

"The one with the little girl voice?"

Celia hadn't thought of her that way before, but suddenly realized Carol's voice in fact sounded like a little girl's. "Yeah, that's her," she said.

116

"What's the matter with her?"

"I'm not sure. Maybe nothing. But I keep thinking about that girl Sidney, Linda's friend, how last spring Linda and Laurie thought there was something off about her and Linda even got Mom to recommend a counselor for her, but she ended up trying to kill herself anyway."

Beth frowned, rubbing her upper arms as though she'd suddenly gotten chilly. "You think Carol wants to commit suicide? Like David?"

"No, no," Celia said hurriedly. "I don't think it's that bad. It's just that she's been so quiet lately, not like her, and then every now and then she gets mad for no reason. And—" Celia caught herself, looking at Beth's worried face. *She seems so mature, but she's really only just turned fourteen. I shouldn't lay this on her.*

Aloud she said, "You know, talking to you makes me realize I really need to ask Mom about this."

Beth's face cleared. "Good idea," she said. "I mean, I'd help if I could, but—"

"No, you have helped. As usual, talking to you makes me realize what I'm thinking. Thanks, Angel."

She leaned forward and kissed Beth's cheek before her sister had a chance to object to the nickname she'd been trying to get them all to stop using.

Beth kissed her back while swatting at her arm in reproach, then turned and trotted up the back stairs, blonde hair bobbing in the ponytail she'd caught it up in to do the dishes.

Celia watched her go, then made her way through the dining room, assuming she'd find Mom in the study. Instead, she was there in the living room, sitting on one of the settees with her back to Celia.

"Oh, there you are," she said. Then she saw that Jamie was sitting on the facing settee. *They must have been talking.* "Sorry, am I interrupting something?"

"No," Jamie said, getting up. "I was just leaving."

Celia watched him stride out of the room, wondering uneasily whether she'd derailed some important conversation, but Mom, head craned around to face her, patted the seat cushion next to her. "Something on your mind, sweetie?"

Celia sat down and snuggled into Mom's side and repeated what she'd just told Beth. She'd half hoped Mom would dismiss it all as typical teenaged angst, but when Celia had finished Mom looked thoughtful and concerned.

"Have you noticed any change in her eating habits?"

Celia sat up. "Yeah!" she exclaimed. "She used to fuss about her figure and watching her weight, but lately she's been stuffing herself. At lunch in the cafeteria she always gets potatoes or macaroni, when she used to pass them by, and sometimes she eats two desserts. Does that mean something?"

"Maybe," Mom said. "What's her relationship like with her parents?"

"Hard to say. I don't see them together much. You know, they have that great big house, but she almost never invites us over." Celia licked her lips, hesitating and twisting her ankles around each other. Then she whispered, "She said once that she hates her mother."

Celia had been shocked. Now Celia thought maybe Carol had seen her shock and it had made her clam up. *I should have just listened without judging, the way Beth does. And Mom.*

Mom now didn't look shocked, she was ruminating with her lips pressed in a thin line. Then she said, "What about her father?"

"She never talks about him at all. Though she once said something about him hitting—I don't know whether she meant herself or her mother."

Mom took Celia's hand and stroked the back of it, gazing across the other settee and out the bay window at the icy drizzle beyond. After a few minutes she said, "I think you should keep me apprised about how she's doing."

"You suspect something specific?"

"'Suspect' is a little strong; let's just say I'm concerned and I'd like to know more."

"You don't think she's going to try to kill herself, like Sidney—or David—do you?"

"Let's not get ahead of ourselves. Just keep being a good friend to her, listen to her if she wants to talk. You could even ask her if there's anything bothering her. I can recommend a counselor, if she doesn't want to talk to me. If she does do anything that looks like it could be self-destructive, let me know *immediately*. Otherwise, unless and until she shares what's going on, there's not much we can do."

Celia felt a weight on her shoulders. This seemed like a lot of responsibility. On the other hand, she was proud that Mom thought she could handle it, and pleased that she was taking Celia's concerns seriously.

But she also had a more frivolous concern: she was missing the football game. *How can the Lions score their usual win against the Packers without me there to cheer them on?*

Before she gave herself over to relaxation, she turned and gave Mom a hard hug. "Thanks," she said. "I can't say I exactly feel better, but it's… a better kind of bad. Know what I mean?"

"Oh, yes, I do," Mom said.

Chapter 23.

Saturday, December 22, 1956

Part 1

"'If I live to be a hundred
I shall never know from where
Came those ribbons, scarlet ribbons,
Scarlet ribbons for her hair.'"

As the chorus finished the song about the father fruitlessly seeking his daughter's heart's desire only to find it miraculously provided for him, Celia realized that Carol, standing on the choir bench beside her, had fallen silent. Mrs. Hunt, turning to bow to the audience with her conductor's baton held across her substantial bosom swathed in black silk, hadn't seemed to notice.

The Christmas program was over. The others were filing off the stage. Celia jerked the sleeve of Carol's choir gown and her friend followed almost mechanically, not answering Celia's sharp whisper, "Are you all right?"

The backstage area was crammed with performers and their families, hugging and laughing, wishing each other Merry Christmas.

Celia got separated from Carol in the crush. Her own family found her, and she absently accepted their congratulations.

Mom leaned to hug her. "Wonderful show, sweetie," she said. "You all really brought Christmas this year. Are you ready to go?"

"No," Celia said, "I have to return my gown to the chorus room. And I need to find Carol; I think she's upset about something."

Mom looked concerned. "Do you want me to go with you?"

Celia was tempted, then thought that whatever was bothering Carol might be something she'd rather not talk about in front of an adult. "That's ok," she said. "You and Dad go on to the party at the Post. Laurie and Linda can take me there."

"Well, if you're sure…" Mom said doubtfully.

"Really." Celia put more confidence in her voice than she felt. *I'm probably making a big deal out of nothing, anyway.*

She went downstairs and hung her robe on the rack with the others. Only a couple of stragglers were still here, and they soon disappeared. Celia scrubbed her hands through her hair and wondered where Carol might be, or if she had already left herself.

She poked her head into the girls' bathroom on this level and called, "Carol? You in here?"

There was silence, but something made her step inside. Glancing along the line of stalls, Celia saw feet in Carol's new black pumps below one of the doors. "Carol? Are you sick? What's going on?"

There was no answer. *Maybe she's crying, and doesn't want me to know.* She moved forward to the stall, but she couldn't hear anything from behind the door. "Carol? Carrie? Come on out, kiddo, tell me what's wrong."

Still silence. "Ok, don't tell me if you don't want to, just come out, will you? You're starting to scare me here."

Not even a rustle. "Well, I hope you're decent, because I'm coming in." Celia shook the rickety door till the latch fell open. Even the rattling and banging hadn't produced a reaction from Carol; Celia was really getting scared now.

She was relieved for a second when she finally pulled the door away. Carol wasn't being sick, and didn't seem hurt. *No blood,* Celia thought, realizing that the story of David's suicide in a hospital bathroom had been at the back of her mind.

Still, something was seriously wrong. Carol was sitting on the toilet seat, fully clothed, hands in her lap and eyes fixed somewhere over Celia's shoulder. She didn't react at all to Celia's frantic questions, or even to her tugging on the sleeve of the choir robe she still wore. Finally, Celia took both Carol's hands and bodily pulled her to her feet.

But as soon as Carol was upright, she tipped forward. Celia thought she was leaning in for a hug and let go of her arms so she could wrap her own around her, but Carol just kept tilting, rotating slowly till she had collapsed bonelessly onto her back on the floor, curly brown hair spread about her head, open eyes staring at the ceiling.

Celia knelt beside her on the cold tiles, calling her name and lightly tapping her face. She wondered whether she should slap her, but found she couldn't bring herself to do it. Instead, she jumped up and filled her cupped hands with water from the sink and splashed it onto her friend's face. To her terror, Carol didn't even twitch.

"I'll be right back," she said. "I'm going to get help. Don't—" She caught herself on the brink of saying, "Don't move." Instead, she said as she backed away from the crumpled figure, "Don't worry. Everything will be all right," hoping desperately that it was true.

Someone had turned off the lights in the chorus dressing room. The stairs were only lit by the dim red glow of the Exit sign. Celia took the steps two at a time and burst into the backstage area. There was no one there. *Where are Laurie and Linda?* she wondered, feeling betrayed and abandoned, then remembered that she hadn't gotten to them to tell them she needed a ride.

She ran onto the darkened stage. In the shadows at the back of the auditorium, she thought she saw someone move. "Help!" she called. "Is someone there? I need help!"

The burst of relief she felt as a flashlight came on and the burly figure of the school janitor, Mr. Demby, shuffled into an aisle, was short lived. "What are you still doing here?" he snapped. "Students are not allowed in the building after hours."

"I was here for the—never mind," she said. "There's a girl who's sick downstairs in the bathroom."

"Well, send her home, then. Students are not allowed—"

"I know, I heard you the first time." Celia realized she should have moderated her tone. Mr. Demby stopped moving toward her and folded his arms across his chest. "Sorry," she forced herself to say more calmly, "I'm just upset. I can't send her home, she can't move."

"Well, she can't stay here," he said stubbornly.

"What am I supposed to do?"

"Not my business. You better do something, though. I'm locking up in ten minutes; after that, you won't be able to get out of the building."

Celia pushed away her disbelief and outrage; she needed to concentrate on how to help Carol. All her family except for Ruby would be at the War College party. Ruby was out for the evening; she'd come to last night's performance. Celia couldn't remember which friend she was visiting tonight. Celia was reluctant to call Carol's parents, thinking that they were more likely to be part of the problem than the solution, but she couldn't think of anyone else.

"Please," she said to Mr. Demby. "I'll try to get help, but please don't lock up till I can find someone to get us out of here."

"Better hurry," he growled.

Celia hopped off the stage and ran up the shadowy aisle. There was a pay phone in the hall outside the auditorium. She pushed the dime in with shaky fingers, dialed Carol's number, then listened as the ringtone echoed hollowly in her ear, over and over. At twenty-five she gave up.

She stood there with her hand holding down the disconnect lever, thinking frantically. Then she remembered that there'd be staff on the night shift at Rolling Meadow. Mom complained sometimes that they were underpaid and under-qualified, but Celia was desperate.

She needed the front desk number, not Mom's office, which of course would be empty now. She fumbled with the phone book on its chain, dropping it twice before she could get it open and tilted toward the phone booth's automatic light. She fished her dime out of the coin return slot and tried the number she found; this time there was an answer.

"This is Cecelia McAlister, Dr. McAlister's daughter," she said at the lackadaisical greeting from the other end.

"Dr. McAlister is not available at this time." The woman's voice was bored.

"I know that. I'm calling because I need some help, and I can't reach my mother. Could I talk to the therapist on duty, please?"

"This is not an emergency psychiatric service. The person you are speaking of is here to attend the residents of this facility."

"I know that," Celia repeated. "It's just that I have an emergency situation and I don't know who else to call. I'm at County High School with a friend and she's just... I don't know how to describe it. She's collapsed, but she doesn't seem to be unconscious, her eyes are open, but she won't answer when I talk to her, and even when I sprinkled cold water on her, she didn't—"

"Why would you pour cold water on her?"

"I didn't *pour* it on, I sprinkled a little, to try to wake her up."

"But you said she wasn't unconscious."

"No, but she's not responding to anything. Please, I don't know what to do."

"What is it you think that I can do?"

"Help me! The janitor says he's locking up the building and we won't be able to get out after that."

"He can't do that."

"Well, can I put him on the phone so you can tell him that? And could you put the therapist on the phone for me?"

"Certainly not. I've said before, this facility does not exist to give advice to random people on the phone. This is not something a teenager should be trying to deal with, in any case. You need to consult an adult."

"That's what I thought I *was* doing!" Celia knew it was a mistake as soon as she said it.

The woman's voice was colder than ever as she said, "I'm sure your mother will know what to do. You should contact her." With a click, the connection was severed.

Celia slumped onto the phone booth's narrow triangular seat. She closed her eyes and prayed, "Please, God, show me what to do."

When she opened her eyes, Mr. Demby was standing outside the phone booth, an unlikely savior. *Any port in a storm.* Celia suddenly understood a phrase she'd heard from Dad. "Mr. Demby?" she quavered, prepared to go back to begging him not to lock them in.

But the man didn't look hostile and aggrieved the way he had before. He was actually wringing his hands. "What's wrong with her?" he quavered at Celia. "I went down there and yelled at her, I thought you kids were playing some kind of prank, but she—what's wrong with her?"

"I don't *know!* What should I do? I can't reach anybody." Celia racked her brain. "I could try to call the Post, I guess, but there's sure to be a mob there, and I don't know if I could convince anyone to go over to the Officer's Club and try to find my parents, and anyway, what could they—"

"An ambulance," Mr. Demby broke in. "Call an ambulance, get her to a hospital."

"Oh, yes," she breathed. "Thank you." *Why didn't I think of that?*

Chapter 24.

Part 2

Afterwards, Celia could never remember much about the ambulance ride. She remembered Mr. Demby convincing the skeptical ambulance attendants that Carol really needed to go to the hospital, and that Celia had to go with her, since she'd be required to give information at the hospital and she had no other way to get there. She remembered him helping her to wrestle off Carol's choir robe and drape her coat over her recumbent figure on the gurney for the short trip from the school door to the ambulance. And she could see him standing in the glow of the streetlight outside the school, arms akimbo, already drawing back over himself the cloak of gruff, aloof competence she was used to. As he'd receded from the view of the rear ambulance window, she'd thought, *Janitor. But some people call them custodians.*

Aside from that moment, she could only recall a confusion of light and shadow, noises and unanswerable questions, jolting, swaying movement and an abrupt stillness. Then she was inside the hospital's dingy waiting room, giving the woman behind the desk Carol's name and address and her parents' names and phone number. Then the woman started on a list of other questions about Carol's medical

127

history and insurance that Celia had no idea about. All she knew was that they'd wheeled her friend down the hall and through some doors.

"I need to go to her," she said desperately.

"Just have a seat and someone will be out to—"

Celia whirled away and ran for the swinging doors. "Stop! Young lady, you get back here right—"

The voice faded as the doors swung shut behind Celia. Ahead she could see a man's feet behind a curtain. She dashed over and slipped inside the curtain herself, expecting to be scolded and sent away, determined not to leave.

Instead, the man—a young man, she vaguely realized, in a short white coat—looked up from Carol and slipped the earpieces of the stethoscope had been using back down around his neck. "What have you girls been up to?" he said sternly.

"What do you mean, 'up to'?"

"Is this some kind of joke? Because I can tell you, we're very busy with people who are actually sick around here."

"Of course it's not a joke! *Look* at her!"

Carol lay on the gurney, one arm twisted awkwardly behind her, unruly hair tousled, open eyes still staring at the ceiling.

The doctor—*probably an intern,* Celia thought—did look, but his expression did not soften. "What is she on?" he asked.

Celia could have stamped her foot with frustration. "She's on a hospital gurney, obviously."

He took a menacing step towards her. "I mean what drugs has she taken?"

"I don't know; none, I think. I mean, we were in a concert and she'd been singing right beside me for an hour and then she suddenly stopped. I lost track of her for a few minutes, and when I caught up with her again she was like this."

The intern had been snapping his fingers in Carol's face as Celia talked. Now he rolled his eyes disbelievingly and moved around Celia to the foot of the gurney. He pulled the sheet up to reveal bare feet. Celia noticed for the first time that Carol was in a hospital gown. *Someone must have undressed her while I was fighting with that gorgon at the desk. Hope it wasn't this jackass.*

The jackass—from this angle, Celia could see the name "Dr. Evans" embroidered on the pocket of his white coat—was opening a small packet he'd fished from a drawer in a cabinet beside him. He pulled out a small needle and... and... *My God, he's poking her foot with it.*

"What are you *doing?*" Celia shouted. "Stop that!"

Instead, he started digging the needle deeper into Carol's toe and grinding it around. After a second he dropped it onto a tray and reached inside the jacket he was wearing under the coat. He pulled out a book of matches, lit one, and held it to the sole of Carol's foot.

"No!" Celia screamed. She lunged forward and knocked his hand away, but he'd already been pulling back. He stood there, mouth agape and eyes bulging, staring at Carol while the match burned down to his fingers.

He flicked it out with a muffled curse and turned on Celia. "What's wrong with her?" he said in a panicked voice.

Celia thought she might explode from frustration and fear. Then an unbelievably welcome voice said from behind her, "Hysterical conversion, unless I miss my guess." Mom moved to Carol's side and said to her unresponsive face, "It's ok, honey, we're going to take care of you."

"She can't hear you," Evans said sharply.

Mom turned on him with a look that had quelled better men than he. "And you're an expert on the condition... *Doctor?*"

"What, this hysterical whatever-you-said? Never heard of it."

"I have no doubt."

"And who are you, anyway? Who let you in here?"

"Dr. Martha McAlister. I am a certified clinician at the Rolling Meadow Juvenile Remedial Institution, with privileges at this hospital. I'm a psychologist and this is a psychological disorder. You can leave her to me now."

"Oh, psychological," Evans said dismissively. "I thought it couldn't be real."

Celia was only dimly following the conversation. Her knees were rubbery with relief and she grasped the bedrail to steady herself.

Mom said, "Honey, you don't need to be here any more. You've done very, very well getting her here and standing by her," now she shot a scornful look at Evans, "but you can let me take over now. Your dad's in the waiting room, why don't you join him? I'll let you know what's happening with Carol when I know more myself."

Celia made her way back to the waiting room on shaky legs and fell into Dad's arms. Finally, she could cry. He stood there rubbing her back and making soft shushing noises, but she couldn't seem to get hold of herself. Finally he sat back down in the chair he'd risen from when she came out, pulling her down onto his lap. Gradually, she calmed down. She thought she ought to be embarrassed at behaving so childishly in a public place, but was too tired to care.

She did lift her head enough to ask, "How did you and Mom find us?"

"When Laurie and Linda showed up at the party without you, we went over to the school. We got there just as Mr. Demby was getting in his car."

Celia nodded and rested her head back on his shoulder.

"How is Carol?" Dad asked.

"I don't know. She couldn't move or talk, Dad, but her eyes were open. I think she knows what's going on. It was awful." She shuddered, and Dad tightened his hold. "Then that stupid intern started poking her with needles, and he lit a match and held it on her *foot!*"

She cried a little again at that, and Dad rocked her in his arms till she quieted. The doors to the outside swished open and a blast of cold air came in. "Ah," Dad said, "here are the Proskys; I called while you two were in there with Carol. They had just gotten home. Stan," he said over Celia's head, "Martha's in with Carol now. Celia says she—"

Celia sat up while Dad was talking and turned to reassure Carol's parents. Her mouth froze open when she saw the fury and disgust on Mr. Prosky's face. "Just who do you think you are, young lady?" he snarled.

Chapter 25.

Celia shrank back against Dad's chest as Mr. Prosky loomed over her. Behind her, she could see Mrs. Prosky disappearing through the doors to the treatment area, leg brace thumping on the hospital linoleum.

Mr. Prosky was still snarling. "Do you have any idea what an ambulance costs? No, of course you don't, you're the pampered princess, aren't you, you and your whole family, sticking your noses in—"

"Now, just a damn minute," Dad said with steel in his voice. "I realize you're upset, Stan, but there's no call to—"

"Don't you tell me what to do, sailor boy. I'm not one of your minions."

Celia felt Dad take a deep breath. Then he said more calmly, "I'm not trying to tell you what to do, Stan. But you must see that Celia did the only thing she could to help. As I understand it, Carol suffered some sort of collapse and the school was about to be locked. There was nothing else Celia could have done."

"My daughter didn't 'suffer' anything, McAlister," Mr. Prosky barked. "She's just being dramatic, as usual."

"Oh, no, Mr. Prosky," Celia said. "It was real. She didn't respond to anything, even when they poked her with needles. Mom said it was… hysteria, or something like that."

"When I want your opinion on my own daughter, I'll ask for it. You've done enough tonight, putting my wife and me to all this trouble and expense."

"I'll pay for the damned ambulance, if that's what's bothering you," Dad snapped. "Now why don't you join your family instead of abusing mine."

"Family," Mr. Prosky scoffed. "Bunch of mongrels and misfits; I know all about your so-called 'family'. And I see you and that phony 'doctor' wife of yours are in a fair way to making this one unfit for human society, too."

Dad gasped, but remained silent as Celia burrowed her head into his chest, trying to escape the hurtful words. Then she heard Carol's high little voice, saying uncertainly, "Daddy?"

Celia's friend was dressed again, in the white blouse and pleated navy skirt the girls had all worn under their choir robes. The concert seemed to have happened a hundred years ago; Celia glanced at the clock and saw it was well after midnight now.

Mom and Mrs. Prosky were holding Carol up on either side. Mom started to move away with an understanding smile at Mr. Prosky, but instead of taking her place, he turned on his heel and stormed out of the building.

"He's upset," Mrs. Prosky quavered.

Mom started to speak, caught Dad's eye, and closed her mouth again.

Carol was looking at Celia as though unaware of anyone else.

"How are you feeling?" Celia asked her.

"Better," Carol said softly. "Thanks. I mean, thank you, Celia, for—you know, taking care of me."

"Yes, thank you," Mrs. Prosky said. "Now I think we could all use some rest." She started to pull Carol towards the exit, but Carol dug her heels in.

"Wait, Mom," she said. "Celia? Would you sleep over tonight? She can, can't she?" she asked her mother.

"Well…" Mrs. Prosky began and Mom said, "I'm not sure that's a good—"

Celia was exhausted, physically and mentally. The last thing she wanted was more drama at Carol's. She thought longingly of her quiet bedroom at home, and Joy sleeping peacefully beside her. But Carol was looking at her pleadingly. *No, it's more than that. She seems almost—frightened.*

Celia took a breath. "It's ok, Mom," she said. "I'll stay with Carol tonight. If that's all right?" she added to Mrs. Prosky.

Mrs. Prosky nodded reluctantly. "I suppose."

"Will you excuse us for a second?" Dad put in. Without waiting for a response, he took Mom aside and started speaking to her in a low voice.

A car horn honked outside. "There's my husband," Mrs. Prosky said. "We have to go." She started for the door, limping heavily on Carol's arm, holding her crutches together in her other hand; it was hard to tell which one of them was supporting the other.

As they reached the doors, Mom and Dad came over to Celia. "I'm not sure about this," Mom said, "especially after what your father just told me about Stan Prosky."

"I'll be ok, Mom," Celia said. "I'll keep out of his way. Really," she insisted as they still looked worried.

"All right," Dad said after glancing at Mom. "But if anything bothers you or upsets you at all—and I mean *anything*—you call us, no matter what time it is. Promise?"

"I promise," she said. Mrs. Prosky and Carol had disappeared. "I'd better run," she said. "I'll talk to you both tomorrow." She kissed them and ran.

She got to the car just as Mr. Prosky was pulling away from the curb. She pulled open the door to the back seat; Mr. Prosky, perforce, stomped on the brake, but he didn't look happy about it. Carol was hysterically crying, shoulder turned away from Celia. Mrs. Prosky was slumped in the front passenger seat, not looking at anyone.

Mr. Prosky said smoothly, as though he hadn't been snarling at Celia just a few minutes before, "I've just been explaining to Carol that when we were in the waiting room you told me you didn't want to spend the night, that you were just being polite when you said you would, but you'd really rather go home."

Her sudden rage washed the exhaustion out of Celia's system and overcame any fear she had of Carol's father. She pulled herself into the back seat and slammed the door shut. "Mr. Prosky," she said firmly, tugging Carol around and into her arms, "I don't know how you could expect me to tell such a lie. Of course I said no such thing. Of course I want to stay with Carol."

Carol quivered and gasped. Mrs. Prosky dropped her head into her hands. Mr. Prosky made a disgusted rasping sound as though he were going to spit, then jammed his foot on the accelerator so the car flew forward with a jerk.

They made the twenty-minute drive to Pine Springs and the Proskys' big, elegant house in silence except for Carol's gradually subsiding sobs. Inside, their maid, a thin, taciturn black woman called Lulabelle, helped Mrs. Prosky get Carol up the stairs. Celia made to follow, but Mr. Prosky jerked his head toward the living room.

Celia went after him and stood uneasily amidst the formal furniture. Even the few times she'd been in this house, they hadn't been allowed in this room. Every flat surface was covered with fiddly china ornaments. The silk upholstery, which looked as though no one had ever sat on it, glowed with a soft sheen from the only light in the room—a glass-fronted curio cabinet holding Mrs. Prosky's collection of what Carol had told Celia were Dresden figurines.

Mr. Prosky reached forward and grasped Celia's upper arm. Startled, she pulled it away, but the movement had turned her toward the light from the cabinet. He stared at her face with a hard hostility mixed with a kind of grudging respect. "Well," he said, "since you seem to have so much influence over her—could you get her to lose some weight?"

Chapter 26.

Celia lay on the floor under the music room window behind the piano, enjoying the winter sunlight on her face and the sound of her brother Rob's music. He'd been practicing hard on Mom's old Spanish guitar, harder than she'd seen him do anything in a long time, and the results of his efforts were clear to hear.

He was singing that Elvis Presley hit, "Heartbreak Hotel," imitating the singer's slurring, bluesy delivery but giving it a resonance all his own.

The way her usually sunny, ebullient younger brother's voice caressed the lyrics of loneliness and loss reminded Celia of the way their parents had found six-year-old Rob and his little sister, Beth: abandoned on the streets of Harrisburg, foraging for food in garbage cans and sleeping in shop doorways. It had taken months for Mom to get Rob to stop secreting food in his dresser drawers—food he always tried to feed to Beth before taking any himself.

"'I get so lonely, I could die,'" he finished on a dying fall.

"That's really good, Robbie," she said. "You're getting good. That song's so sad, though."

"Thanks," he said. "I know it's sad; that's why I like it. I mean, it makes me feel happier, if that makes any sense."

"I think it does," she said. "Playing the piano helps me beat the blues, and the slow, sad pieces can be soothing."

"I've noticed you've been playing those a lot lately." She heard the hollow twang as he set the guitar aside. "I've also noticed you've been squirrelled away with Mommy-o and Daddy-o having deep confabs. What's up?"

Celia frowned as the pressures of the past week or so, dealing with Carol and her insecurities, came rushing back on her. The Proskys hadn't let them see each other much, but they had had some long, fraught phone conversations that left Celia wrung out. "You're the only one who has noticed that, except for Beth. Did she mention it to you?"

"Yeah, Beth sees a lot," he said without irony. "But no, I figured it out all on my ownsome. So what's up?"

Celia sighed. "I really can't tell you," she said. "It's somebody else's… private business, I guess."

"So, nothing I can do?"

"'Fraid not. Thanks for asking, though."

He picked up the guitar again and started plucking strings aimlessly.

There were footsteps on the attic stairs and Dad's head appeared in the stairwell. "Oh," he said, gazing around. "Sorry to disturb you, Rob, we thought Celia was up here."

"I am," she said, poking her head around from behind the spinet.

"Ah," Dad said. "Would you come below, please? Your mother and I need to discuss something with you."

"Come below," she thought. *He only lapses into Navy lingo when he's upset.*

So she tried to keep a pleasant, receptive expression on her face as she hauled herself up from her comfortable berth and followed him down the stairs. Behind them, Robbie's striking up the intro to

"Blueberry Hill" faded as they moved from the attic stairs down to the kitchen and then through the downstairs rooms into the study where Mom was waiting.

She was in the armchair by a bright fire. Dad settled into the big rocker on the other side of the fireplace. Celia started to move toward the sofa opposite them, but Dad reached out and pulled her onto his lap.

She settled in gratefully, even as she realized they were expecting this conversation to be difficult for her. "I assume this is about Carol," she said.

"Yes," Mom answered. "We've just come from a long conversation with the Proskys."

"You mean they actually wanted to talk to you?"

"Their desire to have Carol stay in school and lead a 'normal' life overcame their distaste for having our intrusion into their lives."

"How could you help with that? I thought she was seeing some psychologist in Harrisburg."

"A psychiatrist," Mom corrected her.

"Same difference."

"Not really. In fact, the difference is the crux of this issue we need to discuss. In the first place, Carol should have a full workup to be sure there's not something purely physical wrong with her."

"What kind of physical sickness could cause that?"

"I'm not sure; I'm not an MD myself, remember. Brain tumor, maybe." Mom's face was bleak, her eyes distant. "The confusion of physical and psychological ailments can be deadly. One of my foster brothers had a lot of emotional problems, so when he started complaining of a pain in his hip when there was no evidence of any kind of wound, the social worker called it psychosomatic and had our foster mother drive him over an hour to a state-run mental hospital. I went on that ride; I sat in the back seat behind him and held his head the whole way. He screamed every time the car went over a bump, and sobbed that we hated him in between. It was a relief to turn him over to the hospital, to tell you the truth."

Dad's grip on Celia had tightened as Mom talked. *He must have heard this story before.*

Mom went on, "When we got home, my foster father was waiting to tell us the hospital had called to say they were sending him to a regular hospital in an ambulance. He'd developed osteomyelitis, an infection of the bone from a hypodermic needle that had scraped it. He walked with a cane for the rest of his short life."

Celia didn't even want to ask why his life was short. Mom shook herself and looked at Celia again. "To get back to the point, psychiatrists are MDs, medical doctors. Unlike psychologists, they are authorized to prescribe medications."

"There's some medicine that can cure Carol's problems?"

"Not cure her problems, no; that will take extensive therapy, assuming they don't find a physical cause. But there are some new drugs on the market that will control symptoms like Carol's, that will let her come out of the bouts of catatonia sooner."

"You mean it's going to happen again?"

"It's already happened several times, which is what has alarmed the Proskys. School starts again on Monday, and they know that she's likely to have episodes during the school day."

"But the school nurse could give her this medicine, right?"

Dad put in, "Nurse Hutchins has refused. She says she is not comfortable with handling such powerful drugs, and she doesn't believe the danger is worth the benefits."

Celia could see where this was going. She sat up straight, pulling away from Dad's chest. "So I'm going to give it to her?"

Mom was silent for a long time, staring into the fire while Dad stared at her. Finally she said, "If I agree to supervise, to check on the pills every day to monitor how much she's receiving and hear from you when she got it and how she responded." She turned her face toward Celia. "But your father and I are really doubtful about this. It's a huge responsibility for you, and liable to be disruptive to your studies, to say nothing of your peace of mind."

Dad was now watching Celia's face. "What are you thinking, lassie?"

Celia bit her lip. "This is going to make me sound like a horrible person," she said, "but I have to ask—are you sure this is all real? I mean, that night I spent with Carol, she was really, truly upset, I could see. But there was something else, almost a sort of... triumph, like she was glad she could make this trouble for her parents, like she was punishing them, in a way."

To her surprise, Mom was nodding sympathetically. "It's one of the reasons these conditions are hard to diagnose," she said. "Freud calls it 'symptoms multiply determined'. There are often several factors involved. I have no doubt that Carol has the feelings you noticed; I also have no doubt she feels guilty about having them. On another level, she may be enjoying the attention all this is bringing her; her father's not wrong about that." She raised her hand to stem Celia's protest. "What he is wrong about is in dismissing her very real problems as a result. I tried to explain this to Linda's friend Sydney's parents, as well. It's rather as if a drowning person called for help and the lifeguard said, 'Oh, she just wants attention.' She doesn't just want it, she needs it, desperately, and these episodes are a manifestation of that need."

"At the moment," Dad said, "I'm more concerned with what Celia needs."

Celia leaned over and kissed his cheek. "Don't worry, Dad," she said. "I'm all right. I can handle this."

"I'm not sure I believe you," he answered, "but we can try it."

Chapter 27.

Thursday, January 24, 1957

Miss Palmer was in full flood, talking about the poet Milton's first wife, when the knock came on the classroom door. "Come in," she said a little sharply, which was unusual for her. Celia wondered whether she was annoyed at being interrupted; Celia suspected that her clever, nervous English teacher had something of a crush on the poet and thought she'd have made him a better wife if only she'd lived three hundred years ago.

But maybe it's about me, she amended to herself as a scared-looking student who seemed about twelve years old came in and handed Miss Palmer a note. As Celia expected, the teacher motioned to her, with a scowl on her normally pleasant face. *Is she mad about me missing class again? I've been keeping up with my homework.*

But when she'd scooped up her books and purse and come to the desk for the expected message to go to the nurse's office, Miss Palmer said, "Step out into the hall with me for a minute, please," gave the class an admonitory glare, and ushered Celia out the door. The student messenger scampered off and Celia braced herself for a scolding.

Miss Palmer, though, said in an undertone that wouldn't carry into the classroom, "Celia, I'm worried about you. This is a lot of responsibility to put on a child your age." She raised her hands, stemming the response Celia started to make. "I know, I know, you're very mature, and Carol Prosky is your friend—yes, it didn't take a genius to figure out that whenever you're called out of class, she's also absent; don't worry, I'll keep my conclusion to myself—but still... Are you taking care of yourself?"

Celia felt the band of tension that had formed between her shoulders when the student came in loosen a little. It was a big responsibility to be in charge of dispensing Carol's medication. It was also wearing that most teachers responded to her being called out of class this way with irritation and disapproval; they seemed to think Celia was just showing off.

It was true that when the semester had started two weeks ago, she had felt a little self-important, hurrying out of classes to the curious stares of her classmates. But their curiosity had become burdensome as they scoffed at her refusal to tell them anything about where she went or why, and in fact she was having to hustle a little to keep up with her schoolwork. Miss Palmer was the first person besides her family who seemed to be thinking about how all this might be difficult for Celia.

So she smiled gratefully as she said, "Thanks for asking. My folks are worried about me too, and Ruby—they're all making sure I eat right and get enough sleep; last weekend Ruby—you know, the woman who takes care of us—chased me outside instead of letting me hole up in my room all day. And my mom's a psychologist, you know. She's keeping an eye on me while she monitors Carol's medication."

Miss Palmer looked unconvinced, but Celia said, backing away, "I'm sorry, I really have to go. Thanks again." Then she turned and speed-walked to the nurse's office.

Nurse Hutchins looked up from her desk with her mouth pressed into its usual disapproving grimace. She'd been sour at Celia ever since that kerfuffle with Coach Vaughn about the sweater remark; she thought Celia's complaining about it to her parents had caused unnecessary trouble and given her the added burden of taking over his Health classes. Now she evidently felt her authority was compromised by Celia being the one to administer the medications over her own objections to them. Celia just wished she herself wouldn't get blamed for it.

Every time this had happened, Nurse Hutchins had found something sour to say. Today it was, "Mr. Demby has better things to do with his time than haul your friend into a wheelchair and bring her here."

"I'm sure Carol would rather he didn't have to," Celia answered as pleasantly as she could. Ignoring the woman's snort, she went on into the back room where Carol lay on a cot.

Mom had been furious that the Rolling Meadow front desk person had been so unhelpful the night of the concert. Now she was unhappily resigned to taking a role herself, though her interactions with Carol's psychiatrist had evidently been frustrating her, too.

"These new drugs do seem to have the ability to ameliorate the physical symptoms," Mom had said after their conversation in the study that day. "I just hope they don't start using them as a quick fix and skip the long-term psychological work." She'd sighed. "Well, they've taken it out of my hands, in any case. But that doesn't mean the onus is on you, Cissy. You can help for now, but if it gets to be too much, I want you to let me know."

I wonder how I'm supposed to tell when it's "too much"? Celia put her books down on a chair and opened her purse, taking out the bottles labeled Stelazine and Paranate. She removed a tablet from each, talking softly to Carol as she did so. It turned out that Carol could not only hear everything around her when she was in these states, she could feel as well. Celia shuddered to think what it must have been like being tormented with needles and matches and not even being able to yell, much less twitch away.

"Ok, honey, here we go," she said, moving over to the cot and brushing Carol's hair out of her eyes, fingers catching a little in the curls. As gently as she could, she tilted Carol's head back and pressed her jaw down so that her mouth opened. She slid the tablets into the pouch of her cheek, careful not to place them where they might choke her. Then she pushed the jaw closed again and waited for the medication to dissolve. Carol said it tasted horrible, but there was no other way to get it into her short of an injection, and neither of them wanted Celia messing with hypodermic needles.

Celia moved her books to the floor and drew the metal folding chair closer before sitting on it. For the next few minutes, she talked about schoolwork and light gossip, keeping an upbeat tone. Carol started blinking just as the bell rang for the end of the period.

"My master's voice," Celia said in an exaggeratedly put-upon way, though a traitorous part of her was saying something more like, *Saved by the bell.*

She leaned over and kissed Carol's cheek, thinking of how much more physically affectionate they'd gotten with each other since this all started. That awful night after the concert, Celia had lain at first in the second bed in Carol's storybook-princess bedroom, gazing up at the ruffled canopy above her in the glow of Carol's angel nightlight.

But when Carol started weeping in a sad series of little sobs that sounded like actual boo-hoo-hoos, Celia had gotten up and crawled in with her, the way she would have with Joy. Carol had frozen for a moment and Celia had wondered whether she'd made a mistake. Then Carol had grabbed Celia and clung to her like a limpet the rest of the night.

Since then, Celia had made a point of giving Carol the sorts of frequent caresses she did with her own family. Carol seemed to like it. Now Celia said, "I'll see you later, sweetie," stroking Carol's cheek. In the anteroom she said to the nurse, "I think she's ready for her juice now."

Then she dashed, skidding into her Geometry classroom with seconds to spare. She sorted through her books under Mrs. Ritter's glare. It was matched by one on Barb's face from her desk across the aisle. "You've been with *her* again, haven't you?" she hissed.

Celia sighed. She didn't know what to do with Barb's jealousy of the time Carol and Celia were spending together without her these days. She couldn't explain it without breaking Carol's confidence, and she couldn't convince Carol that Barb wouldn't reject her as some kind of weirdo if she herself told her. *And she might be right, at that.*

Eventually, the day ended. Celia made her way to her locker just in time to see Barb flounce away toward Patty without looking at her, bound for their "Sewing Circle" club, no doubt. But instead of scorn, Celia found herself envying Barb the prospect of an hour talking about simple things with giggling girls whose biggest problems were boys and pimples. *At least I don't have to work at the restaurant on school nights.*

In the bus to Pine Springs and Newville, she looked for Judy but didn't see her. Then she realized she hadn't been in Geometry, either. *Must have the flu or something. I'll call her tonight.* Talking to Judy, even about inconsequential things, always calmed Celia and took her mind off her own problems.

Speaking of which, Carol wasn't here, either. *Probably went straight to Harrisburg to that psychiatrist.*

Looking around for her friends had made Celia one of the last to sit down; the only place left was in the last row on the aisle, just in front of the long bench across the back where the older boys congregated. She closed her eyes and let her head fall back against the seat, half-listening to the joking and verbal jockeying for dominance behind her.

She was just starting to doze off when a voice murmured in her ear, "Hey, sleeping beauty, want a kiss?"

She'd been on a few dates since that disaster with Bobby Jumper; they'd been inoffensive but also unremarkable. At least they'd gotten her past the point where the mere mention of kissing flustered her.

She blinked and turned to see the face behind her. It was that transfer student, Ted something. "I don't know," she said. "If I do, will you turn into a handsome prince?"

"Ouch," he said. "Gribbit, gribbit." He flashed her a smile that wasn't nearly as charming as he evidently thought it was. Still, he was pretty cute and reasonably smart, from what she'd seen in class.

"Sorry," she said. "I'm fresh out of frog food."

"At least you're not surrounded by all your handmaidens for a change," he said. "Maybe you could use some red-blooded male companionship?"

"Maybe I could," she said, and squeezed over to make room for him.

Chapter 28.

"Next time, we're going to see *The Incredible Shrinking Man,*" Ted said firmly as they came out of the Comerford movie theater in Carlisle.

"Ok," Celia said peaceably. Ted had been reasonable about Celia's wanting to see *Funny Face,* but he obviously hadn't enjoyed it as much as she had. In Celia's book, that gave him the more credit for having been such a good sport about seeing a romantic comedy, and a musical at that, instead of the sci-fi horror flick.

"Come on," he said as they came out from under the sleek curves of the art deco canopy and the sleet struck them in the face. "Let's hit the 'Milton."

They dodged across the street and started up toward the restaurant, running into the wind. That was another thing Celia liked about Ted: he always assumed she'd keep up with him, the way her brothers did, not trying to coddle her the way some of her dates had, as though she couldn't stand on her own two feet.

She also appreciated his laid-back approach to making out. Since that encounter on the bus, they'd gone to a couple of school events and stopped for Cokes and fries after school a few times. Celia enjoyed the gentle kisses he'd offered; ever since hearing that Patty was calling her "loose," she'd felt self-conscious about making out, but Ted seemed satisfied to keep the flame burning low.

After the cold and wet outside, and the dark movie theater before that, the noise and light in the restaurant stupefied Celia for a second. The place was full of boisterous Dickinson students, as usual on a Saturday night, but Celia'd barely shed her coat and scarf and stamped the wet off her shoes before Ted had finagled them seats at the end of someone else's table.

She sat there feeling rather smug, as moviegoers who hadn't been as quick off the mark as she and Ted had been milled discontentedly by the door, waiting for empty seats. It was nice, after the pressure and anxiety of dealing with Carol, to have somebody take charge a little, especially since he wasn't obnoxious about it.

The pressure had also been relieved by Carol's being admitted to Parkdale Mental Hospital in Philadelphia, the same place Laurie and Linda's friend Sydney had gone to last year. The high school administration had finally decided that Carol's almost weekly seizures were too disruptive at about the same time Mom and Dad put their collective foot down over the toll the constant interruptions were taking on Celia's schoolwork and frame of mind.

Celia stretched her legs out under the table, relaxing, and accidentally bumped into Ted's. "Playing footsie?" he said, wagging his eyebrows in a comical leer—but Celia felt there was an actual underlying heat there, which warmed her own middle in a way that sat somewhere between pleasurable and scary.

But with reflexes honed by years of banter with her siblings, she just said, "You wish," and went back to studying the list of specials on the chalkboard by the door.

When the waitress came over, Celia asked for coffee and a piece of apple pie. Ted ordered a Hotchee Dog.

"Are you kidding?" Celia exclaimed. "Chili and onions on a hotdog at this time of night?"

Ted preened a little. "I can take it," he said. "Besides, you have to have a Hotchee Dog at the 'Milton; it's a law or something."

"That's right." One of the students at the table nodded. "This kid is hep." He elbowed Ted. "Don't let the chick drag you down."

Celia bristled, but relaxed as Ted said firmly, "She doesn't drag me anywhere I don't want to go."

The older boy laughed suggestively and turned away; Ted gave Celia an apologetic shrug. Then he said, in a low tone meant to carry only to her, "Though it'll be a cold day in June before you get me to a Fred Astaire movie again. Watching some old guy hopping around like a prehistoric rabbit isn't my idea of entertainment."

"Oh, come on," Celia protested. "It wasn't just dancing and singing. That was an interesting story, the way the Audrey Hepburn character wanted to spend time with the professor and be her own person instead of just a model—"

"And found out even smart men only want one thing from a pretty girl," the female student to Celia's right interjected.

Now it was Celia's turn to defend her date. "They're not all like that."

Ted was laughing about something else, though. "Yeah, it was pretty cool when she broke that vase over his head."

The girl by Celia flicked her fingers dismissively toward Ted. "He's a baby," she said. "You both are. Talk to me in a couple of years." She turned back to her friends.

Celia shrugged and attacked her pie.

"Dickinson brats think they're so cool," Ted grumbled. "Wait till I get my license next year, then I can take you someplace where there aren't any of them hanging around, Deer Lodge in Holly, maybe, someplace like that."

"Deer Lodge is nice," Celia agreed, feeling warmed again by his assumption that they'd still be going out in a year.

As though he'd seen the thought in her face, Ted leaned over the table and fixed her with an intent gaze. He worked his fingers up under the cuff of his shirt and pulled his heavy silver ID bracelet down his wrist and over his hand. "I want to be sure you'll still be around then," he said, pitching his voice low under the cacophony all around them. "Will you go steady with me?"

Celia gulped; this was a little more than she'd bargained for. She'd barely started dating—she wasn't at all sure she was ready to limit herself to one boy, and one she hardly knew, at that. They'd kissed and cuddled a little on the bus, to the jeers of the boys on the back bench, and they'd clowned around with the other kids at the drive-in on their after-school Cokes-and-fries jaunts, but they hadn't spent much time alone together, actually getting to know each other.

Still, Ted was nice, if a bit overbearing. He'd been sympathetic to the little she'd felt able to tell him about Carol. And he was smart, good enough in school not to be threatened by Celia's high grades. Celia also admitted to herself that it didn't hurt that he was cute. *I don't judge people by their looks, I don't. Still...* If he'd been a troll or a nerd it would be easier to turn him down.

As it was, she smiled shyly as she extended her own wrist and let him clasp the chain around it, shifting it so the plaque with his name engraved on it lay on top. *He does kiss well.*

"You're mine, now," Ted said, but his voice was gentle, so she didn't take him up on it, though the possessiveness made her a little nervous. *Is this the right thing to do? Maybe I should have waited and talked to Mom about it first. No, I'm not a little kid, I can make my own decisions.* Ted sealed the thought by leaning across the table till their lips met.

The moment was broken when the boy next to Ted snarled, "What's that spade doing here? They won't serve him, will they?"

She looked toward the door to see Laurie standing there, craning around looking for them. She waved and got up as she said coldly, "That's my brother, come to drive us home."

She tried to think of a stinging put-down, but Ted said flatly, "Yeah, so save your breath to cool your coffee, jerk."

Not brilliant, but his heart's in the right place. Everything's going to be great.

Chapter 29.

Mom was in a bad mood today. Celia thought it had something to do with her having turned forty-five this week; Mom seemed to feel that was some sort of turning point: "It's all downhill from here," she'd said, in a tone she hadn't quite carried off as joking. Her gloom was shot through with sparks of irritation today, though, because of the date.

Mom had been a foster child with few connections to her birth roots, but that made her cling the more closely to her identity as someone of Italian descent. St. Patrick's Day observances made her prickly. "Why don't we have celebrations and parades on St. Joseph's Day?" she often said. "Italians have been in Philadelphia at least as long as the Irish."

"Come on, Mom," Laurie cajoled her. "They've been holding a parade in Philadelphia for St. Pat's since before the birth of the Republic."

"My point exactly," Mom said.

Laurie wisely didn't pursue the topic. Instead he said, "Ok, I'm finished sprinkling the ashes. Who's got the peas?"

"Here," Dad said, setting down the covered pail Ruby had carefully preserved the best specimens from last year in.

They were all in the enclosed truck garden behind the house. Ruby, in the section sheltered by the low southern wall, was overseeing Rob, Beth, and Joy as they set out the earliest lettuce seedlings. Jamie was turning over the soil in front of them, getting the rows ready for the plants.

He's probably the only one who hates gardening as much as I do, Celia mused. She enjoyed having the fresh vegetables that were so much better tasting than the ones from the A&P, but there was always the Farmers' Market, even now that the old building in the square had been torn down. And she never had the sense of accomplishment the others seemed to get from growing their own food—the adults had discovered early on that the most effective punishment for Celia when she got into trouble was assigning her garden chores.

Today, though, was traditionally a family activity, so Celia pulled her jacket zipper up a little tighter and knelt to poke the little green spheres into the cold soil with the old dibble. *Gardening is better than worrying about Carol, I suppose. And at least tonight I'll be indoors.* She rubbed her left hand over her right wrist where Ted's ID bracelet lay concealed under her jacket sleeve.

She wasn't hiding from the folks that she and Ted were going steady, but she knew they didn't approve of her focusing on one boy so young, so she tried not to call their attention to it. Tonight Ted was taking her to a St. Patrick's Day party and she was supposed to wear green and bring a green dessert, which wasn't likely to improve Mom's mood any.

By the time they all trooped into the screened porch and sat around waiting their turns to use the mudroom sink to get off the worst of the dirt before going inside, Celia had had more than enough. "I'm going up to wash," she said. "I need to take a quick bath before Ted gets here, anyway."

"Remember, it's a school night—no staying out late," Dad warned.

Celia took a deep breath to keep from snapping at him. It wouldn't help her campaign to get them to think of her as mature if she mouthed off to her parents, but he'd said that twice already about this date.

As it was, he frowned a little at the expression on her face. *Why can't I have less observant parents? And what they don't pick up on, Ruby does. Carol's parents wouldn't notice if she...* Celia bit that thought off before completing it. She really didn't wish she had parents like Carol's.

So instead of scowling, she tilted her head and batted her eyelashes at Dad with a phony simpering smile on her face. He shook his own head and aimed a mock swat at her as she passed, which she deftly dodged and escaped into the kitchen and up the back stairs.

In the tub, she tried to let the oppressive feeling that thinking of Carol and her parents had brought on float away in the warm water. Carol was being released from the hospital next week. Celia was happy for her, and looking forward to seeing her again—really, she was—but she was also not eager to go back to the constant responsibility. They said, and Carol had said in her letters, that she was much better now, but what if the pressure of being back in school and coping with her parents brought on the hysterical conversion bouts again?

She pushed the thought out of her mind as she put on a beige pleated skirt and a Fair Isle sweater in shades of green along with dark green knee socks and her brown loafers. Being with Ted would mean dancing to records, adjusting her body's rhythms to his, letting the music take over, soothing the muscle aches from gardening and the heartache over Carol.

In the kitchen, she found Ruby putting whipped cream on Celia's shamrock-shaped lime Jello mold. "Thanks, Ruby," she said. "I know you're busy with supper." The rich aromas of corned beef and cabbage filled the kitchen. Whosever turn it was to help tonight wasn't here yet, probably still cleaning up after the gardening, so Celia had room to maneuver in the narrow space around the central worktable.

Ruby gave her a speaking look as Celia pulled a jar of green-dyed Maraschino cherries she'd bought for this purpose out of the cupboard.

"What does that mean?" Celia asked.

"Just that I noticed you only have a few minutes before That Boy picks you up."

"His name is Ted," Celia reminded her for the umpteenth time. "Why don't you like him?"

"I don't know him enough to like or dislike him," Ruby said. "I just don't like the idea of you dating." She scowled at Celia's disbelieving laugh and retaliated with a sharp, "Green cherries? You're putting *green* cherries on this nice dessert?"

"I know," Celia admitted, dotting the cherries in a decorative border around the leaves of the shamrock. "They taste like little rubbery globs of petrified sugar with a weird chemical aftertaste. It's like eating pencil erasers soaked in aftershave. But they're pretty, and that's what's important, right?"

Ruby snorted. "Is that what That Boy thinks?"

"You know," Celia said, plopping the aluminum cover over the carry dish and locking it into place, "at this moment, I'm kind of looking forward to a couple of hours not thinking about anything more serious than appearances." She leaned over to pop a kiss onto Ruby's cheek, picked up the covered carry dish in both hands, and backed through the swinging door into the dining room.

As she turned to go the rest of the way to the front hall to wait for Ted to arrive, she thought, *I don't need Ted to take an interest in my troubles. That's what I have my family for. Ted's for relaxing, and being normal.*

Chapter 30.

"Slow down a little, there, Winnie," said Ted's oldest sister, Helen.

From the back seat, Celia could see Ted's shoulders hunch over the steering wheel as he growled, "If I go any slower, the game'll be over before we get there. And I *told* you *not* to call me that any more."

Helen's profile beside him was amused and affectionate in a smug, older-sister sort of way. "But you're our little Teddy Bear, sweet brother. And we'll be even later if you get a ticket and have your Learner's Permit taken away. Slow and steady wins the race, Pooh Bear."

God, is that what I sound like and look like when the others call me "Bossy," Celia wondered, appalled.

Still, it was true that there was plenty of time before the start of the softball game Ted's other big sister, Andy, was to play in as Ted pulled up to the curb in front of the Lamberton School in Carlisle. It had been drizzling on and off all day but not at the moment, so Celia left the hood down on her red raincoat as they hurried around the old brick building to the field behind, their feet crunching on empty cicada husks.

Judy was already there, waiting for them; her brother was serving as umpire. She waved them to the seats she'd saved on the bleachers and Ted and Celia clambered up. Helen sheered off to join a couple of her own friends and give Andy a last-minute pep talk, from the look of it.

"Hey, you cats," Judy said cheerily. "Look, I brought popcorn. Let's eat it before it starts raining again." She pulled a bag out of her knapsack and Celia and Ted grabbed handfuls and started munching. "So what's shakin'?" Judy asked, nudging Celia. "How was your trip to Washington?"

"Oh, it was great," Celia said. "They say there were twenty-five thousand people there, all crammed in front of the Lincoln Memorial. They were doing prayers and gospel songs, you know, so as not to 'embarrass the Eisenhower administration,' they told us, but Congressman Powell didn't really stick to that: he said, 'We are getting more from a dead Republican than we are from a live Republican or a live Democrat.' Then at the end—have you guys heard of the Reverend Martin Luther King, Jr.?" At their headshakes she went on, "Well, you'll hear about him plenty, I'm betting. He gave a real barnburner that had the people stomping and shouting. 'Give us the ballot,' he kept saying at the beginning of every phrase, like the refrain of a song. We were all screaming it with him by the time he finished."

"Wish I could have gone," Judy said. "My parents wouldn't let me skip school. How about you, Ted? Did your folks spring you to take part in a little slice of history?"

Ted shifted uncomfortably and kept his eyes in front of him as the players on the field finished warming up and took their starting positions. His sister Andy threw the first pitch: a smooth but powerful underhand that had the batter swinging futilely just a split second too late. "Strike!" yelled Judy's brother Rick.

They all watched politely through a ball and two more strikes, then as the batter trudged disconsolately off and handed her bat to the next in line, Judy returned to the subject—she had an instinct, Celia thought, for people's weak spots, and could be unscrupulous about prodding them in a sort of clinically interested way.

"How about it, Ted?" she said. "Didn't you want to go?"

Ted took a breath and turned to the girls, but it was Celia he was looking at as he answered, "No, I didn't, really. Look, Celia, I hope you know I'm not prejudiced. I think Laurie's a great guy, and I've got nothing against Negroes in general. But—it's not my fight, you know what I mean? And besides..." He trailed off and turned his face away.

"'And besides' what?" Celia let the few kernels in her hand drop to the ground between the bleacher seats and tugged on Ted's jacket till he turned toward her again.

He met her eyes defiantly. "Twenty-five thousand people, you said. How many of them were white?"

"I have no idea. Not very many, I guess, as far as I saw. But there should have been, Ted. It's our fight, too, no matter what you think. We suffer from the effects of prejudice and discrimination too—it's black people's lives that are mostly affected, but it's our souls that are at risk. Have you read James Baldwin's *Notes of a Native Son?* He talks about how—"

"I don't mean that," Ted interrupted. "We can argue about that later. I just mean I didn't think I'd be comfortable with that many Negroes."

"Oh, right," Judy put in. "All those ministers and politicians and church ladies were going to knock you down and beat you up."

Ted clicked his tongue. "That's not what I'm saying, don't put words in my mouth. It's just... it seemed like it would feel funny, like I didn't belong there."

Judy seemed to be gearing up for another sarcastic remark, but Celia put a quelling hand on her thigh. "Ted," she said gently, "how do you think Laurie feels every time he walks into a classroom at County High, knowing he's likely to be the only black face there? How do you think he felt at the 'Milton that night, knowing that if he wasn't part of our family they wouldn't serve him? Even with him just standing there looking for us, people made crappy remarks. Do you think he doesn't know when that happens? Or when people came up to him at Jamie's synagogue to apologize for Emmett Till, because Laurie was the only Negro they could get close to; don't you think that felt uncomfortable?"

Ted leaned forward with his elbows on his knees. "I guess I never quite thought about it that way," he said slowly. "What it feels like to be the only... whatever. But doesn't that kind of prove my point? People are more comfortable with their own kind." He sat up and flapped a hand at her. "Oh, don't look at me like that, you know what I mean. People who are like them, that's natural, isn't it? Just like the Negroes like to be with other Negroes."

"But that *is* the point," Celia said. "We—human beings—*are* 'our own kind'! Maybe different people like to eat different things or find different things funny or whatever, but that's surface stuff; those differences are fun. Underneath, we're the same."

"I know that," he said, offended.

But Celia thought she was getting through to him anyway. *Maybe Dad wasn't quite right about keeping emotions out of conversations like this,* she thought. *Anger and fear, sure, but love needs passion, and social justice needs love.*

She took Ted's hand. "I know you know we're all equal as humans," she began, but Judy cut her off. "Uh, oh, trouble," she said.

Their voices had risen as they'd talked; Celia had noticed that heads were starting to turn their way, and wondered whether they were being rude. She had no idea what had been happening on the field, and they were here to support Andy and Rick, after all. But Judy wasn't looking at the players, or at the other spectators. Celia followed the line of Judy's gaze to the side of the bleachers.

Carol was standing down there, arms wrapped around her body, weeping in the rain that had just started to pick up, brown curls dripping lank around her chin. "Oh, God," Celia said, and stood up.

Ted, startled, turned to look and got up as well at the same time as Judy did. The three of them threaded past the people sitting next to them on the bleachers. When they got to the end, Ted jumped eight feet or so to the ground, then turned and helped the two girls over the side. As soon as her feet were firmly on the muddy turf, Celia dashed over to Carol.

"What's wrong, Carrie? Did something happen?"

Carol's look wasn't only miserable, it was angry as well, with a little streak of triumph that Celia stored in the back of her mind to think about later. "How could you do this to me?" Carol demanded shrilly. "You said you had to work, and here you are with *them*. I had Lulabelle drop me at the matinée and walked over here because I knew you were lying to me. How could you?"

Celia could feel the sigh she gave coming all the way from her feet.

Chapter 31.

C arol was still crying when Ted's sister dropped her and
Celia off at Celia's house. Celia leaned over to the front
passenger seat to give Ted a quick kiss and a mute look
of appeal. He answered it with a long-suffering roll of the eyes, which
she had to be satisfied with for the moment.

She slid out of the back seat, waited for Carol to follow, then
closed the door with a wave of thanks to Helen. She supported Carol
up the front walk, praying, *Please let Mom be home, please let Mom be
home.*

Her prayer was answered; Mom's purse was sitting on the
credenza in the front hall. She shrugged off her raincoat, one sleeve
at a time, holding Carol with the other arm. Then she hauled her into
the powder room and made her sit on the toilet lid while Celia
toweled her hair dry and peeled her sodden sweater off. Draping a
dry towel over Carol's shoulders, she rapped on the sliding door into
the study, pushed it open, and led Carol into the room.

Mom immediately stood up and came around her desk, face full
of concern. Carol had stopped crying, but her face was still red and
blotchy. Mom shepherded the girls around to the old blue sofa and
sat opposite them in the big rocker, leaning forward with her elbows
on her knees.

163

"Carol, do you want me to call someone?" she asked. "Your parents, or your therapist?"

Carol shook her head.

"Can you tell me what's wrong?"

Carol looked over at Celia, then down at her own lap, fingers twitching, still not speaking.

Celia sighed. "I lied to her," she said steadily. Mom raised an eyebrow and Carol started sobbing again. Celia patted her absently, but she kept her eyes on Mom, willing her to understand. "I said I had to work at the restaurant because I knew she'd get all upset if I left her before the weekend was over. I was just so tired," she said.

"Not too tired to run around with Ted and Judy," Carol said resentfully.

"Not that kind of tired."

"Tired of me, you mean."

"Carol," Mom said gently but firmly, "let's let Celia say what she needs to say." Carol jerked her arms and thrust her head forward awkwardly, but remained silent.

Celia expelled a breath that blew her hair up off her forehead. "You're one of my oldest friends, Carol. I love you; I do. And I want to support you and help you all I can, you know that's true. But sometimes I just feel like it's all too much, like I have to have a break and just be a normal teenager for a couple of hours, go to a game with my boyfriend and eat popcorn and not be all roiled up and emotional. Does that make any sense?" Again she spoke to Mom.

"Of course it does," Mom said. "That said, maybe lying to Carol wasn't the best way to get across what you needed."

"I know. I felt bad about it, but I couldn't think of any way to tell her the truth that wouldn't get her all upset."

"I know I'm a burden," Carol said in a small voice. "I can see why you don't want to be around me. I'm just a mess, my dad's right." Her voice got smaller and higher as she spoke.

"That's not what I'm saying," Celia said as Mom put in, "Carol, that isn't what Celia said."

Celia gestured for Mom to go on. "Carol, you're not my patient, so I have to tread carefully here, but I have to say I'm concerned that you're still so fragile after almost six months of treatment. What does Dr. Blavatsky have to say about your progress, if you don't mind telling me?"

Carol shrugged. "Nothing, really. He doesn't talk to me much."

"Your psychiatrist doesn't talk to you? You mean he encourages you to talk?"

"I guess. But it's all about how the pills are working. Then he jiggers the dosages around and says, 'Let's try this.' It's been worse since you made Celia stop giving me the pills in school and talked Nurse Hutchins into doing it. She's not nice to me, and she doesn't like having to call you up every time, but Dr. Blavatsky says there's no other way."

Mom pressed her lips together and clenched her fists. "I'd say his methods are none of my business, but he and your parents have made it my business by involving me in overseeing your medication. You might want to ask him about these physical tics I see, though; they could be from the drugs." She shook her head, but the red spots high on her cheekbones told Celia her mother was having one of her rare losses of temper. "I really don't see how I can be part of this any more. I'm finding myself pressed into participating in a course of treatment I'm not fully confident of, and being embroiled in your care inappropriately is forcing me to put your needs above my own daughter's."

"Oh, no!" Carol cried. *If her voice gets any higher, only bats will be able to hear her,* Celia thought irreverently. "Dr. Mac, don't say that, they'll send me to some snooty private school, or maybe lock me up in the loony bin again. Please don't give up on me!"

Mom leaned forward to pat her knee. "I'm not going to leave you in the lurch," she said. "But I am going to have to rethink this arrangement. To get back to the immediate topic, and the part of all this that is my business, as Celia's mother: how can we resolve this issue of her needing some time to pursue her own interests? I think we need to establish some boundaries. Carol, can you think about what the most important times are for you to be with Celia, the times you seem to need her most?"

Carol's torso seemed to spasm as she threw her head against the back of the couch and stared at the ceiling. "You mean I have to make an appointment to see her? I'm so rotten she has to ration out the time she spends with me?"

"I think you know that's not what I'm saying. Celia and I are both very concerned for your wellbeing, Carol. But you have to realize, Celia is sixteen years old, just like you. She can't be your doctor, or your full-time caretaker. She can be your friend; she wants to be your friend; she simply needs to have some time to herself as well."

Carol's mouth turned down but she nodded grudgingly. "Maybe," she said slowly. Her voice had come down to its normal high register. "I can manage all right at school. After school?" She looked appealingly at Celia.

"If we can do homework," Celia said. "I can't just sit around talking" *listening to you cry* "all afternoon."

Carol nodded. "I should do more schoolwork anyway, I'm way behind now. And on weekends, I get that you want to be with Ted.

And you have your family thing on Friday nights. Could I have some time Saturdays during the day, when you're not at work? And Sundays?"

"Sundays Celia has to go to church," Mom said firmly. "And I think she deserves a little time just to suit herself, not you or Ted or her job or the family."

Carol sagged a little but nodded. "Okay, then, Saturdays?"

"That's fine," Celia said. Her head was buzzing with excitement. This was the kind of thing Mom was always talking about, attacking complicated emotional situations with practical solutions, almost like a business negotiation. This new arrangement would salve Carol's neediness, allay Mom and Dad's fears about Celia getting in over her head, give Carol's parents less reason to be sour about the time she spent with Celia, and give Celia some much-needed relief from the constant tension. *Now I just have to talk Ted into it,* Celia thought, *and everybody will be happy.*

Chapter 32.

Monday, May 20, 1957

The school cafeteria was hot and noisy, but the day outside was too cold and wet to consider going to the courtyard. *More like March than May,* Celia grumbled to herself, unwrapping the waxed paper from the egg salad sandwich Ruby had packed for her. *Not a great place for a conversation, but we'd better have it sooner than later.*

Last night Ted hadn't wanted to stay on the phone to talk; he'd been cranky and out of sorts over the abrupt ending of their date at the softball game. He didn't look much better now, steaming through the crowd toward her table with a scowl on his face.

Judy was right behind him. Celia moved her head to a slight tilt and Judy immediately understood. She not only veered away toward a different table, she caught Barb's elbow and steered her along, murmuring in her ear till Barb's initial resistance dissolved with a quick glance back at Celia. *Universal girl telepathy. If it had been Carol I wanted to talk to, Barb wouldn't have been deflected, but a boy always takes precedence.*

By then the boy in question was plopping down onto the chair opposite her. He gave her a curt nod and dug into the dubious-looking cafeteria meatloaf. Celia kept him occupied with small talk about classes till he had some food on board.

"Speaking of government negotiations," she ventured when he'd finished telling her about his Civics class discussion, "I had a long talk with my mom and Carol yesterday."

"That must have been thrilling," he said. "Call Dag What's-his-name at the UN. And CBS, too—tell them there's breaking news."

"Don't be snide, Ted. You could at least have asked how she was last night."

"You could at least have asked how *I* was, after you left me sitting there with egg on my face. In front of my sister, too. Imagine how impressed she was that my girlfriend dumped me for some other girl."

Celia struggled to keep her white flare of anger from bursting out and incinerating Ted—or at least, her relationship with him. "Be fair, Ted," she managed to grit out between her teeth. "The girl is in trouble. She needs some extra attention." He glared at her mulishly, but she soldiered on. "Anyway, that's what I wanted to tell you about. Mom helped us negotiate some limits—'boundaries,' Mom called them—so you and I can count on some time together without Carol blossoming in on us. I'm going to do homework with her after school, and spend part of Saturdays with her. That means I'll have Friday nights with the family, Saturday evenings with you, and on Sunday I can just cool it on my own."

His scowl actually deepened. "Wait a minute," he said, and scrabbled through his pile of books beside him on the table. He came up with a notebook and pulled a ballpoint out of his shirt pocket. He opened the notebook, held the pen poised over it, then asked with elaborate courtesy, "What hours were those that I get, again? I want to make sure not to miss my window, or interfere with your time to 'cool it.'"

"Ted," she began helplessly, but he overrode her.

"Oh, you forgot something," he said. "You haven't left any time for working on race relations and…what did you call it? Social justice."

"Right. Making out with you is so much more important than civil rights, or my friend's mental health."

"Who elected you Queen of the Downtrodden? And anyway, I'd like to think I at least make your list of important people."

"Of course you do; I just finished telling you I've made sure we'll have time together. And I don't think I'm the queen of anything, I just think it's important to try to help where we can, whether it's individual people or the world in general." Celia shifted forward in her chair. "I don't want to fight with you, Ted. I do want to spend time with you, but I can't just leave Carol in the lurch. This isn't easy on me, either, you know."

His face softened. "Yeah, all right, I know, I guess." He slapped the notebook closed and put his pen away. "Listen, I told some of the guys I'd meet them in the gym and shoot some hoops. I'll talk to you tonight."

"You're not finished eating," she protested, but he was already gone. She stared disconsolately at the remains of her own lunch. She pulled a grape out of the bottom of the paper bag and nibbled on it.

Judy and Barb, having seen Ted leave, were bringing their own lunches over to join her. She gave them a quick recap of the conversation. Judy looked sympathetic but Barb just shook her head.

"I don't know what you expect, Celia," she said. "You keep people hanging around and try to push them into doing all these weird things, and then when they go away you get all hurt."

"What weird things?"

"Like running around pretending to be boys."

"What on earth are you talking about?"

"And animals and I don't remember what all. You know, that time in the barn."

"Oh, we were supposed to be acting out a story." She turned to Judy. "It was *The Sword in the Stone*. We never actually did it, though," she said to Barb. "You guys decided it would be more fun to go to Carol's house and listen to records."

"And what a mistake that was," Barb said. "Her mother's—well, this won't sound nice to say about a lady who's crippled or whatever, but—kinda creepy. No wonder Carol's got a screw loose."

"Barb!" Celia cried.

"Sorry, but it's true. And you hanging around with her all the time doesn't leave much space for the rest of us. It's why Patty decided to write you off."

"Oh, it is not. Patty wrote me off, as you put it, because she's a narrow-minded little racist jerk."

"Fine, I get it, you're better than everybody." Barb stuffed her Tupperware container of salad into her handbag and flounced away from the table.

Celia set her hands on top of each other and sank her forehead to rest on them with a groan.

Judy patted her shoulder, but then she said, "I have to ask, Celia. Why are you still friends with her?"

"You've got me," Celia admitted. "Inertia, I guess. We've been… we used to say, 'best' friends, since we were six."

Judy nodded. "It's like old shoes, isn't it? They gradually get smaller and smaller without you noticing, then you realize not only have your feet grown while they haven't, they're not even attractive any more."

Celia laughed guiltily as Judy went on, "And what possessed you to try to get that particular group of space cadets to act out any story, much less T. H. White?"

"I was desperate," Celia said. "I didn't have you then, after all."

"Right, I'm the Universal Panacea."

"I'm glad somebody is. I'm tired of the job, myself." Celia gave up on her lunch and started gathering her books for class.

Chapter 33.

Sunday, July 14, 1957

Celia slid into the booth in the Pine Springs diner, deliberately bumping knees with Ted in an attempt to dislodge the scowl on his face. *Nothing can make me blue today.* "Sorry I'm late," she said. "Mass ran long this morning, Father Shea was on a tear about the new Elvis movie... what's this?"

Ted had pushed a plate with an unappealingly congealing mass on it against her elbow. "It's your lunch," he said. "I ordered because you said you'd be here at noon."

"Well, I didn't mean necessarily to the minute." She prodded the leathery top layer. "Tuna melt? Why did you order this?"

"I thought you liked them."

"I guess I do, sometimes, but how did you know I'd be in the mood for this today?"

Ted grabbed the plate away from her and dumped it on top of his own unfinished burger. "I don't know," he snapped. "I don't know anything about your moods any more, or your tastes, or anything else. I guess I'm just supposed to be grateful you're here at all on one of your precious 'free time' Sundays."

"Well, I did skip Dad's pancakes to be with you," Celia said, her good mood rapidly eroding. "What's your problem today, anyway?"

173

"Me? I don't have any problems. After all, I'm not black, or crazy, or a member of your family, what problems could I have?"

"Ted, what's going on?"

"You tell me. What was so important you had to cancel our date last night? What activity did your family have that was better than being with me?"

"Oh, Ted. It wasn't that something was better—or worse, for that matter—than being with you. It wasn't even an activity that was so important; we just listened to my mother read aloud, actually, since we hadn't done it Friday night as usual. We just needed some family time. But that's the thing, Ted." She hitched forward on her seat and reached across to grasp his wrist.

"The thing we had to talk about Friday night instead of our usual routine, it's so exciting. We're going to get another brother!"

"I don't suppose you mean your mom is pregnant; you'd have no way of knowing whether it was going to be a boy or not, anyway."

"No, no, another adopted brother."

His face didn't loosen into the smile she'd hoped for. "It's all decided already? When were you going to mention this to me?"

"I just found out myself."

"You told me that other time, your folks had the kid come and visit on the weekends. That's how you knew he was a loony-tune in time to get rid of him."

The brutality of the remark set Celia back enough for her to register Ted's stiff shoulders and jutting chin. At the look on her face, he softened his posture a little, but said, "I just mean, couldn't this be another problem?"

"It's possible, yes," she admitted. "But there are special circumstances. Do you remember reading in the papers about that boy who had been kept locked up in a room for ten years by his cousin, who tortured and abused him till the boy ended up stabbing him to death?"

Now Ted recoiled, a look of horror on his face. "That's who your parents are bringing into your house?"

"Yes, but listen: Mom has been working with him for months, and she and Dad—and Ruby, too—all think he's got a lot of promise. He loves music, and he's trying really hard, Mom says. The problem is, there are people at Rolling Meadow who think he's either retarded, which Mom says is absolutely not true, or going to be a troublemaker, which she doesn't believe, either. They want him either moved into the secure facility for delinquents or over into long-term custodial care in the hospital. We have to get him out of there before either of those things happens."

"Why?"

The word stopped Celia in full spate. She didn't understand what he meant. "Why what?"

"Why do you have to get him out of there? I mean, why you—your family—specifically? Isn't there anybody else to save the world again?"

"But… but we're the ones who're right here! I mean, Mom is, and the rest of us are ready to back her up. Why should somebody else do it when we're right there? And there might be other people somewhere who could help, but I don't see them stepping up. Don't you see, with all the practice we've gotten dealing with the problems some of us have, we're the right ones to help this Steve?"

Ted leaned his elbows on the table and hid his eyes with one hand. "And where am I in this?" he asked wearily.

Celia chewed her lip. "If you want to be part of it, I'm sure Mom would think that was a good idea. I mean, this kid has never had friends before—can you believe that?—so he could use some contacts outside the family. That would be really nice of you."

Ted dropped his hand and looked at her bleakly. "Except that's not what I meant. I meant where does all this leave you and me?" At her blank expression he smiled wryly and went on, "See, Celia, part of my problem is that you make me feel like some kind of selfish troll. You're always caught up in crusades for other people, and what kind of jerk am I to resent that? But I do. I do resent it, Celia. You're a great girl; I really like you, and I admire you, too. And I can see that it's not fair to ask you to be somebody different, just a… oh hell, I'll say it: just a normal girlfriend. But that's what I want, what I need. Isn't what I need important, too?"

"Of course it's important, Ted. It's only—"

"Not *as* important?"

"No, that's not true. I was going to say, not as urgent."

"Uh huh."

Celia dropped her own arm to the table and slowly slid Ted's ID bracelet off her wrist. They both stared at it where it lay coiled next to their uneaten food.

Hesitantly, delicately, almost as if it were made of some fragile material instead of heavy metal, Ted's fingers pulled it closer to his side of the table. Then his hand closed decisively over it and it disappeared into his pocket.

"I wish you all the best, Celia. And I hope everything with this kid and Carol and your brother Jamie and, and, the civil rights movement and everything else you're involved with works out the way you want it to."

"I wish you the best, too, Ted. You know that, don't you?"

"Sure, Celia. Like you wish everybody. I know."

Then he was gone. *Guess I was wrong,* Celia thought, pushing herself to her feet. *There was something that could make me feel blue.*

Chapter 34.

Saturday, August 25, 1957

Celia let the screen door to the kitchen slam behind her as she came in, then winced as Mom's voice came from the screened porch to her right: "*Don't* let the door slam!"

"Right," she muttered under her breath. "The world is gonna end because I slammed a door."

"What was that, young lady?" came Dad's voice.

Celia sighed and went through the side door to them. They were sitting with Ruby, drinking iced tea and eating poppy seed cake, listening to *The Mikado*, if Celia remembered her Gilbert and Sullivan, coming through the open window to Ruby's sitting room.

"Sorry," she said, pouring herself a glass from the pitcher Ruby shoved toward her and sinking into a wicker armchair beside the table. "I'm in a bad mood. After being best friends since we were sprouts, I think I just broke up with Barb."

Then she flinched; the ambiguous phrase reminded her of the sharp remark Barb had flung at her.

"She's still upset that you spend so much time with Carol?" Mom asked. "I thought she'd be pleased when I told her you were out back."

"You might think that. What you didn't know is that Carol was there, too, out by the barn. I was sitting under the old tire-swing tree and Carol was lying there with her head in my lap. When Barb saw us, she said, 'What is this, Peyton Place?'"

Mom clicked her tongue, Dad looked half amused and half irritated, Ruby cocked her head in confusion.

"It's from that book everybody's reading," Mom said. "About sex in a small New England town?"

"Oh, that trash," Ruby said. "I've heard talk. But what does that have to do with Celia and Carol? Oh. *Oh!*" She turned to Celia, outrage on her face. "Celia, child, now don't you let that kind of mess upset you. She's got no business sayin something like that about you." Ruby always reverted to her Georgia childhood and started dropping g's when she was angry or upset.

"That's not the point, Ruby," Celia said. "It didn't bother me. But it bothered Carol; she ran away crying, in that little boo-hoo way she has. And then Barb and I got into a shouting match." She put her empty glass down on the floor beside her chair and drew her feet up to rest her chin on her knees.

"She feels insecure," Mom said. "Not only because she's afraid of losing you, but probably because your closeness to Carol arouses feelings in her that she doesn't know how to deal with."

"Give her a couple of days," Dad suggested. "Let her cool down a little. Then you can call her and—"

"No, I don't think I will," Celia interrupted.

"I wasn't finished speaking." Dad's tone was mild, but there was a warning glint in his eye.

Mom reached a hand to his arm. "Sean," she said soothingly, "I think Celia needs to—"

Celia stood up. "Well, *I* think Celia needs to manage her relationships on her own for once. I'm sorry," she went on at the aghast looks on all the adults' faces. "I don't mean to be rude, really I don't. But I don't need you all getting involved in every single thing I ever do." The adults' open mouths brought her up sharply. *Stop yelling, it's not their fault,* she reminded herself.

"It'll probably blow over on its own," she said. *I still sounded kind of snarky. Oh, who cares, I have a right to my own feelings.* "Or maybe it won't. Maybe my friendship with Barb is over—has been over for a long time, really, to be honest, only I didn't want to see it. We really don't have anything in common any more; we get together more out of habit than because we have anything to say to each other."

She yanked the rubber band off her ponytail and pulled the loose bits of damp hair back off her face more tightly, rewinding the band around it again. Then she bent to pick up her glass and said more mildly, "I appreciate your wanting to help, really I do. But when Ted broke up with me, he made me see how important it is to know what you need in a relationship, and not be afraid to move on if there's no way you're going to get it. I have more in common with Judy now, which might be another part of Barb's problem. But that's where I am now with Barb, and that's the end of it."

There was a short silence in the room while the window emitted Nanki-Poo brightly chirping, "The flowers that bloom in the spring, tra-la!" Then Mom said, "Someone should call the Proskys and make sure Carol got home all right."

"Will you do that, Mom? I'm done for today." She and Mom exchanged wry smiles acknowledging that Celia did want her help for some things.

Dad was still looking a little miffed, so Celia leaned over and kissed his cheek. "I'm sorry I cut you off, Daddy. I just can't talk about it any more, ok?"

She took her glass into the kitchen, pretending not to hear Ruby's plaintive, "Don't you want some cake?" as she set it in the sink and made her way up the back stairs.

She almost collided with Steve on the landing as he came down from the attic. He'd been going up there a lot the past few days; Celia suspected that Jamie had showed him his own hiding place up there, that they all pretended not to know about.

She smiled at Steve when he flinched away from her, then stood back to let him pass into the upstairs hall. He went but looked back at her, eyes wide and white in his pale face. He was shivering a little, as though something had frightened him.

Probably heard me yelling, she thought guiltily. The violence in his past made him panic at any sign of anger. She recalled the first day he came here, a month ago—how she and Laurie and Rob had found him in the playground being bullied by some young hoodlums. Celia had enjoyed the feeling of strength and power she got from defending him, but she also remembered how scared he'd been.

Now she almost gave him another reassuring smile. *But Mom said never to lie to him. That would be a kind of lie, pretending nothing is wrong.* So instead she said, "I got a little upset just now."

He shrank back. "About me?"

"Oh, no, honey. I wasn't even thinking about you." *That didn't come out right.* She opened her mouth to soften what she had said, but realized that he didn't look hurt; he looked relieved.

He started to back away from her, toward the room he shared with Jamie.

I should invite him to do something with me, the way the boys have. But she really didn't want to deal with anybody else's emotions right now. *Soon,* she promised herself. *Just not today.*

She turned away from him and went into her own room.

CHAPTER 35.

TUESDAY, SEPTEMBER 3, 1957

Celia snapped the last course divider into her ring binder and sat back, satisfied. She loved getting things all arranged at the beginning of the school year; it made her feel in control, and hopeful. The ring binder was new and clean, filled with blank lined paper and pristine cardboard dividers, the course names neatly inked onto their tabs.

By Christmas, she knew, there would be smudges and doodles and scratch-outs, memories of cranky teachers and essays she could have written better and tests she'd wish she'd scored higher on, but for now it was all possibility and potential. This feeling of new beginnings combined with the great time she'd had with Steve this afternoon—plus a bellyful of Ruby's incomparable pot roast—left her brimming with hope. Life was good.

When the phone rang, she jumped up from the desk and dashed into the hall for it. "I've got it," she yelled. "Hello?"

"Celia?"

"Oh, Judy, you're a mind reader. I was just thinking I'd call you. The greatest thing happened today." She hauled the phone on its long cord into her bedroom as she talked, closed the door on the cord and flung herself onto her bed, toeing off her loafers and kicking them from her feet into the air, not caring where they landed.

"It's Steve," she went on. Judy had met Steve briefly when she came to the house the other day and had been friendly to him without overwhelming him or being put off by his odd ways. Still, Celia quickly discarded her original idea of telling Judy how she'd found Steve cleaning the girls' bathroom with his own toothbrush this afternoon—a holdover from what his mad cousin had made him do during his years of imprisonment by the man. It seemed that to repeat that to Judy would be compromising Steve's privacy. *Besides, I want to emphasize the positive.*

So instead she said, "He sat with me in my room, listening to music and talking. It's the first time we've really been able to connect. I answered a few of his questions about school and about the family; I even told him about my fight with Barb, though natch I didn't get into what her problem was. In fact, I made it seem like it was nothing and would blow over. But he talked, Judy; he actually talked to me. He hardly talks to anybody but Joy."

"That's wonderful," Judy said.

"Yeah, and the music thing—Joy came in and wanted to play Pat Boone and Steve and I sort of upchucked at that, and Joy said, 'So you know everything, huh?' So Steve says, 'I know more than you about music, anyway.' Then he got this funny look on his face and says, 'That's the first time I ever told anybody I knew more than them about anything.' Can you feature that? And then—this is the most amazing thing—he let us tickle him!"

"Really?"

Judy's voice sounded polite, not as enthusiastic as Celia wanted her to be, so she tried to explain. "He's had so much bad treatment in his life; I know you saw those stories in the paper about how he'd been... I guess 'tortured' is really the only word for it. So he hardly ever lets anybody touch him. Dad and Mom are slowly getting him used to being hugged, but in some ways this is even better than that. Not so solemn, you know what I mean? This was just touch for fun."

"I see," Judy said, sounding a little more engaged. "That is important, isn't it? I'm glad things are going well with him, Celia."

"Well, we've still got a long way to go, but it's a start. And Carol's been doing a little better lately."

"I heard they're sending her to boarding school."

"Yeah, some fancy girls' school up near Penn State. She was upset about it at first, but her doctor said she'd do better somewhere people don't have preconceptions about her, and Mom thinks she'll do well without the added pressure of having boys around. They do have dances with boys from another school nearby, and they have neat stuff like horseback riding and fencing. She got excited over the idea eventually."

"That sounds good."

"Yeah, and to tell you the truth, I'm just as happy. I don't want to sound heartless, but I didn't feel like I was doing her any good, and my folks were worried about the pressure on me."

"I don't think you're heartless."

"Thanks. I think, in a funny way, Ted breaking up with me has been helping me figure out what I need from other people, and that it's ok for me to think about that—you know, not selfish or anything." Judy made a little sound at that which Celia took for assent. She sat up, lifting the telephone off her stomach. "Well, I better go. I promised my brother Rob I'd help him with his freshman algebra. Can you imagine, me helping somebody with algebra? The sun's going to rise in the West tomorrow. Anyway, I'll see you at school. Bye."

Judy's screech of "Wait!" halted Celia's lowering the receiver.

She put it back up to her ear. "What is it?"

Judy huffed. "I was the one who called you, remember?"

"Yeah. So?"

"So didn't it occur to you that I might have something to say?"

Celia could feel herself flush. "I'm sorry, Judy. I guess I did get carried away with my own stuff. I didn't mean to rattle on like that. What's wrong?"

"Nothing's wrong. Or anyway, nothing's wrong with me. It's just—"

Celia tried to decipher the silence that followed. *Is she breaking up with me, too?* "You mean there's something wrong with me?" she croaked.

"No." Now Judy sounded impatient. "Not the way you mean."

"What way, then?"

"It's only that I don't want you to be upset."

Celia planted both her feet on the rug beside her bed. "What am I going to be upset about?"

"Maybe nothing. I mean, you said some good things had come out of you and Ted breaking up."

"So what does that have to do with the price of tea in China? Come on, Judy, you don't usually beat around the bush. Just spit it out."

"Ted and I are seeing each other."

"Oh." *Oh.*

"What do you mean, 'Oh'?" Judy asked cautiously.

What do I mean? "I mean, uh, that's great."

"Really?"

"I don't know. Maybe not. Judy, I need a few breaths to take this in, ok?"

The following silence stretched on. Finally Judy said, "I can hear you breathing, you know."

That got a chuckle out of Celia. "Yeah, I've had my few breaths, I get it. Ok, yeah, it's fine, Judy. I mean, what kind of dog in the manger would I be to get upset? He's a great guy and I don't have any claim on him. And you're—you know what, I just realized: you're my best friend. So go, fly, little birds. Be free, build a nest, whatever. I'm fine."

"There'll be no nest building," Judy said with a touch of acid. "I didn't even think I liked him when I first met him. Flying, we'll see. Anyway, I'm glad I'm still your best friend." She gave an exaggerated sigh of relief. "You'd better go rescue your algebra-phobic brother."

"Right. Ok. Bye."

Celia hung up and fell back on her bed, balancing the phone on her chest and taking stock of her mental state. *Is life still good? Yeah, it is.*

Chapter 36.

The problem was, Ray was just so handsome. Celia thought she herself was reasonably attractive: she had a good figure, if a little hip-heavy, *thanks a lot, Mom;* her dark hair was thick and glossy; her brown eyes were big and long-lashed. Still, she was no great beauty, no traffic-stopper.

But Ray almost literally was a traffic-stopper. He was tall and lean but well-muscled, an accomplished high school wrestler. His blond hair shone nearly silver in some lights, cut in a modified ducktail with a forelock artfully curved over his brow like a comma punctuating his movie-star regular features. Most of all, he had a way of carrying himself that seemed to say to the world, "I'm on top of things, nothing bothers me; I know you're admiring me because that's my due, but I'm a humble good-hearted guy, really."

The reason all this was a problem was that Celia suspected his heart wasn't actually all that good—sometimes she wasn't even sure she liked him. His air of entitlement usually amused her, but once in a while she saw a flash of something that made her uneasy, a hint that he really did think the world owed him its admiration.

She stifled that thought; she was determined to enjoy herself tonight. Her contentment after her conversation with Judy hadn't survived the lonely weeks that followed. After Ted and then Barb dumped her, and on top of that Ted and Judy got together, she was feeling rejected and rather bruised. They were all busy now, and Carol was off at boarding school—Celia was lonely, as well. And she still felt embarrassed by how self-centered she'd been in that phone conversation with Judy, as though she'd been presumptuous in her conviction that she knew how other people felt, that she was attuned to other people's needs.

So when the handsome wrestling champion strolled up to her in the cafeteria one day and said, "This seat taken, princess?" she'd been both flattered and flustered. She'd seen Ray around—everyone had—but she didn't know him; his family had only come to live in Mount Holly Springs a year or so ago.

He'd never spoken a word to her before, but she wasn't going to worry too hard about what had sparked his interest all of a sudden. She let him lead the conversation, that day in the cafeteria and later, when they'd chatted in the hall or when they'd gone for Cokes after school. *He doesn't need to hear about my troubles, or to tell me his if he doesn't feel like it, for that matter. If he wants to talk about the wrestling team or how dumb his English teacher is, I can just listen for a change.*

Tonight was their first formal date, the Homecoming dance. It was also the first day of wrestling season, and Ray had excelled in the dual meet with Carlisle High this afternoon. Cumberland County High had beat Dauphin County in last night's football game, as well, so the atmosphere in the gym was effervescent.

Ray opened the gym door and ushered Celia in with a flourish. Celia knew her dress flattered her; the layers of pale yellow tulle camouflaged those troublesome hips while the wide satin belt accentuated her trim waist. Since it was a strapless gown—her first—Ray had gotten her a wrist corsage of yellow roses. It all went well with the autumn theme of the decorations, without making Celia feel like a glorified pumpkin.

As the door swished closed behind them, she looked up at Ray with a smile.

He returned it and said, "You look gorgeous." He'd said that already, when he'd picked her up at the house, but she didn't mind hearing it again.

"So do you," she said. The slim, tailored lines of his tux accentuated the muscles she'd seen straining and slick with sweat earlier today as he'd struggled on the mat with his opponent. The image, overlaid on his current cool, correct one, made her face flush and her stomach swoop.

He gave a dismissive tilt of the head and swept her onto the dance floor. The band was playing the Pat Boone song, "April Love"; Celia shared her new brother Steve's contempt for the goopy tune and sentimental lyrics but at the moment she couldn't care about that. She was a competent dancer but Ray made her feel like Ginger Rogers. He led so forcefully and surely that her feet seemed to follow his without her having to think about it.

He twirled her out from himself and reeled her back in and she felt like a kite, alternately flying in the sky and nestled safe against his firm chest. As the song ended, he bent her in an extravagant dip, lowering his face to hers till she was sure he was about to kiss her, then giving her a mischievous grin and pulling her upright again.

The band went into Presley's "All Shook Up" and Ray seamlessly shifted his hands to her waist and lifted her into the air. No one had done that since she was about seven years old. She threw her head back and laughed aloud. He brought her back down and twirled her out again; this time it felt like fireworks and fizz. Her feet moved faster than she'd known they could and for the first time she felt she really understood the lyrics to "Rock Around the Clock"—*I really could do this all night.*

Eventually, they stopped for a breather. He planted her on one of the chairs along the side of the gym and went to get some punch. She took the opportunity to kick off her high-heeled satin pumps, dyed to match her dress, and worked her toes in their nylon stockings against the cool floor. She sighed in relief and cast her eyes up to see Patty Lebo glaring at her. The glare looked ludicrous with her round freckled face and carefully pin-curled blonde hair, but it took Celia aback nonetheless.

What now? she wondered. She hadn't spoken to the girl in over a year, since that idiot Bobby Jumper told her she'd been telling people Celia was "loose," so she couldn't think what was getting her so worked up now. She watched as Patty leaned over to whisper to the girl next to her, someone Celia didn't know, and they both sniggered and glared at her with pinched, jealous faces.

Jealous, that's it, she realized. Patty was put out that Celia was here with a catch like Ray. Celia pointedly turned a shoulder to the two girls, lifted a foot to her knee with elaborate unconcern, and started rubbing the burning sole.

"Here, let me do that," Ray said, arriving beside her and setting their paper cups of punch on the seat of an empty chair.

"No!" she cried in horror, but watched helplessly as he sank to the floor in front of her, took her sweaty, probably smelly, foot in his hands and started to rub. After a second, she gave in.

I shouldn't let him do it, but it just feels so good.

Chapter 37.

Saturday, January 4, 1958 Part 1

I t had been a long time since Celia had been in Carol's house. Now she felt a strong sense of déjà vu as Mr. Prosky drew her from the front door into the living room. Outside, it was a clear, cold, sunny day, but heavy drapes had been drawn across the windows so that the room was as shadowy and oppressive as it had been that night a year ago, when he'd pulled her in here to natter about his desperately ill daughter's weight.

His intent glare was the same, too. "I don't want any more nonsense," he snapped.

"I don't think there was ever any 'nonsense,' sir," Celia said firmly. "Carol needed—"

"I'm her father; I decide what she needs. And what she doesn't need is a lot of people staring at her like a monkey in the zoo. What she doesn't need is everybody talking about her. What she doesn't need is outsiders poking their noses in where they don't belong." His voice lowered menacingly on each sentence. His face flushed dark in the gloomy room, and his eyes bulged.

Celia forced herself to meet them and tried to control her breath. *People seeing, talking, outsiders: that's what he's afraid of. Not what's wrong with Carol but what other people might think about it. All those times she had to be taken out of class because she'd gone into hysterical paralysis. That's why they sent her away to school: too many people here knew something was wrong. And me—I knew too much.*

She backed away from Mr. Prosky and watched his face crumple. "She's in her room," he muttered, defeated, and turned away from her.

"Entrée!" came the fluting voice from behind Carol's door. Celia fixed a smile on her face and pushed it open. The storybook princess furniture was all the same: the twin canopied beds, the ruffled skirt on the vanity, the heart-shaped mirror above it, the row of elegant international dolls, never to be played with, on the shelf over the spindly escritoire.

Only the girl sitting at it was different. Her unruly brown curls had been somehow tamed and gelled into a smooth carapace belling over her head to a stiff little upflip at the ends. Her face was completely, expertly made up, though it was only ten o'clock on a Saturday morning. She wore dark blue tailored slacks and a crisp blue-and-white striped shirt; a blue silk scarf was threaded through the button-down collar and tied in a square knot at her throat.

She jumped up and came toward Celia, arms outstretched. Celia wasn't sure whether to expect the backslapping rough greeting of their childhood or the limpet-clinging of their last months together. She wasn't expecting what she got: Carol pulled her to half arms' length and air-kissed each of Celia's cheeks, like a cinema Frenchman. "Darling," she trilled. "*So* good to see you."

She drew Celia to sit on the chintz-cushioned vanity bench and reseated herself on the delicate escritoire chair, stretching her feet out and wiggling them a little. She had nylons on under her highly polished cordovan loafers, Celia noticed. *And she's lost that weight her father was so worried about.*

"You look marvelous," she said honestly.

Carol's toes made a gleeful little twirl. "I do, don't I?" she said with innocent delight. "It's all the activity we do at the Grier. Not all those tiresome gym exercises, but riding and fencing. And dancing of course; there's a dance with the Academy or the Institute almost every month. So many boys! And speaking of dancing and boys, who was that gorgeous hunk I saw you with New Years' Eve?"

Celia told her a little about Ray and let the conversation stay in the realm of girly gossip for a while. She listened as Carol rattled on about the boys she'd dated and the girls she hung around with. Eventually, though, Celia put forward a hand and pressed Carol's arm, stemming the spate of chatter.

"How are you, Carrie?" she asked. "I mean, really?"

"I'm absolutely terrific, Celia. Haven't I just been telling you that? There's nothing in the world wrong with me. I don't know why you'd think otherwise."

That last sentence was a mistake, Celia thought. *And you know it, too, judging by the way you're flushing.*

She opened her mouth to say why she might think Carol wasn't "absolutely terrific." Then she looked at her eyes. There was an almost desperate appeal in them, before they shifted away from Celia and fixed on those shiny shoes.

She's self-conscious. More than that, she's embarrassed. I've seen too much, I know too much about her, I've been there when she was weak and suffering. But she shouldn't be, it's nothing to be ashamed of. I shouldn't let her close herself off like this, I should push till she lets me in.

Then Celia thought again. She tried to put herself in Carol's place and suddenly she could see the brittle shell her friend had erected not so much as a barrier to be overcome as a shield to protect herself. *She must be doing better or she wouldn't be able to stay in that school. Maybe she knows better than I do what she needs.*

"Oh, you know me," Celia said lightly. "With my family history, I'm always sniffing out trouble. Like with Ray, for instance. He is good looking, and to tell you the truth, he does things to me physically that make me feel like he's Prince Charming and I'm Cinderella, like the luckiest girl in the world. But sometimes I feel like he's not really there with me, you know what I mean?"

Carol shot Celia a grateful look and shifted over to sprawl on her bed. "Not really," she said avidly. "Do tell."

So Celia talked about her uneasiness over Ray, and then about Ruby's nephew Henry Still, who'd visited at Thanksgiving, and then about Beth's new boyfriend, until she ran out of gossip.

There was a short silence, then Carol jumped up in alarm. "Look at the time!" she said. "I have to take my pill." She pulled a medicine bottle off her bedside table that said "Miltown" on it, shook out a tablet, and swallowed it with water from a glass topping the carafe that sat beside it. "This stuff is really fabulous," she told Celia. "I've only had a couple of my little… episodes since I started taking it."

"Little episodes," eh? That's not how I would have described them. But she does seem better. It looks like this stuff really works. Celia quashed a lingering uneasiness and let herself feel relieved. *If this is the life she wants, it's not up to me to try to talk her out of it.*

"Well, I guess I'd better go," she said.

A few months ago, that would have brought a pout or even tears. Carol just said, "It was fabulous to see you, darling," and jumped up from her bed to give Celia more of those air kisses.

At the last minute, though, Celia pulled her into a real hug. "I'm always here for you, if you ever need me," she whispered.

Carol squeezed her back just a bit, then let her go and opened the door for Celia to leave.

In the hall, Mrs. Prosky sat in her wheelchair, out of sight of Carol's doorway but where Celia couldn't miss her as she headed for the stairs. They looked at each other for a moment.

"Take care of her," Celia said softly.

"I'm her mother."

"Yes, you are." Celia left.

Chapter 38.

Saturday, January 4, 1958 Part 2

"You're putting on a girdle to go to watch a wrestling meet?" Joy said disbelievingly.

"We'll go for a burger or something later," Celia said. "Ray's always hungry, after." *Hungry for more than one thing.* She smoothed her hands over her hips, encased in stretchy elasticized mesh. "Besides, I'm going to be wearing a straight skirt."

"So what?"

Almost fourteen, but she's still a child in some ways. "A straight skirt shows too much," she explained kindly.

But Joy surprised her, saying dismissively, "Who wants an ass with no crack?" just as there was a tap on the door and Mom came in.

"Such language," she said to Joy. Then, to Celia, "Here's the sweater clip you wanted to borrow."

"Thanks, Mom. It'll look great with that set you got me for Christmas."

As Celia wriggled into her pencil-slim plaid skirt and her new blue cashmere sweater set, clipping the cardigan across her front with Mom's paired gold little hands and linking chain, Mom settled onto her bed to talk.

"How did it go with Carol today?"

"Pretty good, I think, though it was a little weird. I mean, she was much more, I don't know, put together than usual. I mean, made up and dressed to the nines in a Seven-Sisters sort of way. She seemed happy as a clam. But manic, if you know what I mean. Laughing and gabbing nineteen to the dozen. I guess it's better than before, though. She says she's only had a couple of what she called her 'little episodes' this year."

Mom snorted at the term. "I know," Celia said. "But she says she takes these pills, Miltown, they're called, that keep her on an even keel."

"Hm," Mom said. "I've seen ads for that. It's a brand name for Meprobomate. They're calling it a miracle drug, like penicillin. I'm a little uneasy about it, though."

"Why's that, Mom?" Joy asked from her perch on the desk.

"Well, it's similar to the way I felt about the psychotropic drugs she was taking to counteract the paralysis. It seems to me there's more to the human psyche than brain chemistry, that someone with serious psychological problems needs to get to the root causes rather than simply treating the symptoms."

Joy said, "I don't get the difference."

Mom explained, "Imagine you have a cough. You can take cough syrup to suppress it, and usually that's fine. But what if it's actually caused by allergies that you keep exposing yourself to without knowing it? Or an infection of some kind? Or even like Laurie's poor birth mother, cancer? She probably dosed herself with nostrums for some time before she saw a doctor who could diagnose the real problem. And a psychologist has to look at emotional problems and psychological issues that can cause physical symptoms as well as mental ones."

Joy swung herself around to lie across the desk, one wrist on her forehead, and declaimed dramatically, "Oh, Dr. Freud, it's all the fault of my toilet training!"

Mom chuckled and lofted one of Celia's discarded bobby socks at her, but went on, "There's something about this particular drug that bothers me, too. The ads I've seen: they're all directed at women. Or rather, at men regarding women. 'Does she react too strongly to everything?' 'Is her PMS out of control?' 'When she can't take a week in the Bahamas, give her Miltown instead.' Of course, it's nothing new in psychology that women are viewed as somehow inherently defective compared to men, but I don't like this tendency to medicate us out of our troubles."

Mom drew one knee up, locking her hands around it. "At my reunion at Smith last year, one of the younger alumnae, named Betty Goldstein—it's Friedan now—was passing out questionnaires. She's a journalist, but she studied psychology as an undergrad. She's trying to explore this whole business of women's unhappiness and the causes of it and the reasons it's ignored or minimized by our male-dominated society. Filling out her form has made me wonder, in cases like Carol's, whether we're sweeping the real problems under the rug with drugs and emotional Band-Aids."

Celia finished patting her thick, dark bob into place and propped a hip on the foot of her bed, facing Mom. The relief she'd been feeling since she left Proskys' was draining away, to be replaced by a familiar burning band across her shoulders.

Mom responded immediately to her expression. "I'm not saying this is something you need to deal with, Cissy. Carol is your friend, not your patient or your responsibility. Just keep being her friend; let her parents and her doctor worry about her treatment."

"Really? But after we've been through so much together…"

"Did she seem disposed to revisit that time with you?"

"No, the opposite. She wanted to change the subject when I brought it up."

Mom nodded. "That boat has sailed. Let it go. You're in different waters with her now."

The band across Celia's shoulders loosened. "Ok," she breathed. "I've been thinking, though, Mom. I think I want to work with people like Carol, people with problems like that."

"Be a psychologist, you mean?"

Celia squirmed a little. "Not exactly. No offense, Mom, I think you're great, and what you do is great, but I was thinking I'd be a real doctor." At the expression on Mom's face she added hurriedly, "I mean an MD, a psychiatrist. Somebody who can prescribe medicine. Like you said that time in the study, do it the right way, with talk therapy along with it. Control the symptoms *and* get to the root causes."

Mom's expression softened at the anxiety in Celia's. "That sounds marvelous, darling. You know it will be a lot of work. You've tended to focus on the humanities in your studies, on literature and history. You'll need a solid grounding in science to get a medical degree, and a special focus on chemistry if you're interested in the pharmacological aspect."

Joy rolled off the desk and bounced over to sit on her own bed. "Ooh, Cissy," she said. "Looks like someone's going to be cracking the books."

"Quiet, shrimp," Celia said. "I'll start studying tomorrow. Right now, I need to get downstairs. I don't want to keep Ray waiting; he's always nervous before a match."

She wondered what Ray would think of her new resolve. *I'll wait till after the match to mention it. He'll have his own stuff on his mind right now.*

Chapter 39.

It was lunchtime, but for once, Celia wasn't hungry. Judy had been understanding when she'd said she wanted to be alone to think; Ray had been less so, but she'd persevered in the face of his disapproval. He'd been unsympathetic to her new resolve to buckle down in the sciences, and mocking of her ambition to be an MD. When she'd been hurt and disappointed at his attitude, he'd chaffed her for being humorless and self-absorbed.

But she didn't want to think about Ray now. She wanted to think about Steve. It was drizzly outside, but warm enough, so she tucked herself under the overhang over the cafeteria door, sitting cross-legged in the corner of the concrete stoop where she couldn't be seen through the glass from inside but wouldn't be in the way of someone coming through.

Last night, Steve had gone through a major crisis; Celia and Joy had been awakened in the middle of the night by shouting and crying upstairs in the music room, then before they'd had a chance to investigate, by the sound of crashing and glass smashing. She and her sister had stood in their bedroom doorway, arms around each other's waists, watching as Mom and Dad came from the attic stairway, supporting Steve between them, while Jamie followed on their heels into the room the two boys shared. Just before disappearing inside,

Dad had told Laurie and Rob, who'd just come out of their room, to get the mattress off the spare room bed.

Celia was still half asleep; she couldn't imagine why they'd need another mattress. Then Jamie came out of his room carrying a bundle of bed linens. Celia could smell the acrid tang of urine from where she stood, and the penny dropped. As Jamie carried the sheets downstairs, she disengaged from Joy and went to the linen closet for fresh ones. "Come on," she said to Joy.

In Steve and Jamie's room, Mom was alone, wrestling with the mattress on Steve's bed; it had a big stain in the middle, one that had been growing for some nights by the look and smell of it. Celia opened a window and helped Mom prop the mattress against the window seat just as the boys hauled in the fresh mattress. While they maneuvered it into place and Mom and Joy started putting on the fresh sheets Celia had brought, Celia shoved the old mattress out the window onto the garage walkway below.

Jamie came in and said that Ruby was awake and taking care of the laundry. Then the bathroom door opened and Dad came out, bare-chested, carrying Steve like a baby, wrapped in a big towel. Celia realized she'd been hearing the shower running till just now.

Dad laid Steve gently on the newly clean bed and started to dry him while Mom got out clean pajamas. Celia and the others said good night and left; Steve was obviously in no shape for more interactions, however loving. Feeling confident that Mom and Dad had the situation well in hand, Celia fell quickly into a dreamless sleep.

This morning, the parents had been nowhere in evidence in the kitchen. Ruby'd said they were taking the day off, along with Steve and Jamie. Then it was time for the bus, and the others had to scramble.

This was the first minute Celia'd had alone with time to think. She knew from news reports at the time that Steve had killed the cousin who'd imprisoned and tortured him for ten years. She knew from Beth, who was already at school for the week, that Steve had recently confessed that to her, not realizing they all already knew. *What must that have been like, thinking he had such a terrible secret?*

Obviously, it had been preying on him, if he'd been wetting the bed. That must be where Jamie came in: he must have told the folks what was happening. And they'd all gone up to get Steve out of his attic hideaway, and there'd been some kind of confrontation. And that smashing and crashing sound? Celia pictured the music room in her mind. There'd been no other sounds involved, no strings twanging or piano keys clashing, so it wouldn't have been an instrument. Then she remembered the knickknack shelf on the wall, with its china figurines.

Somebody must have knocked it down. Steve? *No, that doesn't seem like him. He's too afraid of his own anger. And Jamie's too buttoned down. Mom—I can't even imagine her doing such a thing.* That left Dad. Whatever Steve had told them had made Dad angry enough to start smashing things. What could it have been? *Whatever made Steve finally snap and kill that Bert,* she guessed. *Something he did, or threatened to do.*

She shivered and drew her knees up to her chest. Those withdrawal periods of his, like Carol's in a way—Mom called them by the same name, hysterical conversion, though Steve's didn't include the paralysis. What had Steve gone through to make him close off like that? Part of her was filled with sympathy for Steve, and horror at what this said about what his life had been like. But another part was... admiration. Whatever Bert had done, Steve had stood up to him. A traumatized, abused, skinny little thirteen-year-old—*no, he'd only been twelve at the time*—had faced down a full-grown man and ended it the only way he could.

Where did that kind of strength come from? And what would they do about the aftershocks now? Mom and Dad could each give something different to Steve.

Mom could talk to him about how he felt and help him deal with the guilt; Dad could be the protector and the strong shield against Steve's own turmoil. I hope he wasn't scared by Dad losing his temper and smashing the shelf. If he is, they'll help him get over it. And Jamie was the witness, standing by through it all; I bet that was hard for him. As for the rest of us, we did what we could to help through the material, external things. They're important, too: a clean bed to sleep in, the warm milk with honey Ruby always makes when Jamie has a nightmare. We let him know we love him without having to bother him by saying so.

But what comes next? He never believes us when we say we admire him; it just makes him mad. How can I show him?

The answer came to Celia with a calm certainty. *By being strong myself, and letting him know he's inspired me. I can have sympathy, I can show love. But I can stand up for people, and for myself, too. And Ray will just have to learn to live with it.*

The bell rang. Celia pushed herself up off the damp concrete. *Gym this period. Maybe I can cram a few bites of my sandwich in while I change.*

Chapter 40.

Saturday, May 31, 1958

It had drizzled a little this morning, but a summery sun shone golden on the fresh-washed foliage now as Celia guided Mom's blue Dodge down the shady streets of Mt. Holly Springs to Ray's house. The winter had been the coldest since 1950, and Celia felt as though she were bursting out of a cocoon, ready to spread her wings.

"'Arise, my love, my fair one, and come away; for lo, the winter is past and gone: the time of the singing of birds is come, and the voice of the turtle is heard in the land,'" she quoted softly. Then she giggled a little. That "voice of the turtle" always tickled her, thinking what a turtle's voice might sound like, though she knew it was an Elizabethan term for "turtledove."

Then she remembered why she was driving instead of letting Ray pick her up, as he preferred, and her euphoria abruptly vanished. She was going to break up with him tonight. But her dejection didn't last, either. Instead, she felt a firm resolve. *If I could feel that happy, knowing what I'm going to do, then it must be the right thing.*

This double date with Ted and Judy had been postponed from last night to suit her schedule, so she hadn't felt able to cancel it; the other couple would meet them here, then they'd go to the Deer Lodge for dinner, followed by *Vertigo* at the Carlisle movie house.

They were supposed to finish up with Cokes at the Pine Springs diner; that was where Celia planned to break the news to Ray. *That place is getting to be the one where all my romantic disasters happen,* she reflected.

She knew Ray would be angry and upset, so she thought it would be wise to have her own transportation home. But it couldn't be helped. She'd had a conversation with Steve last night that had cemented her resolve. Ray was getting more and more demanding— of her time, and of her physical involvement. They had started some fairly heavy petting, which Celia had to admit she enjoyed, but he clearly wanted to take it farther, and she definitely was not up for that. Then he'd kicked up a fuss about her not wanting to do this date on a Friday night and miss Shabbat dinner and the family evening.

"You could join us," she'd suggested, as she had before when he'd tried to get her to go out on a Friday night.

Ray had scoffed at the idea yet again. "Sit around saying a bunch of prayers in a language I don't understand, then spend the rest of the night listening to your mother read some book out loud? No, thanks."

Then he'd made another lunge for her bra fastener. Since they were sitting in the open in her living room, and she'd just seen Steve pass on his way to the door at the back of the front hall, she'd slapped his hand away. "Really, Ray."

He'd left soon after, accepting her suggestion that they do the dinner and a movie date tonight, but with an ill grace. Then, setting the table with Steve, she'd found out that Steve thought Ray disliked their family. "He talks to me like I'm a moron and he looks at Laurie like he thinks he's going to steal his wallet," Steve had said.

It all made Celia wonder why Ray was interested in her in the first place. There were obviously prettier girls than Celia—ones with more voluptuous figures and more biddable attitudes, if that's all he was after. He certainly never seemed interested in what Celia thought or had to say about anything. She remembered how he'd met her announcement last winter about her decision to get a medical degree with barely concealed amusement, and the extra time she'd spent since on trying to catch up in science with mounting impatience.

She was ashamed to realize it was his stunning looks and the way their make-out sessions made her feel that had kept her in the relationship this long (and maybe, just a little bit, the jealous, incredulous glares of the other girls); they really had nothing in common.

Strengthened in her resolve to end it before she got too enmeshed, Celia pulled up to Ray's family's trim white frame bungalow. Ted's car was already in the driveway, so she parked on the narrow street a few doors away and walked back to the house.

Hearing the boys' voices and the unmistakable *thwock- thwock-thwock* of a basketball on concrete, she started around the side to the back yard. Halfway there, she stopped.

"You know how it is," Ray was saying. "That's why you bilged her, right? Because of her freak family and how obsessed she is with them?"

"Not exactly," Ted said. Celia could hear the discomfort in his voice. "I didn't like taking a back seat all the time, being the also-ran in her life drama. But I liked her family fine, and it's really out of line to call them freaks, Ray."

The ball dribbled a couple of times, then there was a swish as it evidently went through the hoop affixed to the back of the garage where the sidewalk widened out to a sort of patio.

Celia started forward but stopped again at the venom in Ray's voice. "I call 'em like I see 'em. Besides, I'm not even getting in her pants, so it's a bit rich that she thinks she can just make me wait till she can fit me into her precious schedule before I'm allowed to spend money on her."

The sound of the ball stopped. "But why are you still with her if you feel that way?" Ted said. He sounded both confused and angry, which reflected Celia's own feelings.

Ray made an exasperated noise. "Why do you think? Her old man is the commandant at the Depot. You know what that could have meant for my dad, if I got together with her? But now that Dad's moved on to the War College... Oh, right, you're not military, are you? Judy's father is, though; she'd get what I mean."

"Oh, I get it, all right," came Judy's voice. Celia heard the back screen door smack against its frame; Judy's voice got clearer as she evidently came outside. "You know, Ted, I've suddenly lost my appetite for dinner. Would you take me home now, please?"

"I sure will," Ted said.

"Wait, what?" Ray sounded as panicked as Celia had ever heard him. "Telling Celia we're through is one thing, explaining you leaving is something else. You can't go, what will I tell her?"

"I'm sure you'll think of something," Judy said coldly. "I know I'll have plenty to tell her later tonight."

"Don't you dare," Ray snarled.

"Step back from my girlfriend," Ted growled in turn, "before I rearrange your pretty face."

"Ted, you don't need to go all caveman," Judy snapped. "I'm not afraid of this jackass. It's Celia I'm worried about; I don't think she should go off with him alone when he's in this mood."

Celia's feet finally unstuck themselves from where they'd frozen on the sparse grass by the side of the house, and her brain engaged again. "Don't worry," she said, striding forward around the house. "I'm not planning to be alone with him any more. I had thought I would break up with him at the diner tonight after you guys left, but he's just saved me the trouble."

"*You're* going to break up with *me?*" Ray said incredulously. His face was white except for his turkey-red cheeks.

"Doesn't miss a trick, does he?" Celia said to the other two. "Man's a mental giant. I don't know what I was thinking to stick with him this long; my head must have been in the clouds."

"I don't think it's your head you were thinking with," Judy said wryly.

Ted said, "Judy, really," but Celia nodded ruefully at her friend.

Celia was shaking a little. Still, she took more strength from Judy's sarcasm and the firm stance she took beside Celia than from Ted's anxious solicitude.

"Are you going to be all right to drive home alone?" Ted asked.

"She's not going to drive home alone," Judy said before Celia had a chance to answer. "She's driving to my house with me, where we're going to make peanut butter and marshmallow fluff sandwiches and sit around and abuse the male race for a few hours. You don't mind, do you, honey?"

Ted hesitated for a second, then said, "No, sure, I don't mind. Have a good girl talk." He leaned over and kissed Judy briefly on the mouth, then gave Celia a peck on the cheek.

The three of them moved together toward the front of the house. No one looked back at Ray.

CHAPTER 41.

SUNDAY, JUNE 1, 1957

This was the first time Celia had ever asked for a family meeting. It was silly to feel nervous about it, she knew, but knowing that didn't stop the butterflies in her stomach as they all looked at her expectantly. The remains of Sunday brunch still littered the table but she hadn't wanted to wait till everything was cleared up.

She took a breath and looked around at them all again. Laurie, who suspected what this was about, reached over and gave her hand a reassuring squeeze. Jamie, whom she'd talked to last night about this, looked gloomy but resigned. For his part, Steve, who'd also been around for her conversation with Laurie this morning before church, was starting to look anxious. *Time to get started.*

She cleared her throat. "We all know about Laurie's problem with Dean Dunkelman threatening to keep him from taking Linda to the prom by giving her a bad college rec," she began. The others nodded; they'd come together to comfort him when he'd broken down over it the day Steve's adoption had become final. Heartened by both memories, she went on, "Well, I think I may have a solution."

Immediately, the atmosphere in the room lightened. *They thought I was going to tell them something bad,* she realized. So she quickly went on,

"What if Laurie goes with me as his date, and Jamie takes Linda? The dean wouldn't have a leg to stand on going after Linda; she couldn't claim that garbage about 'not thinking of the good of the community' she was going to try if Linda and Laurie went together. And she couldn't very well object to me going with my own brother, even if we are different races. It would make it too obvious that it was really her bigotry at play."

"Hmm, interesting idea," Mom said. "I don't know that it really solves the problem, though. People are still going to be riled up over this; they already are."

Celia nodded. "It's been awful, I know. Those anonymous hate calls, and egging Dad's car a couple of weeks ago. We're not going to banish racial prejudice overnight no matter what we do. But we can make a sort of statement by arranging things so that Laurie and Linda can still have their evening together and Dean Dunkelman can't ruin Linda's life over it."

"What do you think, Laurie?" Dad asked.

Laurie pushed his hands into his hair and pulled a little, looking down at his syrup-smeared plate. "I'm torn. Part of me wants to do this, not to let the racist jerks win, and not to let anybody get between me and my girl. But another part of me just wants to protect Linda. Maybe I should just forget about it. Maybe I shouldn't be trying to keep going with her at all. Maybe—"

"You stop right there, young man." Celia gaped; she hadn't heard Ruby take that tone with Laurie in years. She saw his head come up to stare as Ruby went on, "You know I was of two minds about this whole business at the beginning. But it's gone too far to back out now. You'll hate yourself if you do, and you won't help Linda, either. Everybody knows how she feels about you. If you don't go to this dance, they'll still be makin nasty calls to her house, but they'll be laughin at her, too."

Ruby's voice was fierce but her lips were trembling. She raised her hands to cover them and glared around the table with brimming eyes. Beth got up and bent over her, putting her arms around Ruby's shoulders; Ruby moved a hand to pat one of Beth's, then visibly pulled herself together. Beth went back to her seat.

"Ok, Ruby," Laurie said meekly. "I see what you're saying."

Dad said, "Well, I think we have the sense of the meeting, as Beth's Friends would say. Your mother and I will talk it over some more, and of course we'll have to consult with Linda's parents, and Laurie will want to talk to her and to them as well. I'm not completely convinced; I'm worried about the potential for troublemakers to cause something serious, but this was a good and generous idea, Cissy. Thank you."

"Wait a minute," Joy suddenly put in. "Speaking of 'generous,' what about your own dates? Are they going to go with each other or something?"

"Rima is going to Cape May with her parents," Jamie said. "She's not really interested in a high school dance in any case, now that she's started at Franklin and Marshall, and I wasn't exactly brokenhearted at the prospect of skipping prom myself. I don't mind going with Linda if it helps Laurie, though."

"I appreciate it, Hymele," Laurie said. Jamie shrugged off the thanks, looking embarrassed.

"What about you, Celia?" Mom asked. "Won't Ray be disappointed?"

"I broke up with Ray yesterday," Celia said.

"All right!" Steve crowed. The adults turned to stare at him, it was so uncharacteristic of him to speak out in the group this way.

But Rob said, "About time," and Joy nodded vigorously.

Celia was flabbergasted. "Do you all feel this way about him? How long has this been going on?"

"Almost since the beginning, in my case," Beth said. "I didn't want to interfere, Celia, but I've always heard a... tone in his voice that made me uneasy. I'm afraid he's... not always very nice."

That was a blistering denunciation coming from Beth. They all looked taken aback a little. Then Laurie said, "Do you feel like telling us what happened, Ceecee?" deliberately repeating the childhood nickname he'd used this morning.

"No, I don't mind," she said. "In fact, I'd appreciate some help understanding what happened myself. I spent the rest of the evening at Judy's, stuffing ourselves and complaining about boys, but we didn't really get to the heart of the problem. When Ray and I first started going together, he seemed to get it when I explained that our time together would be limited—and, especially, that I had a commitment to spend Friday nights with the family."

"You don't have to give up your fun for me," Jamie said stiffly.

"I don't do it for you, or not mostly. I love our Shabbat ritual: the meal, the prayers, Mom reading by the fire—all of it. I'm so glad you started us on it, Jamie, and I wouldn't give it up now. I hope we'll keep doing it even after you leave for college." The others all nodded and Jamie sat back, relaxing.

Celia went on, "But lately he's been giving me a hard time about it, pressuring me to do something with him instead." She thought for a minute, then shook her head. "You know, I started to have misgivings way back at Thanksgiving. You remember, when Ruby's nephew came to visit? Henry was so nice and, I don't know, direct, I guess. I mean, it was obvious he was nervous about being here, but he... he paid attention to everyone, he was really here with us, you know what I mean? And I thought, this is what I'm missing with Ray. Ray could be really kind of extravagantly romantic, but something about it didn't ring true the way everything that Henry said did."

Celia picked up a strawberry hull from her plate and started pulling the leaves apart.

"And," Mom put in, "Henry is also a very good-looking boy, so the contrast in behavior would be sharper."

"I didn't think of that," Celia said, then added, blushing, "but I have to admit that Ray's looks are part of the reason I kept on with him so long. I mean, it was flattering, right? Why would someone like that be interested in me?" She flapped a hand at the hisses and eye-rolling around the table. "Yeah, yeah, you all think I'm gorgeous, I know. But getting back to the point, this Friday he suddenly went all Neanderthal on me, insisting we had to go out with Ted and Judy for dinner and a movie that night. I got him to postpone it till Saturday and I thought it was solved, but then I talked to Steve."

"Me?" Steve squeaked with some alarm.

Celia nodded to him. "You really helped, telling me you felt like Ray didn't like the family." She smiled as Steve got an expression as though someone had given him an unexpected present. *That's one thing good that's come out of this.* Then she sighed and continued, "So I went to Ray's yesterday thinking I was going to break up with him anyway—and I feel really good that I got it in before he did—but as I was coming around the house I overheard him telling Ted that... that the only reason he stuck with me was because it might help his dad's position at the Depot."

"Why, that little sh-weasel," Dad growled.

"'Sh-weasel'?" Celia teased. "I don't think I know that species." But her nose started prickling and she knew she'd be crying in a minute.

Dad leaned across Mom to take Celia's hand; Mom shifted her chair back out of the way. "I've never liked Charlie Angstrom," he said.

"Angstrom!" Laurie exclaimed. "That jerk? You remember, Jamie, the guy I told you about who was so obnoxious to me? That's who Ray's father is?"

Dad nodded. "A bully and a lickspittle, and a bigot to boot."

"Why didn't you say anything, Dad?"

"I didn't want to visit the sins of the father on the son; as long as Ray seemed to be behaving himself decently, I tried to separate the two in my mind. I did notice some unpleasant attitudes in him towards us from time to time, but you seemed happy and I hoped that exposure to us, along with feelings for you, would wean him away from the way he'd been raised." He shook his head. "I never thought of this angle, though; it never occurred to me that a high school kid would be that calculating."

"But why would Ray suddenly get all, like, 'Rumble, rumble, I'm a tank' with Celia?" Rob said.

"Because I got sick enough of Charlie that I finally managed to get him transferred to the War College," Dad said. "He doesn't need to fawn on me anymore. So I suppose this breakup is my fault, Cissy."

"Thank God," Celia said. "I declare this meeting adjourned."

CHAPTER 42.

SATURDAY, JUNE 7, 1958

There was blood on Celia's dress. Looking at herself in the bathroom mirror, she thought back to the day of her first menstrual period, four years ago. That blood had felt like an emblem of adult womanhood. This blood was empowering in an entirely different way.

The bathroom door to Beth's room opened a crack and her sister's voice said softly, "Cissy? Are you all right?"

"Yeah, come on in, Bethie. I'm ok, just a little weak in the knees and my stomach's a bit upset. Reaction, I guess."

Beth started to reach for her, then pulled her hand back in alarm. "I smell blood. Are you hurt?"

"No, it's not my blood."

"What?" squawked a voice behind her. Joy had opened the door to her and Celia's bedroom on the other side of the bathroom. "What happened? Whose blood is it?"

Celia drew a breath to say something placating and bland to both of them, then thought, *I really do want to talk about it.*

She drew Beth after her into the bedroom behind Joy. Once they got there, Joy unpinned the ruins of Celia's gardenia corsage from her shoulder while Beth stepped around her and started unclipping the hook-and-eye fastenings down the back of her dress. Joy lifted the

214

gardenia and questioned Celia with a raised eyebrow; Celia shook her head and Joy tossed it into the wastebasket. *The last thing I need is a memento of this night.*

As Joy began drawing Celia's blue sash from around her waist, she eyed the white silk organza covering Celia's chest critically. "This dress is done for," she said. "Spatters and smears, and all dried."

"Sorry," Celia said. "I know you liked it."

"Yeah, I did, but look on the bright side: it means I'll get a new one for my prom instead of wearing your hand-me-down. Now, enough fashion chat. Spill."

Celia untied the drawstring at the waist of her crinoline petticoat and stepped out of it as she said, "I think the smears are Jamie's; he helped me into the car, and his cheek was bleeding from that chain of Tom Varner's. The spatters are from when Laurie smashed Travis Thumper's nose."

Beth gasped and Joy's eyes widened. Celia sank back onto her own bed and started undoing another set of hooks and eyes, this down the front of her "merry widow" corselet, then she pulled down the zipper beneath the placket. As the stiff structure of wire and mesh and plastic stays fell away from her upper body, she sighed in relief and let herself sag into Beth's arms where she waited behind Celia. Joy undid the garters holding the garment to Celia's stockings and peeled it away, frowning at the red lines the thing had left on Celia's flesh. "Start at the beginning," she demanded.

So Celia told them about the prom: about the tension and the awkwardness, the frowns from Dean Dunkelman, the hostility from some of the other kids, the moral support from a few others, and, finally, the jostling of Laurie and Linda by Varner and Thumper and their dance partners. The incident was clearly orchestrated by the boys, though.

"You remember my telling you about them; they were the ones, with some other lunkhead, who pestered Steve in the playground his first day here. The other creep has dropped out and gone into a hole somewhere, but those two are sticking out their last year—evidently just so they could hang around and give us grief. Coach Perkins and Dean Jumper put them out of the dance but they were waiting for us in the parking lot."

Joy tossed Celia a nightgown and Celia hitched up from Beth enough to pull it over her head and shimmy into it before she continued. "So Laurie sent Linda back into the gym to get adult help. He was going to try that on me, too, but I just gave him a look and he backed down."

Joy nodded approvingly but Beth breathed, "Oh, Celia." It was sympathy rather than reproach; still, it made Celia uneasy.

"I couldn't just leave the boys there alone, Bethie. It's not in me. When we backed up against each other to hold them off, I felt—*good,* Beth. I felt strong and brave. I also felt scared shitless, by the way," (Joy giggled at the word and Celia waggled her eyebrows at her) "but that was somehow less important than the other ways I was feeling. The actual fight only lasted a minute; Laurie smashed his head into Thumper's nose, Varner clipped Jamie's cheek with that chain and Jamie punched him in the stomach, and I stomped on Varner's instep and ripped that damn chain right out of his hand. Then Dad and Mr. Marks showed up and the cowards ran off."

"Wow," Joy said. She'd peeled off Celia's hose and flung them aside. Now she stood up and said, "I have to pee. Don't say anything till I get back."

But as soon as she was out of the room, Celia said, "I know you're disappointed in me, Beth."

Beth squeezed her around the waist. "Have I said or done something that makes you think I'm judging you?" she asked mildly.

"No, but I know you don't believe in violence."

"I wasn't there. It's like I told Steve this spring, when he had that breakdown. I don't know how I would have behaved in his situation and I don't know that about yours, either." She paused for a second, then said, "If you're looking for my advice, I'd just say don't... don't glory in that memory, in that feeling of triumph. Accept it; it happened, it's part of you. But pass through it, or let it pass through you. Does that make any sense?"

"I think it does. I'll mull it over, anyway. Thank you, Angel."

Beth huffed at the nickname and moved aside to pull down Celia's covers and help her into bed.

"I should shower," Celia said vaguely. "I stink."

"Yes, you do, rather," Beth agreed. "But I think it could wait till tomorrow."

Joy came back into the room and looked at her two sisters leaning on each other on Celia's bed. Her avid expression softened. "Poor Celia. You look wiped out. What an awful experience for your junior prom. I hope your senior one will be better: at least that you'll have a decent date now that you've split with Ray."

Celia shrugged, eyelids drooping. "He was there tonight, stag. Never danced with the same one twice, but rubbed up on them all like a dog in rut. I don't care. I'll never date a guy just because he's good looking and everyone else is jealous again. Tonight was better than a date, anyway. I was strong, I stood up for something important. And I don't just mean those jerks at the end. Jamie and I, we were there for Laurie." Her voice was starting to wobble and the room was fading.

Someone knocked at the door and Joy opened it. Ruby was there, with a tray full of her patented nostrum in cases of injury or trauma: warm milk and honey.

"Your dad's with Laurie and your mother is helping Jamie get his mind settled," she said. "I thought I'd check with you. I see you're getting some help already, though."

"Yes, I am," Celia said, smiling at her. "But this will help, too." She took one of the mugs and held it in both hands, enjoying the warmth and breathing in the aroma of the nutmeg floating on the surface of the milk. She bent her head and took a sip. Somehow it seemed like too much work to raise her head again afterwards.

She felt the mug slipping out of her hands; someone took it away. Then Ruby's brown hand came into her vision and tipped her chin up. She fought to keep her eyes open enough to meet Ruby's sharp, evaluating gaze, then gave up the battle.

Ruby put a hand·behind Celia's head and guided it down to the pillow. "Enough talk for now," she said. "Sleep, child."

"Yes, ma'am," Celia mumbled, and went out like a candle.

Chapter 43.

Saturday, July 5, 1958

Judy stared across at Celia from where she lay on her stomach on Joy's bed, chin on her folded hands. "I still don't get what's bugging you so much about this," she said. "You stepped up to the plate and the bad guys whiffed. Why shouldn't you feel good about that?"

"I know, you're right, but—" Celia turned onto her back and stared at the ceiling, hands behind her head. "That's what Jamie says, too. He says what we did after the prom, standing up to those bullies, made him feel powerful, strong. It made me feel that way, too, that night. It's different for me, though. I didn't see Nazis murder my parents and then have to live in a concentration camp feeling frightened and powerless all the time."

"So because you didn't grow up in a nightmare, you have to be all sweetness and light?"

"That's not it. My sister Beth said I should accept my feelings about it but not glory in them, to let them pass through me."

"I don't know what that means."

"I'm still puzzling it out myself, but I think it means that I shouldn't let those feelings of, of *triumph* take over."

"I don't know, Celia. It seems to me you ask an awful lot of yourself."

Celia hummed a little in half-hearted agreement, but she was thinking, *"Every one to whom much is given, of him will much be required."*

While she was trying to think of a way to say that without sounding unbearably pious, the sound of a car horn drifted up through the noise of her window fan.

Judy leaped up. "There's Rick," she said. "I've told him not to do that, to come to the front door like a civilized person, but you know how brothers are…"

"Yeah, I know," Celia said, getting up herself. "Uncivilizable. Is that a word?"

"It should be."

After Celia saw Judy out the front door and closed it behind her, she stood there leaning against it for a minute, deciding what to do. She could hear the murmur of Mom and Dad's voices and—was that Jamie? *Good. Maybe they're talking about all this.*

She stuck her head in the open study door but the room was empty and she realized the voices were coming from the TV room, where the new window air conditioner battled the humid heat of the waning day.

She circled the stairs and pushed the door open, mind busy with what she wanted to say, in time to hear Jamie's voice: "What if MIT finds out I'm queer?"

Celia's breath rushed out of her lungs. She stood half in, half out of the room, her own problems swept out of her mind. *But yes,* she thought, as illumination replaced the murk. *That would explain it: the way his reactions often seem slightly off, the tension between him and Rima that's not quite like the tension between boys and me. What should I do? How can I help him?*

Jamie evidently wasn't thinking in terms of Celia being any use to him, though. He gritted out, "Cissy, I swear to God," and she realized he was afraid she'd let his secret out.

She came all the way into the room and shut the door. She flapped her hands at him, trying to sweep the fear out of the air and off his face. "I won't say anything, I promise. I'm sorry I butted in, I just wanted to talk to Mom about—well, never mind, it's not important. Just... Really? Jamie, you really think you're... that way?"

Dad said, "This is still pretty new. I don't think Jamie's ready to talk about it with you just yet," as he came over and hugged Celia to his side with one arm.

Jamie nodded in agreement. "Too many people already know. Beth. And Rima, she's the one who—"

"Kevin," Dad broke in. "You need to talk to Kevin."

They kept talking; Dad went over to hug Jamie. Celia moved to Mom on the couch and perched next to her.

"What should I do?" she asked her. "How can I help?"

Mom pulled Celia's head forward and kissed her forehead. "You don't need to do anything, sweetheart. Just be your usual self with him; try to help him see that this won't change the way we feel about him." She leaned back and locked her eyes on Celia's. "Was there a reason you came in here just now?"

"Yeah, I wanted to talk about what happened after prom, but this has sort of driven that off the front burner. We can do that some other time."

Mom nodded. "I do think your father and I have to focus on Jamie right now. If you're not in immediate distress "

Celia gave a fond little laugh. "I'm not 'in distress' at all, just thinking things through. To be continued." She kissed Mom's cheek, got up, and left the room, circling around Dad and Jamie, who were still clasped in each other's arms. As she turned to close the door behind her, Dad raised his eyes and met hers with a twitch of his eyebrows that somehow conveyed love, understanding, and appreciation all at once.

That night, lying in bed listening to Joy's soft sleeping breath, Celia ran a sort of inventory of all that had been happening to her in the past couple of years.

Maybe thinking it all over will help me see how I can help Jamie find his way. Coping with all Carol's problems, and with lesser aggravations like Mr. Prosky and that obnoxious intern, helped me see that it's possible to keep your feet even when trouble seems like an overwhelming flood. And taking it step by step instead of trying to deal with it all at once gets you through in the end. I suppose coping with the different problems and people at work gave me some confidence that I could manage stress without falling apart.

She sighed and turned her pillow over, searching for a cool spot. *And the boys: realizing that my family was a higher priority for me than my relationship with Ted, and that what I had with Ray wasn't a relationship at all. Steve helped me see that.*

And Steve is someone with more to cope with than I'll ever have. He's actually killed someone. Jamie told us that when Steve had that breakdown this spring, he said he was afraid he'd want to kill us if we rejected him—that he was afraid he was a bad person. But it's so obvious he's not; he's got such a good heart, when he can let go enough to let it show. I don't have a boyfriend any more, or many girlfriends, either, for that matter—Barb's done with me, and Carol has avoided me this summer since she got back from that school; thank goodness I've still got Judy. Sort of. She's so taken up with Ted lately... So I can focus more on Steve.

She nibbled on her thumbnail. *It's easy to love Steve, to understand what drove him to what he did. I wonder what drives people like Thumper and Varner?* Travis and Tom, she corrected herself. *They're people, too, individuals with names and with histories I know nothing about. "Love those that hate you." It'd be pretty hard to love them, but I suppose Jesus didn't mean I have to like them. He certainly didn't mean we have to let hateful people—people who are full of hate—do whatever they want. That would be as bad for them as for us. Okay, there it is. That's where Beth's "not glorying" comes in. I'm going*

222

to be a person who doesn't hold on to anger, who stops people from doing bad things when I can but doesn't stay angry and closed off to them. Let it go, let it pass through.

Celia felt the tension bleed out of her like water. She brought her hands together and said her prayers, starting with Tom Varner and Travis Thumper.

Chapter 44.

Tuesday, September 2, 1958

*I*t's your imagination, Celia told herself sternly. *The house does not seem empty. There are eight people here, for heaven's sake.* Yet it did seem empty, somehow. Laurie and Jamie were both gone: Laurie to Haverford and Jamie to MIT, early admission.

Celia had offered to take a shift at the restaurant, even though it was a school night, deliberately to avoid coming home to half-empty bedrooms in the afternoon and empty seats at the dinner table. But this was worse, somehow. *Everybody should be safe at home after dark.*

People were scattered at their usual evening pursuits. She could hear gunfire coming from the TV room; Rob and Joy were probably watching a Western, with Beth, whose boarding school wouldn't start for the year till next week, sitting companionably by while they narrated the action for her. Beyond that, the plummy tones of Arthur Godfrey filtered through: Ruby's television in her sitting room. Nearer at hand, she could hear the sound of a typewriter and a brief, low-voiced exchange—Mom and Dad at their everlasting paperwork.

Where's Steve? she wondered. He seldom watched TV, except for variety shows; he certainly didn't care for shoot-'em-ups. *Probably up in the music room.*

She called a greeting to her parents and made her way up the front stairs and down the hall to the back stairs, where she cocked an ear toward the upper level. But there was no sound of guitar or piano, or of Steve's plangent, plaintive voice. She'd glanced into the bedroom he and Jamie shared as she'd passed its open door; it was dark and empty. *He must be in the cabinet,* she realized.

When he'd first joined the family, more than a year ago now, Jamie had ceded his own hiding place to Steve; the family had all been pleased that Jamie didn't feel he needed it any more, and recognized that the bustle and the varied temperaments that filled the house would be hard for a child raised in isolation to cope with all the time. Then last spring, when his guilt and fear over having killed his tormentor and—just as challengingly, that he was now surrounded by people who loved and cared for him—had come to a head in that emotional tornado, the exact location of the hiding place had come to light.

Except for when Mom and Dad and Jamie had gone up there in the middle of the night that time to confront and succor Steve, everyone had acted as though they still didn't know. But a strong instinct was pulling Celia that way now. She climbed the steps to the music room and went through the low door into the attic space. Then she sat cross-legged on the floor in front of the cabinet door. Light from Steve's battery lantern leaked through the cracks, and she could hear the faint sounds of the transistor radio the folks gave him for Christmas.

She knew he would have heard her come in; she wondered whether she should call to him. But after a few seconds, the door clicked open and he stared out at her.

"Oh, it's you," he said dully.

"Did you want someone else? Should I get Mom or Dad for you?"

"No, it was... no, it doesn't matter." He shrugged, but Celia could see even in the dim light that his eyes were swollen and his hands were shaking, though his face was as blank as it had been when he first came to them.

"What is it, honey? Are you upset because Laurie and Jamie are gone?"

His face crumpled, though he didn't cry again. "I don't like it when things change," he whispered.

"Me, neither," she said. "Really," she insisted to his skeptical look. "Change doesn't scare me the way I think it does you, but so much of my life outside this family is always jerking around, and jerking *me* around, that I wish everything here would just stay put."

"Stay safe," he said.

"That, too. But really, nothing stays the same forever. And they'll be back, and they'll still love us."

"They'll be different, though."

"I know. I don't think closing yourself off from the rest of us is going to make you feel better, though."

His eyebrows raised and his eyes focused on her for the first time. "How did you know that's what I was doing?"

"I like to watch how people feel, and figure out what makes them tick."

"Like Mom."

Celia flushed with pleasure. "Yeah, like Mom. Like Ruby, too; she told me to listen."

"I guess you practice on your crazy friends."

Now the blood suffusing Celia's cheeks felt less comfortable. "I don't think that's what I'm doing. I don't mean to, anyway. And besides, it's just Carol who's... sort of unbalanced."

Steve snorted. "'Sort of,'" he agreed. "But that Ray was a little bit crazy, too."

"I guess so, but I'm not seeing him any more, remember? And there's nothing wrong with Judy."

"True, she's normal."

He's right, Celia thought. *She keeps me grounded, brings me back down to earth. And she's not... needy.* Then another thought struck her. "Hey, how did this get to be a conversation about me? We were talking about you, what's bothering you!"

Steve shrugged again. "I don't like talking about me so much," he said. "I don't know how to do talking to fix stuff the way the rest of you do."

"So what do you need?"

He opened his mouth, then seemed to have a second thought and closed it again. Finally he said, "I guess music."

He started to wriggle out of the cabinet and Celia shifted back to give him room. Then she got up and followed him out into the cooler music room. As he picked up the Spanish guitar Rob had taught him to play and started to tune it, she settled on the piano bench beside him. So she saw Joy's head appear in the stairwell before he did. He raised his head almost immediately, though, while his fingers began to pluck out the tune to "It's All in the Game."

Joy said, "I was waiting to hear that you came out," as though in answer to a question he hadn't asked.

He nodded, and Celia saw his shoulders loosen. Joy came in and sat on the floor beside him, leaning against his leg and looking up into his face. His hands moved to strumming full chords, and he started to sing softly, "Many a tear has to fall/But it's all in the game..."

Celia quietly got up, slipped out of the room, and left them to it.

Chapter 45.

At last year's Homecoming dance, Celia had felt swept off her feet by Ray. Tonight, her date—a boy named Bill Heckman she'd known since kindergarten—was less exciting, which suited Celia fine. She'd had enough of excitement for the moment. She was looking forward to a pleasant, easy evening enjoying herself like a normal teenager. Instead of the standard chiffon confection, she was wearing a slubbed silk sheath with a pattern of autumn leaves that she'd bought with money she earned at the restaurant; it made her feel independent and sophisticated.

She stood contentedly next to Bill amidst the orange-and-black crepe paper festooning the gym, watching Rob and Steve on the bandstand tuning their guitars. This was their first important public gig, after months of performing at private parties; Principal Masland's wife had seen them at young Scott Feldman's bar mitzvah and recommended them to her husband.

Robbie seemed excited but Steve looked a little green around the gills. His eyes kept flicking to one side of the stage. Celia looked that way and saw Tom Varner, who'd been kept back a year, taking a nip from a pocket flask. She started to send him a death glare, then recollected her resolve not to hold onto anger and changed her expression to one she thought was calm but firm. Somewhat to her surprise, he flinched and backed into the shadows where she thought she could see a couple other lurking figures.

Then she forgot them as the boys swung into their signature song, "Heartbreak Hotel." They kept it from being an Elvis parody, bringing up the tempo a little and hitting the notes more crisply. Steve took the lead and the piercing, yearning sadness in his voice stilled the chattering crowd. Some people started dancing; more gathered around the bandstand just to listen. *They're going to be all right,* she saw, and stopped worrying to sink into Bill's arms and sway to the music.

Robbie came to the fore in the next song, "Peggy Sue," and Celia prepared to enjoy herself in a faster, swinging dance. But Bill said, "Can I talk to you?" and drew her aside to a bleacher bench as far from the bandstand as possible. Celia swallowed her disappointment as she registered the look on his face: at once bleak and nervous.

"Is something wrong, Bill? Did I do or say something to upset you?" *God, I hope he's not going to tell me he's a homosexual or something.* She'd been thinking a lot about Jamie's revelation of the past summer, worrying about how he was coping at MIT and trying to reconcile her conviction of her brother's essential integrity with the implacable hostility of the Church and society. Part of the result was that she now looked for signs of homosexuality in every boy she knew.

"No, no, it's not you at all." She waited patiently while he gathered himself, then he said, "It's my dad."

"Your dad?" *That came out of left field.* She racked her brain for what she could remember of Mr. Heckman but only came up with a vague image of a man in a suit—some kind of business executive, she thought.

"He just doesn't get me," Bill said. "I mean, like, he wouldn't let me go to that march for school integration in Washington today. I don't think he's prejudiced, it's not that, he just doesn't believe in marching or protesting or whatever; he thinks only Commies do stuff like that."

"But it's a peaceful way to change people's minds and get politicians to change the laws."

"I know that, but he doesn't see it. I'm surprised you didn't go."

"No, my brother Laurie didn't want us to. It's like he's decided he wants to deal with all that on his own. I don't think he's right, though, and when he comes home for Thanksgiving—"

"And then when that woman stabbed Dr. King last month," Bill broke in, "Dad goes, 'See?' I mean, what does that mean? It had nothing to do with the march or protests or anything. She was a Negro herself, for God's sake. And off her rocker, from what they're saying."

"I know. It's just—"

"And it's not only that." He turned a little aside and started fiddling with the buttons on his maroon sport coat. "I tried to grow my hair a little longer and he said no son of his was going to go around like a beatnik or a greaser or a, a sissy boy."

Celia looked at Bill's unfashionable buzz cut and twisted her mouth sympathetically.

Bill shook his head as though she'd disagreed with him and said, "But I lo- I mean, I care about what he thinks." Then, as though confessing something shameful, "All right, all right, I love him, ok? And I guess he loves me. But it's like there's a wall between us and I can never get through it, or over it, and make him actually see me the way I am. And then I get scared that if he did see me the way I am, he wouldn't like it. It was simpler when I was little…"

He kept talking, and her mind started to wander. *This is about Carol,* she realized. *I've got a reputation now for taking on lame ducks and people in trouble. I suppose it's the downside of being like Mom. But she's a professional—this is her job. Do people buttonhole her like this when she's at parties or at the market or whatever? Does this kind of thing have to happen in the middle of a dance?*

Around them, people were jitterbugging now to "Come On, Let's Go"; the McAlister Brothers were smoking hot. Celia had overheard several admiring remarks about them from dancers who swung close to where they sat. Other couples were sneaking behind the bandstand to make out. The metal edge of the bleacher bench was cutting into the backs of Celia's thighs. She shifted a little, and arched her back to relieve the ache of sitting with it unsupported for so long.

"Offer it up," Sister Jonathan would say, she remembered. It was a foundation stone of what they'd been taught in Catechism class: that even minor suffering could count toward one's salvation, if proffered as a sacrifice. Then she thought of something Jamie had said once, that Christianity was vertical—people looked up to God and thought about the state of their souls—where Judaism was horizontal, looking for the divine in social justice and repairing the world.

I suppose it's possible to try repairing the world soul by soul, she thought. *I wish it didn't have to be tonight, though.*

Bill was still talking. With an inward sigh, she gave up on thoughts of a simple, enjoyable evening and set herself to listen to him. "Sometimes I wish I could just crawl into his lap and cry," he muttered, flushing darkly.

Celia, whose own brothers were capable of doing that very thing even as old as they were, felt her heart opening almost against her will. She thought of Ray, who seemed incapable of thinking such a thing, much less admitting it; she could see him on the dance floor now, sashaying around with his newest conquest. *I guess there are worse things than getting a reputation as a sort of junior shrink,* she thought, repressing a sigh. *But if he tells me he thinks of me as a sister, I'm going to scream.*

Chapter 46.

Tuesday, October 28, 1958

The phone in the downstairs hall rang just as Celia got in from school. She dumped her books onto the credenza, slung her coat over the banister rail, and sank onto the chair by the telephone table. Then she used the excuse of having to catch her breath to put off picking it up. That only took a few seconds, but still she sat while the clangor shrilled on.

I'll answer if it's still going after fifteen rings, she told herself. *Maybe it's not even for me.*

But she knew it was, and what's more, she knew who it was. *You have to talk to her eventually.* With a sigh, she picked up the receiver. "Hello?"

"Oh, so now it's hello, is it? I only had to chase you down three hallways and try to trap you on the bus—how *did* you get home, anyway?—and then let the phone ring for *hours* before you deign to speak with me?"

"Judy, it's not like that."

"Really? What is it like?"

"I caught a ride home with Bill Heckman. I had to talk to him."

"Lucky him."

"I knew I had to talk to you, too. I, uh, just needed to think over how I was going to tell you...." Her voice petered out.

233

"Tell me what? You've decided to become a cowgirl? You're secretly a Russian spy? You have a disease that will cause you to expire while gracefully drooping amidst a cloud of camellias and adoring swains? You're going to be dating my brother?"

Celia squeaked, then stammered, "Th-that last one. How did you know?"

Judy blew a cloud of static through the phone. "Jesus, Cee, you have brothers. You know how it is. He came in Sunday suppertime walking like he had springs in his shoes and this sappy grin on his face and when I asked where he'd been he said, 'Oh, just helping Commander McAlister put up Halloween decorations in their yard.' At the same time, you mysteriously failed to show up for our study session for the chemistry midterm that afternoon."

Celia was giggling too hard to interrupt this catalogue, so listened helplessly as Judy went on, "Finally, before he left for Shippensburg yesterday, he said in this moony voice, 'Tell Celia I'll be watching the lunar eclipse tonight.' Well, I would have told you if you'd been anywhere in the same spiral arm of the galaxy with me. But I'd have had to be in a coma not to have figured it out."

"And you're ok with it?"

"Are you planning to toy with his affections, compromise his virtue, and leave him a sobbing wreck?"

"Of course not!"

"Oh, damn. Well, all right, I guess I can deal with happily ever after."

"Not that, either. Judy, for God's sake, we're just going to go out on weekends a little. I'm not even sure it's a boyfriend-girlfriend thing."

"Then what is it, the Cumberland County chapter of the Athenaeum Club? Because I have to tell you, I love my brother, but there's a reason he's going to a small local college rather than up in the academic stratosphere like your brothers. Besides, I thought that guy Bill was your new boyfriend."

"I did too, for about a minute, but he told me at the dance the other night that he thinks of me more like a sister."

"Ouch."

"Yeah, and he's got all these parent issues. I think I gave him some good advice about communicating; he said in the car today that he'd had a good conversation with his dad. So maybe I did some good there, but it wasn't much of a date. I mean, I feel for him, and I'm glad he could confide in me and feel better about it all, but Rick is—he's a grownup."

"Wait a minute, we must be talking about different guys named Rick."

"Har-de-har-har. I mean it, Jude. He knows who he is. I don't have to walk on eggshells around him in case I hurt his feelings or bruise his fragile ego or something. We just have a good time together, and it's such a relief."

"Hmm. Well, ok, I guess I can see that. What was the problem, did you think I was going to be jealous or something?"

Celia made a dismissive sound but didn't actually say anything.

Judy pounced. "You did, didn't you? Which one of you did you think I'd be unhappy about?"

Blushing hard but feeling she owed her friend an honest answer, Celia said, "That's it, really. It's that it's both of us. I was afraid you'd feel, I don't know, left out of things."

"The thing is, Celia, sometimes you just think too much. You're the one who's been feeling left out. What does your mom call that? Projection, isn't it? Besides, I'm not one of your lame ducks, you know. I have a boyfriend—one I snagged from you, if you remember—and a life, and I like being on my own sometimes just fine. I'm a big girl."

"I know that. I do. It's one of the reasons I'm so glad we're friends. I just worried this would be different. I should have had more faith in you."

The front door swung open and Joy dashed in on a tide of cool air and dry leaves. "Did you hear?" she demanded.

"I'm on the phone," Celia pointed out.

"Yeah, but this is important. Is that Judy?"

At Celia's nod, Joy threw her jacket next to Celia's on the balustrade, grabbed the receiver from her hand, and plopped herself onto Celia's lap without ceremony. Holding the phone so Judy could hear, Joy exclaimed, "We have a new pope!"

"Really?" Celia was excited. Pope Pius XII had died a couple of weeks ago and the conclave of cardinals to elect a new one had been in session since Saturday. "Who was it? Mindszenty? That would be one in the eye for the Commies."

"No, Roncalli," Joy said.

She was holding the receiver tilted away from her ear, so Celia could hear Judy say, "Never heard of him."

"That's 'cause you don't have a Jewish brother," Joy informed her loftily. Then, in her more typical eager way, "This guy was great during the Holocaust, when he was an archbishop. He got people freed from concentration camps, helped them escape hostile countries, issued false baptismal certificates, had children shipped to Palestine, all kinds of stuff while the Vatican sat on its hands."

"He's old, though, don't I remember?" Celia put in.

"Yeah, seventy-three. I was listening to the news over at Susie's. They think the cardinals couldn't find anybody they agreed on, so they picked somebody who's likely to die soon, before he can make waves."

"What's he going to call himself?" Celia asked.

"John XXIII. So I guess he's already making waves, since no pope's been called John since that guy in the, what was it, fourteen hundreds, who got tossed out."

"And maybe, before he kicks off, he'll do something about the Church and the Jews." Celia nodded. *New beginnings all around.*

CHAPTER 47.

MONDAY, DECEMBER 8, 1958

Celia wasn't sure whether what she was feeling was the giddiest relief or the most profound rage of her life. *Maybe both.* For the past week, her emotions had been swinging like a pendulum, and sometimes flying off the clock altogether. Her frustration with being treated like a confessor rather than a date by Bill; her delight that she'd started going with Judy's brother, Rick; her worry about what that might mean for her relationship with Judy—all those concerns that had seemed so pressing a week ago had vanished like newspaper in the fireplace at Mom's news last Monday.

Mom's supervisor at Rolling Meadow, from a combination of officiousness and professional jealousy and sheer bureaucratic idiocy, had decided to press charges against Steve for the murder of his cousin Bert, the man who'd imprisoned and tortured him throughout his childhood till Steve had finally snapped. Steve had been beside himself with fear and anger, of course; Mom and Dad had been absorbed in shoring up his fragile sense of security and preparing for the hearing with his lawyer; Ruby had grimly set about making sure that the household routines ran smoothly so that there was at least a superficial sense of peace and order and normality. It had been left to

Celia, with the older boys away at college, to allay the panic and soothe the anxieties of her younger siblings.

And she had done it. She had found the right balance of brisk reassurance and sympathetic comfort that they seemed to need. But it had come at the cost of her repressing her own moods, which had veered from despair to hope to confidence and back again a dozen times a day. At night after Joy fell asleep, Celia had wept and prayed and cudgeled her brain for ways to cope with the pressure for one more day. Her lifeline had been the telephone: Rick and Judy had both called often to express support and let her vent. Still, she didn't know how much longer she could have kept it up, or what she would have done if the result of the hearing had been bad.

But it hadn't been bad. Though the process itself had been excruciating, the juvenile court judge's decision had been that Steve acted in self-defense, and that his best chance of becoming a functioning member of society was to stay with his adoptive family. Sitting in the station wagon now with Joy and Laurie in the back seat and Ruby beside her at the wheel, Celia focused on that outcome and tried to still the flailing in her chest.

Behind her, Joy was uncharacteristically silent. Celia could hear Laurie's low, steady voice reassuring her; they'd always had a special bond. *The oldest and the youngest,* Celia thought, with a slight but ancient pang of wistfulness. But then Ruby said to her in a low voice, "Would you like to join your mother and me tonight?" and she nodded in gratitude.

Celia was the only one of the children who knew about Mom and Ruby's habit of saying the rosary together in Ruby's rooms after everyone else had gone to bed, whenever the day had been particularly difficult or joyous. It had started when Dad was still on active duty in Korea. Now that he was back home and posted at the Navy Depot, they didn't do it as often, but Mom had told Celia the practice was still a source of comfort to her. This was the first time Celia had been asked to join; the prospect acted like a balm, soothing her unrest and helping her focus.

Ruby pulled into the parking lot of the Harrisburg bus and train depot. Laurie leaned over the back seat to kiss Ruby's and Celia's cheeks, then gave Joy a tight squeeze goodbye. He grabbed the overnight bag he'd brought from Haverford and the knapsack of birthday presents out of the station wagon's rear compartment. Then he jumped out and ran—he didn't have much time to spare before the next train left. "Bye, Happy birthday!" they all called after him.

There was quiet in the car till Joy said, "I wish he could have stayed longer."

"He needed to get back; exams are coming up," Ruby said.

"I know. But still."

As Ruby backed the old wagon and headed for Front Street and the way home, Celia said, "I thought we were going to go to a pay phone and tell Jamie how it came out."

"Change of plan," Ruby said. "Your mother decided to tell him herself. She thinks he was more upset by this than he was letting on, and she wants to hear his voice and get a fix on him."

"That makes sense," Celia said, thinking, *"A fix on him": that's a good way to put what Mom does.*

"Of course he was upset," Joy put in. "It's all so awful. I sort of knew what had happened to him, but hearing about it today, and seeing those horrible pictures... And then, seeing Steve's face. I don't know what to say to him about it. Do you think he'll want to talk about it, or should I just leave that to Mom and Dr. Benson?"

"I noticed it's easier for him to talk to you than to any of the rest of us," Ruby said. "But I'd let him take the lead—you can bring it up, but if he closes you off, just let it alone."

The two of them went on talking and Celia went back to her thoughts. She had talked to Mom after that disappointing date with Bill and Mom had reassured her that she'd soon be mingling with older boys who would be less inclined to see her as either a mother figure or a threatening brainiac. Then, that very day, her relationship with Rick had changed from casual acquaintanceship to romantic interest. *How does Mom know that stuff? Part of being a psychologist, I suppose.*

Like today. I always thought trials and legal hearings were about the lawyers involved, like a combat between gladiators. She reminded herself that Mom had a law degree herself, something she seldom thought about since Mom almost never spoke of it. *But what happened today was more about psychology and the psychologists, Mom and that moron Mrs. French.* She refused to let herself feel even a little guilty about using Steve's word to describe the woman who'd failed both him and Sydney so spectacularly. *Except she's not really a psychologist, just some sort of counselor,* she reminded herself. *Mom says she was in over her head. Like that Henderson guy, Mom's boss, who forced this whole situation. But he looked sick at the end, as though he'd suddenly realized what he was doing, how close he came to wrecking Steve's life. Good, he should feel sick about it.*

With an effort, Celia disengaged from the satisfaction of contemplating the comeuppance of Marty Henderson and brought her mind back to the main point.

Mom, and Dr. Benson, laid out what would have happened in Steve's mind during those years of isolation and abuse. Those disgusting pictures of Steve's bruises and scars were hardly necessary; they made it all so clear with their words. They made the judge see the truth of Steve, the damage done to him, and how it could be helped.

Oh my God, this is how serious what I want to do is. I never saw it so clearly before. It's not only helping individual people cope with their problems, it's a different way of looking at what's wrong with society and combating violence and irrationality by uprooting the causes, one person at a time. And as a psychiatrist, I will have the power to use medications, use them the proper way, to help with the work instead of using them as crutches. And with an MD, I'd have more respect from people like judges and other doctors. She thought about how that intern had dismissed Mom—and Carol's problems—when he heard the word "psychologist."

But when I'm a regular doctor, they'll have to listen to me. Then a wave of uncertainty washed over her. *Who do I think I am? And how could I think I could do more than Mom? But it wouldn't be more than Mom,* she corrected herself. *I'm not getting a law degree on top of a medical one. Even so, can I handle the workload? Can I handle the pressure? Mom was almost wrecked by this today. It was like when we lost David. And other times, when she's come home soul-tired from not being able to help some kid.*

And yet, how wonderful to be able to do it, to make a real difference. She reminded herself of the days when Mom came home exhilarated from some success or breakthrough one of her Rolling Meadow kids had made. The station wagon was coasting into the garage now. Mom's blue Dodge was already there; the others had made it home before them, without the stop to drop Laurie off.

Celia clenched her fists, renewing her commitment to the course she'd chosen and casting her mind ahead to the rest of the evening. *Joy and I are on to help Ruby get dinner on the table tonight. Then we'll be lighting the Hanukkah candles; I'll sit and play and sing with the others for that, and see whether Steve needs anything from me. And later tonight, I'll say the rosary with Mom and Ruby.*

But in between, I'm studying chemistry.

Chapter 48.

Tuesday, December 23, 1958

The boys were home. Celia was almost sorry she'd invited Rick over for the afternoon; even after a weekend with them, she found herself reluctant to get very far from Laurie and Jamie. And they were sticking close to home, too, she realized. They were all still reverberating from the blow to their security that Steve's hearing had been. Add to that the fact that it was taking a little bit of adjustment on everyone's part to reintegrate her brothers after a semester's absence, and the sum was that Celia felt as though this ought to be family time.

Still, Rick had been willing to compromise his original suggestion that they go out somewhere today and had agreed to come here instead, so she shouldn't really complain. It wasn't as if she would actually be doing something with the family.

Jamie was all excited about this new communications satellite the US had launched. The family had listened to President Eisenhower's recorded Christmas message that the satellite had broadcast over the planet, of course, but Jamie was interested in the broader implications. This was the world's first radio transmission from space, a little over a year since the Soviets shocked the world by launching Sputnik. This had been a top-secret project, so there was little or no information on it available, but Jamie was trying to ferret

243

out what he could. There was something a little frantic about his preoccupation with it, Celia thought. *I think he's using it to avoid something else. Maybe something to do with Laurie.*

For his part, Laurie—who was at Linda's today, on his first foray out of the house since he'd gotten home—was treating Jamie with a sort of gingerly respect that Celia didn't think was just the result of their both having started college. It seemed to her that, silly as it sounded in her head, he passed Jamie the orange juice differently this morning: with a grave look and a brush of the fingers. *I bet Jamie's told Laurie he's gay.* She hoped so. The more members of the family who knew about it, the sooner Celia could stop worrying about keeping the secret. If she was right, it was only Rob, Joy, and Steve who didn't know, anyway. *He'd better tell them soon; they'll be hurt if they realize they were the only ones left out. And Mom always says secrets are corrosive if held too long.*

Maybe she'd talk to Mom about it later. For Mom and Dad, this was a regular work day. Beth and Joy were in Carlisle doing some last-minute Christmas shopping. Rob and Steve were ensconced in the music room upstairs, practicing. Steve wasn't much fun to be with these days in any case; he'd been acting like a brat since the hearing, which Mom said was a natural reaction and one she'd been expecting.

So stop obsessing about the family and pay attention to Rick, she commanded herself severely as she went to answer his ring. She smiled with uncomplicated pleasure at the sight of him on the doorstep, sheltered from the winter rain by the portico, propped casually against one of the white pillars that flanked it. "Stop leaning there with that look of negligent woodcraft," she couldn't help saying.

He gave her a crooked grin as he straightened and moved toward her. "Sounds like a quote," he said.

"*The Once and Future King.* T. H. White. About King Arthur. Mom's read the different parts of it out loud to us over the years, but the whole thing collected together just came out."

"My little bookworm," he said, but he said it fondly and not with the condescending tone Ray would have used. Celia appreciated that, and admired the lean lines of his body as he stripped off his hooded rain jacket and toed his sodden sneakers off onto the doormat before coming forward to kiss her.

She led him into the living room. "Ruby has some spiced cider keeping warm on the stove," she said. "Want some?"

"Mm," he agreed. "And maybe a few of those gingerbread cookies? Or are those only for the tree?"

"No, we always make enough to eat as well as hang. Make yourself at home; I'll be right back."

When she returned with a laden tray, she found him just rising from setting a fire he'd evidently expertly laid in the hearth while she was gone. As usual, she liked his competence and his confidence. They snuggled onto one of the settees, the one facing the windows so they could see the tree presiding over one of the bays, and took up their mugs of hot cider.

"Oh, this is nice," he said with a comfortable grunt. "I'm glad you talked me out of going someplace else."

"I'm happy you're glad. I was just thinking it was kind of unnecessary; my family's all busy today, anyway."

"That's all right. I have something to tell you, and it's probably better to do it here where it's quiet."

"I do have a drink in my hand to throw in your face if I don't like it," she teased.

He gave a short laugh and nuzzled her ear. "Nothing that should induce drink-throwing, I'm fairly sure. Though you might not be too happy about it."

"Oh?" *What could it be? Judy's upset about us after all? No, she would have told me herself. He's met someone else? No, he wouldn't be cuddling like this with me.* "Well, out with it, then."

"I'm transferring to Duke."

That, she hadn't expected. "But Duke's a first-rate school," she blurted, thinking of Judy's slighting opinion of Rick's brainpower. "That came out wrong, I don't mean to say you're not smart enough for Duke…"

He patted her hand. "Don't worry about it. I know I'm no mental giant. But I'm not stupid. I just don't 'apply myself,' like the school counselors used to say. Made me feel like I was some sort of glue, and should be spreading myself on the books. But this is all your fault, anyway."

"How so?"

"You've inspired me, since you decided to go to med school and be a lady doctor. Not only that you're taking the hard science courses and studying all the time—just the idea that you could decide you wanted your life to go in a different direction and then just do it. I realized I've just been marking time at Ship. There's nothing wrong with it, it just doesn't offer what I'm going to need for the direction I've picked."

Celia blushed with pleasure. "What direction are you going in?"

"Business. Duke's got a good business school. And they're interested in me as a baseball player, too. They've offered me a scholarship. I didn't want to tell you about it till it was definite."

"So you'll be going next fall?"

"No, right away. I start second semester; they want me there for spring training."

"That's terrific, Rick. I'm happy for you."

But he seemed to hear the undertone in her voice. "You can come and visit," he said. "There's this girl—did you ever meet

Ginger Murdoch? She's a year ahead of you. Well, anyway, she goes there, and I ran into her this weekend and she said if you come you could stay with her."

Celia pursed her lips. She was gratified he'd been planning ahead for her, but not sure about staying with some total stranger, even if she was from around here.

Misunderstanding her look, Rick said, "She's just this girl I know; there's nothing between us."

She shook her head. "No, no. We've always said we're not exclusive, anyway. I was just thinking it might be awkward. But that's a silly thing to get shook up about. I'm happy for you, I really am."

"Some good news?" Laurie said from the dining room door. They hadn't even heard him come in through the kitchen.

"Rick's transferring to Duke," Celia told him.

His expression was polite but reserved. "Congratulations," he said coolly.

Rick only said "Thanks," but Celia knew Laurie better than he did. "What's the matter?"

Laurie shrugged. "My roommate at Haverford comes from North Carolina. He says he decided against Duke because it's segregated."

Now it was Rick's turn to blush, and not with pleasure. "I didn't even think about that. I guess I should have."

Laurie's look softened. He gave Rick a light cuff on the shoulder as he leaned over them to snag a cookie from the tray on the coffee table. "Maybe you can be part of getting that changed."

"Yeah, maybe I can. Could you give me some advice about how to do that?"

"Sure," Laurie said. "Now? I don't want to… interrupt anything." He looked at Celia under his eyebrows.

She jabbed him in the ribs. "You're not interrupting anything, Mr. Tact. Sit down over there and tell us how to change the world."

"Sure thing, Little Sister," Laurie said, and settled onto the other settee. "You change the world one mind at a time," he began, "but first you have to get their attention."

Snuggling with Rick and *interacting with family,* Celia thought. *This is more like it.*

Chapter 49.

Saturday, March 28, 1959

"**Y**ou're going to an all-girls school? *You?*" Carol was incredulous.

"You're going to one," Celia pointed out.

"Yeah, for prep school. For college, I want a place with boys around, not a nunnery."

Carol, home on spring break, had come over to help with the McAlisters' annual Easter egg dyeing session. Laurie was home from Haverford on his spring break, though Jamie had decided to wait and take time off from MIT at Passover. But Laurie's longtime girlfriend, Linda, was going to Dickinson right here in Carlisle, so she was able to join them as well. *Almost like old times.* Even Carol had come down a bit from the frantic insistence that all was well in her world and always had been that she'd shown last year. Her parents had taken her on a European tour at Christmas time; her conversation today was all about boys she'd talked to rather than anything she'd seen.

Rick had just gotten in from North Carolina last night, so neither he nor Judy had been able to get away for the Easter prep here. Celia understood, but was still feeling a little scratchy about it—especially since the original plan had been for her to visit him at Duke this week. His deciding to come home instead had short-circuited an argument she'd been having with her parents about where she would stay on campus, since he'd quarreled with the girl he'd thought would house her. She was partially relieved about that, partially frustrated that they wouldn't have an air-clearing dispute that would establish her as capable of making adult decisions. She hoped.

So she was shorter than she might have been now when she answered Carol. "Barnard is hardly a nunnery. They even have classes with Columbia boys, and vice versa. But I'm going there to study, Carol. I don't need to have boys around to live a fulfilling life."

"What's this? Heresy? Who says you don't need boys?" came a voice from the door of the TV room where the two girls were holed up.

"Rick! I didn't hear the door—and I thought you weren't coming over today."

"Well, sorry to disappoint. I met Rob on the walk and he let me in. I could go away again if you're busy."

He pretended to be huffy, but Celia was already on her feet and in his arms, to Carol's amusement. "It's nice to see how independent you are," she said slyly. "An inspiration to feminists everywhere."

"Feminists!" Rick exclaimed, steering Celia back to the shabby TV room couch and sitting down with a proprietary arm around her shoulders. "Does that mean I have to be a, what, masculinist? Women already have the vote, haven't you heard? Let's not start another fuss. I have enough aggravation dealing with the race issue."

"Oh?" Celia asked, ignoring the jab about feminism. "Something happening at Duke?"

"The trustees just shot down a couple of petitions from grad schools for integration; the student paper ran an editorial that consisted of a paragraph criticizing them, ending with 'If not now:' and then a whole column of just the repeated word, 'when.' But there's been talk about the FBI investigating anybody who signed the petition. The administration says that's not happening, but it scared some people."

"That doesn't sound like much of a start."

"Baby steps," he said. "Besides, Duke Ellington and Lionel Hampton are going to perform on campus in May, so it's not like nobody appreciates Negroes at Duke."

"Yeah? Where are they going to sleep?"

"What do you mean?"

"What I said: where are they going to sleep?" Celia repeated. "It's a common thing in Jim Crow states—they're happy to have talented Negroes entertain them, but they still have to come in the back door and eat in the kitchen rather than the dining hall and camp out with volunteer families at night."

Rick looked sour. Celia was sorry to have punctured his easy optimism about progress but this was a subject she wasn't inclined to compromise over.

Then Steve, who'd been sitting by the window, so quiet she'd forgotten he was there, piped up. "Do you usually have great musicians coming around to play?"

"Sure. A couple of weeks ago, the Kingston Trio came to campus."

"Wow," Steve said. "It'd almost be worth all the studying to be someplace where you could hear live music."

They all laughed and Celia decided to let the subject of integration lapse for the moment. "Carol," she said, "tell Rick about Paris."

"Paris, *France?*" Rick said with exaggerated awe.

"No, Paris, Texas," Celia deadpanned, giving him a shove.

Carol rolled her eyes. "Yes, gay Paree," she said. "Home of the cutest guys on the planet."

"Is that all you saw, cute guys?" Rick asked.

"Well, we couldn't see a lot of the sights, with my dumb mother along."

"Carol!" Celia protested. She'd never figured out what Carol had against her mother, especially when it was her father who seemed so obnoxious.

"But she can't do *anything*. We couldn't go up the Eiffel Tower, or onto the upper levels of Notre Dame, and she got tired of the Louvre after about ten minutes."

"It's hardly her fault that they don't have a way for people on crutches to get around more easily."

"I didn't say it was her fault, I just said it was dumb."

"No, you said *she* was dumb."

"Well, she is. We did get into the Folies Bergère, though. You should see what those girls wear!"

"I thought it was more about what they don't wear," Rick put in with a waggle of the eyebrows.

"Oo, la, la," Carol agreed. "Mom was shocked, but Dad and I thought it was great."

Celia took a deep breath. *How Carol feels about her mother and why she feels that way isn't my problem,* she reminded herself. *I need to practice what Mom told me, to separate my day-to-day relationships from things I'm learning— and later, practicing—about psychology. I wonder if they'll be impressed at Barnard that I'm already reading Melanie Klein?*

Chapter 50.

"Got it?" Dad asked.

"Got it," Celia said, shifting her feet to take the weight of the storm window more securely. Together, they lowered it to the ground.

With one accord, they stepped back and looked up at the house with satisfaction. The windows were all cleared of their heavy winter protection; as soon as Ruby and Jamie finished washing them, the screens would go up and they'd be ready for summer.

Celia felt her shoulders straighten as though a load had been lifted from her own back.

Dad reached a hand around to rub them. "Sore?" he asked.

"No," she said, "though that feels good; don't stop. I was actually thinking that I feel... lighter, somehow."

He nodded, then moved around to massage her shoulders with both hands. "You've had a challenging winter," he agreed. "Getting involved with Rick, only to have him go off to Duke; deciding on colleges to apply to yourself and waiting to hear you'd gotten into Barnard—"

She joined the litany. "Finding out about Jamie, worrying about how he was going to cope with realizing he was homosexual and going off to MIT at the same time; missing him and Laurie; getting

253

more involved in the Civil Rights movement—that rally this spring with Dr. King was amazing, wasn't it? All those young people: 'Not the "Beat" generation, but the generation of integration.' And of course, the big upheaval, Steve's hearing. I'd known more or less what he'd gone through, but seeing those pictures of his scars, hearing the testimony! Even though it turned out the way we wanted it to, I feel, I don't know, somehow *wounded* by it. And the backlash, poor Steve trying to cope and acting up, testing his boundaries with you and Mom and all of us. How's he feeling now, anyway? Is that flu letting up? He's been keeping to himself so much lately, I haven't set eyes on him in days."

Dad gave her a last pat and pulled the waiting wheelbarrow closer to the pile of storm windows. The two of them started loading them into it as Dad said, "He's feeling better. Ruby made him go outside today." He hesitated for a moment, then went on, "I'm not surprised you haven't seen him lately, though. Did you know he tried to keep it from us that he was sick?"

"He did? Why?"

Dad's voice was grim. "He thought we'd lock him in his room so he wouldn't contaminate us."

Celia almost dropped her end of the window they were adding to the stack in the wheelbarrow. *"What?* He didn't really!"

"On one level, no. He understood rationally that we wouldn't do that. But viscerally, he was afraid. I think some part of him will always be afraid that those days will come back." Dad tested the stability of the stack with the side of his hand and said, "I think we have enough for this load, let's take it down to the barn."

He started to push the wheelbarrow around the lilacs and down the bumpy lawn. Celia walked beside it, steadying the pile so it wouldn't slide off. "What did you do to make him understand?" she asked.

"Held him in my arms. Told him some of my own fears and weaknesses. Gave him that peacock feather picture David drew for your mother."

He might not have a psychology degree, but he knows what to do for people. Aloud, she said, "Is that the navy?"

It took him a second, then he followed her thought. "I suppose so. Commanding men, if you're good at it, means understanding what makes them tick and how to help them deal with their fears and get the best out of them."

They trundled into the cool shade of the old barn and began unloading the windows, leaning them against a side wall. "I have boss parents," she said, using the slang term deliberately.

He huffed a laugh. "That's good, right?" He slung an arm around her as they left the barn and climbed the slope, Celia pushing the empty barrow. "But we're not out of the woods yet. I'm still worried about Steve. Beth told your mother and me at Easter that she thought he was drinking on the sly—that's in confidence, Cissy." At her nod, he went on, "And something's off between him and Joy, too."

"That night we found out those singers died in that plane crash, she got in bed with me; something was upsetting her. I thought at the time it was the accident, but now that you mention it, there has been something different in the way she is with him since then."

"And we're worried about Jamie, and about Laurie, and for other reasons about Beth and Rob." Dad stopped walking to look at her. "You're the only one we don't worry about, Cissy. I wonder whether that's fair to you."

Celia shrugged. "Squeaky wheel and all that, I guess. You guys got me over some rough times when I was younger, remember? When it started to seem like everybody hated me all of a sudden because I was smart, and when I was trying to figure out how to deal with jerks like Coach Vaughn. And when Carol was in such trouble, you helped me deal with all the pressure and pulled me out of it when it got to be too much. You've been there when I needed you, Dad, don't worry."

They hove to by the remaining storm windows and started piling them into the wheelbarrow. Dad said, "Just don't feel like you have to put on a stiff upper lip or pretend you're fine when you're not. We never really talked about how you felt after that scuffle in the parking lot after prom last year, for instance."

"I actually felt good about that. I mean, kind of sick from the violence, but strong, too. It made me feel like I could take care of myself, and help out in a bad situation rather than just being some damsel in distress. Then Beth helped me figure out how to take pleasure in that while still remembering that those guys are human beings with their own needs and fears."

"Amazing," Dad said. "I know plenty of adults who can't walk that fine line. I've wondered whether you were so shaken by that experience that you didn't want to go to your own prom."

"No," Celia said, hissing and shaking her hand in the air after catching her fingers between two windows. "I just couldn't be bothered. Especially since everybody these days seems to think the point is to lose your virginity afterwards." She made a face at Dad's horrified expression. "And Rick was away at Duke, anyway. Not that they would have let him come if he had been here. Girls who've graduated are allowed in, but not boys."

"The idea is that older boys are... only after one thing," Dad said. "Of course, we *know* that Rick wouldn't have been."

"Doesn't matter if he had been," Celia said briskly. "I have no intention of having sex with Rick Hartzell, or with anyone else till I'm good and ready."

"Don't hold back, Cissy," Dad laughed. "Tell me what you really think."

"I'm never holding back on what I think again," Celia said. "I've decided I'm finished with trying to hide my brains, or my ambitions, or my feelings. If people don't like it, it's their problem."

Dad nodded. "So maybe things have changed for you in the past few years. After Laurie and I had our crisis over the whole David disaster, I remember you said you sometimes felt that nobody could see who you really were, and might not like you if they did."

Touched that he remembered that after all these years, Celia said, "It's true, I used to feel like there was something wrong with me, some indefinable way that I wasn't normal."

"And now?"

She laughed, realizing the truth. "Now I think that 'normal' is overrated. I'm fine, Dad. Better all the time."

Chapter 51.

"Bless me, Father, for I have sinned. It has been... um, about four hours since my last confession."

On the other side of the grille, Father Shea sighed. In a voice ragged with fatigue from hours of sitting in this dark booth listening to the woes of his parishioners, he said, "And what brings you back so soon, Celia? Have you murdered someone this afternoon?"

Celia gulped. "I'm sorry to be a bother," she began, but cut off as she dimly saw through the scrim dividing them that he'd waved a dismissive hand.

"I'm sorry, daughter," he said wearily. "That was most inappropriate. Give me a minute, please." He bowed his head and began to mutter under his breath, a prayer for strength or patience or understanding or all three, no doubt.

Celia deliberately withdrew her attention from what he was saying and thought over how she would explain what brought her here for the second time in one day. When he turned to her again, she was ready.

"I broke a confidence with one of my brothers to another brother," she said. "An important one. I hurt both their feelings, and now they're both mad at me."

He waited a beat to be sure she was finished speaking, then asked, "Did you intend to hurt their feelings?"

"No!" she wailed softly. "I was trying to help."

"Which one did you think would be helped by your betraying a trust?"

"I didn't think of it like that. He asked me a direct question and it was either answer it or lie."

"You couldn't explain that whatever this was wasn't yours to tell?"

Celia thought that over. Steve had been asking her about sex, specifically about whether she had been having it with Rick, which she had answered with a firm negative; as she'd told Dad, wherever their relationship was going, she was sure by now that it would never be deep enough for such a commitment from her. Then Steve had asked about Laurie and Linda, and finally about Jamie and Rima. Laurie and Linda seemed half broken up already, she knew, but his bringing up Rima showed that Steve was so far out of the loop that he'd be bound to feel betrayed when he learned the truth about Jamie, and that others in the family had known it for months now.

"I don't think I could have, no, Father. He wouldn't be put off when I tried to deflect him, and I thought it was time for him to know, anyway. I mean, my mother always says that secrets are corrosive. I thought if it all got out in the open, everyone would feel better."

"But they didn't."

"No." Jamie had been horrified, embarrassed and then furious, venting a rant about the disadvantages and dangers of being a homosexual in American society, a rant it sounded as though he'd been storing up for some time. To her surprise, Steve had been angry in his turn: he'd felt judged as inadequate, too weak to know this truth about the brother he shared a room with, and a past that had produced both physical and mental scars for both of them.

"Yet you say that your intent was good. Of what sin are you accusing yourself?"

She had come here thinking her sin was breaking the confidence. Now the truth washed over her face and down into her heart with a flush of shame. "Arrogance," she whispered. "Thinking I know better than everybody else what's good for them."

"And do you?"

"Of course not."

He was silent, forcing her to think over her answer again. "Sometimes?" she temporized.

"And how can you know the difference?"

She shifted uneasily on the thinly padded kneeler. "By… by prayer?"

"Prayer will certainly help. But in the middle of a conversation, perhaps not always practicable. And so?"

"I don't know. I—oh!" A thought came to her. "I want to be a psychiatrist, you know, I think I've told you that, so—I need to study more, learn about when it's good to tell people things and when they need to figure them out for themselves."

"But more immediately?"

She couldn't imagine what he was hinting at, and beginning to feel a little resentful that he wouldn't just *tell* her.

"Think, Celia."

"I'm *trying* to!" she snapped. "Oh, sorry, I'm sorry, Father. It's just so frustrating, not knowing the answer."

"I'm giving you the answer: think."

"I still don't get it."

She could see him rubbing the space between his eyes with the fingertips of one hand and felt a pang of guilt at giving him a literal headache.

So she was taken by surprise when he said, "This is like that silly Abbot and Costello routine, 'Who's on first?' I'm telling you that the answer is that you must think about what you say before you say it."

"That simple?"

"That simple, and that difficult. You have a great gift, Celia—two great gifts, really. One is your ability to articulate quickly and clearly, often while other people are still gathering their thoughts. The other is your insight into other people's needs and feelings, and your compassion for them, your desire to help. But the one gift can get in the way of the other. To pursue your chosen field, and to avoid the sort of mistake you made today, you need to learn to listen better, and to reflect before you speak."

"I see."

"You say that your brothers are angry at you. I want you to accept that anger, don't try to deflect or ameliorate it. You may apologize; in fact, you should. But give their feelings the respect of accepting their validity."

"I will."

"Now, for your penance I want you to do something other than the usual assignment of prayers. For the next two weeks, you are to do as you are required by those in authority over you, at work and at home, without complaint or argument. But for those of your friends and family who are your equals, you are to listen without judgment and *without trying to fix them.* If they outright ask for your advice, tell them you need time to consider their problem, and address it after the two weeks are up."

"Wow. Ok, I understand. Thank you."

He gave a heavy sigh and began the words of absolution while she recited the Act of Contrition. But just as he was sliding the grille shut, she said, "Uh, Father? I think you should go back to the rectory and take a little nap after this."

His laughter followed her out of the confessional.

Chapter 52.

Friday, September 25, 1959

*D*ear folks, she wrote.

So, after my first week at Barnard, I'm starting to believe I'm really here. I wasn't sure I'd make it when I left Jamie waiting for the Boston train at Grand Central. I have to admit, I chickened out on using those bus and subway directions Dad so carefully wrote out for me. I stood on the sidewalk on Park Avenue—Park Avenue!—just drinking in the sights and sounds of the city, excited and happy but nervous as heck about plunging into it, like a novice swimmer looking at the Atlantic for the first time. Then, like an answer to prayer, an empty cab pulled up at a light and I just grabbed it and yelled, "Take me to Barnard!" I think he was laughing at me.

Anyway, I got here, somewhat the poorer for my loss of nerve, and picked up my orientation materials. The upperclasswomen (?) there laughed at me, too, for having bought all my books new. But I laughed right back at them and told them I was part of the wave of the future. We're the largest freshman class in Barnard history. I have a dorm room, but some girls are living in a hotel. There's a new dorm coming, and a new library, and a new arts center—very exciting atmosphere, even if I did get lost coming out of the bookstore.

Then I found my dorm room, and my roommate. And her typewriter. Her typewriter, yes. She's got a full size standard, a big Germanic-looking gray thing that makes the darling blue portable you got me look like a kitten in the lion's den. And its owner had kind of the same effect: she's tall and blonde and Nordic,

263

exactly the looks I've always wished I had. And she's cool and self-contained and very, very neat. I gulped a little, then reminded myself I hadn't actually exchanged a word with her yet except our names (hers is Christine).

So I started asking her about herself and, guess what, she's really nice, not standoffish at all; maybe a little shy, but she warmed up quickly. I think we're going to be good friends, especially if I remember to put my dirty socks in my laundry bag instead of over the back of my desk chair.

We both got the same assignment for Community Orientation Day, serving lunch to residents at a Jewish nursing home. Another day we heard a panel of faculty and students talk about Barnard's principles and programs and had a chance to question them. And there was an impressive signing-in ceremony in President McIntosh's office. The most fun was a boat ride around Manhattan Island to show us highlights of the city and dances and parties and all kinds of stuff. It was all coed; I'll have to tell Carol, she was so worried I was going to a "nunnery."

"Enough," I hear you saying. "We're not paying almost $2,000 to read this drivel. What about your classes?"

Well, that's the most amazing thing: exactly as I'd hoped. I can't believe the difference being in a roomful of girls—er, women—makes. There are some male students from Columbia, and male faculty, but most of the other students are female. That means that nobody rolls their eyes when I know the answer to something, or snickers when I say I'm pre-med.

I even like not being the smartest student in the room. Hmm, is that a lie? Not really. It stings a little, having someone else come up with an answer faster than I do, or say something really insightful that I hadn't thought of, but mostly it's like... like playing basketball again without those stupid "girls' rules." I can stretch myself, test my ability and push it beyond where it's been; what pain there is means I'm getting stronger.

There's another thing I'd been looking forward to and am surprised to find gives me a twinge. I talked about this with Mom once, how I wanted to be someplace where no one called me "Cissy" or thought of me as an older sister.

Now I have that. No one knows me or has any preconceived notions about me, the men or the women. So nobody automatically asks my advice or tells me their troubles. Christine certainly doesn't need me to be her big sister.

But that leaves me feeling kind of blank sometimes. If I'm not that, who am I? (I can hear Jamie quoting Rabbi Hillel: "If I am not for myself, who will be for me? But if I am only for myself, who am I? And if not now, when?") I suppose part of what I have to learn is who I am when I'm not Cissy McAlister, Universal Sympathizer and Bossy Know-It-All, but Cecelia McAlister, Glamorous Woman of Mystery. (Stop laughing, Robbie.)

And that leads me to the larger ache, the one where I'm not part of the family. You know what I mean, not around you all every day. Part of that means that when I give an opinion on, say, race relations, people around me don't dismiss it with that look on their face that says, "Oh, she's got that Negro brother, of course she thinks that." But I also don't have the people who think, "Oh, she's got that Negro brother, she must know what she's talking about." So I have to be ready to defend my opinions on my own ground, from my own knowledge.

I also think I never quite realized how much difference my literal name made in how people looked at me, what being a McAlister in Cumberland County meant in terms of respect and sometimes resentment. I say my name here and people just nod, remembering it or not depending on whether they think I'm worth remembering. Nobody knew my grandparents, or worries about whether alienating me will affect their father's military career, or wonders whether Mom can read their minds (remember that silly girl Patty, Mom?).

I'm walking on the tightrope now without a net. I still have the balance bar you taught me to use, though. And I trust I'll get to the other platform safely, wherever it is. (Beth, you know what I'm talking about.)

Self-conscious metaphors aside, I miss you all like fury. (Yes, even you, Joy.) Steve, you should know that I was going around humming "Bright, Warm Home" till Christine finally asked me to either sing it properly or shut up. So I sang it, and she actually got tears in her eyes, which I don't think has happened to her since the Truman Administration. "Your little brother wrote that?" she said.

Even when I'm not humming or singing it, I'm carrying it in my heart, along with all of you. I can hardly wait to see you again, but I don't want to be anywhere but here.

(Remember Emerson: "A foolish consistency is the hobgoblin of little minds.")

Love and kisses,

Celia

Chapter 53.

Thursday, November 26, 1959

As they got up from the Thanksgiving table, Claiborne Barringer, Laurie's former roommate from Haverford, pulled Celia aside. "What's her name again, your gal?" he asked in an undertone.

"Jones," Celia said stiffly.

His face twisted in incredulity. "You call her 'Jones'?"

"No, of course not, *we* call her Ruby."

His face cleared. "Thanks for the dinner, Ruby," he called out in his North Carolina drawl. "It was prime."

Ruby nodded coldly as she followed Laurie and Rob into the kitchen.

Clai turned back to Celia. "I say somethin wrong?"

Celia took a deep breath. *Laurie likes him enough to have invited him here, don't make assumptions. He just doesn't get it.* Aloud she said, "You don't really know her well enough to call her by her first name."

His brow creased as though she'd presented him with a conundrum. "She's the help," he said uncertainly.

"She's old enough to be our grandmother," she pointed out.

"You call her Ruby."

"I've known her since I was born."

He stared at her a minute, lips pressed together in a thin line, then turned on his heel and strode into the kitchen.

Celia scurried after him, alarmed.

But when he got there, he stood foursquare by the breakfast nook and said to Ruby's back at the refrigerator, "I meant no offense, Miz Jones. It's the way I was raised."

Ruby's hands paused on the bowl of leftover stuffing she was pushing onto a shelf, then she closed the fridge and turned to look, not at Barringer, but at Laurie, scraping dishes by the sink.

He met her eye and nodded once.

She turned further till she was facing Barringer and said neutrally, "I understand. Maybe you wouldn't mind helping Celia take the cloth off the table, Mr. Barringer?"

"Sure thing," he said on a gusty breath of relief. "And call me Clai."

Back in the dining room, they each took an end of the tablecloth and walked toward each other, trapping the crumbs in the middle.

"So you're really Mac's sister," he said.

It wasn't a question, but she answered anyway. "I really am."

"He told me about y'all when we roomed together the last couple years, but I couldn't quite believe it."

She shrugged. "There are people we've known for years who don't really believe it. But Laurie was part of my family before I was born. He's always been my big brother."

"And that girl, Linda, who was here last night, she 'uz his girlfriend?"

"All through high school, yes. He's got a new girlfriend now, though."

He nodded as their fingers met and she took the cloth from him. She brought it to the window, hoisted the sash with linen-covered fingers, and shook the crumbs into the hydrangeas. Behind her, he said, "Julia Hawkins. I've met her. Feisty little thang. Somethin tells me she had a hard time believin the way things are here, too."

He'd taken the protective pads off the table and set them against the sideboard. Celia left the soiled tablecloth on a chair, ready to go to the laundry, and set out the candlesticks and the fall centerpiece of gourds and dried thistles onto the exposed glossy wood.

Celia remembered how it had been when she'd come home for Fall Break in October and Laurie had brought Julia for the weekend. "You're right about Julia," she agreed. "There was a little bit of a flap when she took something Rob said to Laurie as racist. She hasn't known many white people; she's kind of defensive, still. She'll get used to us."

She thought of leading him back into the kitchen to keep the chore-doers company and put him back with Laurie as someone he already felt comfortable with, but on second thought decided she'd like the chance to get to know him a little better. She cocked her head toward the swinging door into the living room and he pushed it open for her with a bow.

She gave him an exaggeratedly imperious nod as she passed through, then returned his friendly grin.

Once they'd settled onto facing settees, he said, "So how did that work out?"

"Basically, we talked about it. We do a lot of talking in this family. Talking, and hugging."

"Italians," he said wisely.

"I beg your pardon?"

"Somethin Mac said to me, back when we first met. Your mama's Italian extraction, right? He said they act real affectionate. I'd seen him kiss that brother, the one that isn't here now, and thought they were queer." He chortled.

Celia drew herself up. "What if he had been?"

269

"'What if he…'? What you talkin about? Mac's no homo."

"No, he's not."

Clai nodded decisively. "That gal of his, prettiest little Negress I ever set eyes on."

Celia let her jaw fall open and set both hands on top of her head.

Clai flushed a deep, mottled red. "Wrong thing again?"

"Clai, my God, 'Negress'? Nobody even uses that word any more."

"I was tryin a be polite."

She let her hands fall into her lap, rolling her eyes and shaking her head.

He got even redder, but now he looked mulish. He leaned forward, hands braced on muscular thighs. "Is every word I say here goin a be a test?"

"No," she said. "No, I'm sorry, I'm being a very poor hostess, aren't I?"

He stared at her a second, eyes narrowed. "Your boyfriend goes to Duke, Mac told me," he said. "You know they're segregated, right?"

"I do know that. And that you decided not to go there because of that. He's working on it."

"Well, I'm workin on it, too. In my own way."

She nodded. *You're doing it again,* she realized. *Don't make this like that awful conversation with Steve and Jamie. It's not your job to fix everybody, or make them over into your own image.* "I see that," she said.

Laurie came into the room, still drying his hands on a dishtowel. "Hey, what're you two doing lollygagging around in here? The game's about to start!"

Celia yelped and jumped up and the three of them charged off to the TV room.

CHAPTER 54.

WEDNESDAY, DECEMBER 31, 1959

"Take my hand and show me
How to break my bonds and go free
And I will always see my sweet angel on the tree."

As Steve's clear tenor and Rob's echoing baritone faded into silence along with their guitars, the stillness seemed to ripple out from them as though the hundred or so couples in the Navy Depot Officers Club were spellbound. Then the spell broke as the applause erupted.

Rick and Celia smiled at each other from where they leaned against two of the room's adjacent square support pillars. "And the McAlister Brothers are on their way," Rick said. "Those boys are really something. And that song is boss—did Steve write it to be about Beth?"

"Yes, she cried the first time she heard it, then later scolded him for thinking of her that way. But she didn't give him as hard a time over idealizing her as she would have one of the rest of us; she knows it's important whenever he's able to express emotions at all."

Steve and Rob had left the bandstand, taking a rest after their long set. Some bland canned music made soothing background noise as the crowd milled around, chatting and lining up at the bar to snag champagne in preparation for the New Year's toast.

Rick had already gotten glasses for the two of them. Celia ran her finger around the rim of hers, thinking about Steve and expressing emotions. Rick was a good guy, and she enjoyed being with him most of the time, but she didn't have any strong feelings about him since she'd started at Barnard. She'd been giddy over being with him at the beginning, but now she wasn't really worrying about guys at all. *Am I just using him as a convenience? Is that fair to him?*

She glanced up to find his eyes focused on nothing, turned away from hers.

"You want to hear something funny?" he asked, bringing his attention back. "Well, more ironic than humorous, I guess, but I laughed out loud when I heard about it."

"Now I'm intrigued. Tell me."

"Duke had a Moslem guest speaker come to talk about interfaith relations this semester. But they didn't want this brown guy to see an all-white audience, so they imported black students from North Carolina College for the evening."

"Oh, my God. And nobody saw the hypocrisy?"

"Some people did. There was a lot of talk about it, and ridicule of the administration. You know, most of the time the campus is either focusing on internal stuff like what frat houses are in trouble this week, or else obsessing about Khrushchev and the Soviets. But the whole desegregation problem keeps cropping up more and more. They're not going to be able to ignore it much longer, however deep President Edens keeps his head buried in the sand."

"I don't understand why they've held out this long. I can't think of another big university that's still segregated."

He shifted his shoulders to face her; the crowd was getting noisier and it was harder to hear each other. "That cuts both ways," he said. "Some people feel like Duke is the last best hope for white supremacy in academia. But they're losing national prestige, Northern scholars don't want to be on the faculty, and they're losing federal money. On the other hand, they're afraid they'll lose alumni support and that enrollments will go down if they do integrate. Meanwhile, Edens is trying to placate the trustees and not rock the boat. He'll probably lose his own job; they're saying there's pressure on him to resign."

"Huh. At Barnard last spring they protested segregated universities in South Africa. Maybe I should try to get them to shine a little light closer to home."

"Maybe you should. I don't get this whole Southern thing about race, anyway. It's more like a religion than a philosophy; you can't reason with some of them about it. Speaking of religion, I heard one of the statues in the doorway of the chapel is supposed to be Robert E. Lee. Couldn't prove it by me, but it seems crazy. For one thing, what's a Civil War general got to do with the church?"

Celia shrugged. "In the North it's not so emotional, I think partly because we keep our racism all neatly tucked away and harder to identify. Barnard was founded on principles of racial equality and academic freedom, but I've only seen a handful of black faces on campus. Better than none, I suppose."

Rick nodded. "We had Harry Golden, that guy who wrote the book about the history of Jews in America—"

"We did, too!" Celia said.

"One thing he said about racism in America really struck me. Something like, 'In the North, they tell Negroes they can go high but don't *come close*, while the South tells them they can come close...'"

"'But don't rise up,'" Celia finished for him. "Yeah, Laurie likes that line, too."

They both laughed a little in mutual sympathy. Then Rick took a breath and said, "I really have to thank you, Celia."

"Oh?"

"You've made me see a lot of things I would've missed if I hadn't known you. Going all the way back to when Judy told me about this crazy girl in her gym class who raised a fuss about those stupid girls' basketball rules. You were just somebody my kid sister liked, and I was all involved with finding my own friends at a new school, but I kept thinking about that, and about how people look at girls and women. And Duke; I don't think I would ever have pushed myself to get into a higher ranked school if I hadn't seen you dig your teeth in to the pre-med idea. Then this whole business about segregation: I might have thought about it if I hadn't known you, but I wouldn't have actually gotten involved. If I ever make anything of myself, I'm going to owe some of it to you."

Celia was touched, but she said, "You're sounding kind of past-tense there, Rick."

He looked at her sadly. "I feel like I'm kind of ready to move on. Don't you?"

"I do," she admitted. "I'm meeting new guys, new people in general, people who don't think of me as a sister—or a sister's friend—and learning new things about myself, figuring out who I am outside of my family, and it seems like time for a new start."

Around them, the countdown to midnight had started. Celia could barely hear Rick as he agreed, "New year, new decade—I wonder what the '60s will be like?—new paths to travel down… but we won't lose track of each other."

"No," she said as the room erupted in streamers and balloons and cries of "Happy New Year." She stepped away from her pillar; Rick met her between them and they kissed one last time.

Steve and Rob were back on the bandstand. They led the crowd and Celia and Rick joined in, linking arms and swaying softly together, singing, "'Should auld acquaintance be forgot...'" while confetti fell into their forgotten champagne.

Chapter 55.

Sunday, March 13, 1960

The rhythmic rattling of the train over the railroad ties almost hypnotized Celia as she leaned her head against the window. Outside, the dark landscape rushed by, telephone poles seeming to rise out of the ground and sink back again as Celia hung motionless and helplessly watching.

Hanging. She shuddered, thinking of the young man named Felton Turner who'd been beaten and hung upside down in a tree with the letters KKK carved into his chest by Texas toughs angry at the recent upsurge of sit-ins and demonstrations against segregation. Celia and her roommate, Christine, had joined in the on-campus civil rights group, but it had seemed rather academic—the real dangers were down South, far from the casual liberalism of the New York City scene.

Thinking about the South and the maelstrom Laurie was going into made Celia's stomach roil. She pulled her mind away from it and onto more general thoughts about herself and Barnard. She was starting to feel comfortable with both the urban setting and the challenging academic atmosphere. There was always something interesting to do or see, but having a studious roommate helped keep her focused on her studies. The coursework was hard, especially the science courses, but she could keep her head above water.

She often thought about Izola Curry, the black woman who'd tried to assassinate Dr. King a couple of years ago. She was mentally disturbed, in an institution now. But the incident drove home to Celia how her working with the mentally ill could affect not only the lives of the people who came to her but could work to the benefit of society at large. But after what had just happened at home, that sort of long-term planning no longer seemed to be enough.

In any case, concentrating on her goals didn't quite ease the ache of longing for home, for the easy acceptance and affection of her family and the familiarity of places she'd known all her life, a comfort and ease that had been rattled by this trip.

When Laurie had asked her to come home this weekend, even though it was still a month till Barnard's spring break, she'd assumed that Julia would be with him. She'd looked forward to seeing her again and to hearing what she'd thought must be good news. It was a little soon for them to be getting engaged, but she'd seen in October how smitten Laurie was and she knew from his letters that they'd been growing rapidly closer. And what better time to announce it than Mom's birthday?

She'd caught an early train yesterday morning, knowing she'd have to trek back tonight but feeling it was worth it to be part of what promised to be a landmark event in the family's life. She was puzzled when nothing was said all day, and that Julia was nowhere in evidence; she was coming later in the week, Laurie said, but Celia would have left by then. Still, at least that meant they hadn't broken up. So why was Laurie so edgy? He'd kept looking at everyone as though he were trying to memorize them.

Then, this morning after pancakes, Laurie had dropped the bombshell. He hadn't wanted to share happy news at all: he'd wanted to tell them that he was taking a leave from Haverford and that he and Julia—and evidently Linda, too—were going down to Nashville to take part in the lunch counter sit-ins there. Mom and Dad had fussed and cried and protested, they all had, but Laurie had been adamant. He needed to do this, and what's more, he needed to do it on his own; he didn't want any of them coming with him.

On top of that, Ruby had announced that she was going down to Atlanta with her sister Pearl to help organize efforts there. It felt as though the world was ending: Ruby wouldn't be there at the center of the house, radiating calmness and order and strength. She wouldn't be putting herself at as much obvious risk as Laurie but still… How could Ruby leave the family? Did this mean she didn't care about them?

Celia was unmoored, floating anchorless through the dark night. The safety of home and family had been breached and the feeling of security waiting to receive her whenever she needed it was gone. *Is this what it means to be an adult?* she wondered. *Am I going to be on my own from now on?*

Stop that, she told herself sternly. *The world doesn't revolve around you. There are bigger issues than your comfort, and Ruby caring about them doesn't mean she doesn't care about us. Any more than Laurie putting himself in harm's way means he wants to suffer.* She pulled herself upright on the worn plush seat. This was no time to be feeling sorry for herself. Laurie and Ruby were going into danger; the least she could do was show some backbone.

By the time she got back to her dorm room, she'd managed to get herself together, or so she thought.

But Christine looked at her straight back and determined face through narrowed eyes. "It wasn't your brother getting engaged, was it?" she said shrewdly.

Celia slumped down onto her desk chair, giving up for the moment. "No," she said, and explained what had happened.

"Nashville?" Christine said. "Maybe he'll meet that activist, that Lawson guy. Vanderbilt just expelled him for being active in non-violent resistance, you know."

"Laurie told us that," Celia said, "once we all stopped freaking out about him going. CORE—you know, the Congress of Racial Equality?—has been running sit-ins since the 1940s but they never drew so much attention before."

Christine briskly crossed to her desk and pulled the cover off her imposing standard typewriter. "Your brother didn't want the family going with him, you said. That makes sense; we all have to learn to stand on our own two feet. But that doesn't mean you can't do something. I've been thinking about this ever since Mrs. Roosevelt spoke here last month on morality in politics. Let's draft a statement in support."

As usual, Celia found her roommate's calm practicality both bracing and comforting. "Good idea," she said. "Hey, do we still have that copy of Barnard's announcement refusing federal money because of the loyalty oath they pegged it to? Maybe we can use that as a template."

"Second drawer of my bureau in the folder on the right," Christine said, rolling a sheet of paper into the machine's carriage. "Maybe we can light a fire under the NSA that supposedly represents us students, get them off the dime about supporting the sit-ins."

Sending a silent prayer her brother's way, Celia cracked her knuckles and got to work.

Chapter 56.

"Thanks, Mrs. Sossdorf." Celia nodded to the rectory housekeeper as she accepted the cup of coffee and settled back on the worn corduroy of the armchair. This was her first interaction with Father Shea as an adult, and outside the strict realm of liturgy and sacrament. It felt both a little daring and as comfortable and familiar as meeting an old friend in a strange place.

They'd already chatted about Celia's grades and Father Shea's sister in New York, and discussed Senator Kennedy's run for the presidency and what that might mean for American Catholics. Celia sipped the bitter brew Mrs. Sossdorf had provided, wishing she'd asked for milk and thinking that by the time she finished drinking it, it would be time to let the busy priest get back about his business for the day.

She looked up to see him watching her keenly. "Was there something particular you wanted to talk to me about, Celia?"

She felt herself flush a little. "You always see through me, Father. Yes, a couple of things have been on my mind, actually. I know what my parents think about them, but I'd like another perspective, if you don't mind."

At his encouraging nod, she set her cup down on the coffee table and laced her fingers around one knee. "First, I wanted to ask you a sort of personal question."

She laughed at his wary look. "Not *that* kind of personal," she assured him. "I just wondered, being a priest, dealing with people's problems all the time, how do you stay so calm? You always seem ready to listen to anyone who comes to you and then just go on without letting it bring you down. My mother says she's had to learn to keep the different parts of her life in different compartments; that's how she copes. And she says I'll learn more in graduate school about different techniques. But the box image doesn't seem to do much for me. Do you have something like that?"

"I do," he said. "I learned it in seminary. My teacher told us to picture ourselves as funnels. People pour their troubles into us and we let them fill us, but then we let them flow on out so that we're ready for the next task or claim on our attention."

"'Funnel,' huh. Yes, I can see that; it reminds me of something my sister Beth said to me once, about letting anger flow through and out of me, not holding onto it. Well, thanks, that helps." She twisted the napkin in her lap, gathering her courage for her next question. "I also wanted to talk to you about something in confidence."

He put his own cup aside. "Perhaps we should continue this conversation under the aegis of the Sacrament?"

"No, thanks, I don't mean under the Seal of the Confessional." She smiled at him. "If they're threatening to pull out your fingernails if you don't tell them my dark secret, go ahead and tell. I just mean ordinary confidentiality, and it's more for my brother's sake than mine."

"Ah," he said, taking up his cup again. "That I can certainly promise you. Just out of curiosity, is anyone actually likely to want to tear out my fingernails to learn this dark secret?"

"No, it's not that kind of dark. It's just that it could cause him a lot of pain and trouble if it got to be generally known. It's that my brother Jamie is a homosexual."

Celia watched as he processed the information, going from surprised to troubled to speculative. She spoke in response to the last expression. "Yes, it's what I was talking about in Confession last summer when I had to pester you twice in one day. I've been thinking about some things he said when he was angry that day, about how society rejects people like him, how it could affect his professional life and even put him at risk from the law. But lately it's occurred to me to wonder about the Church's attitude. He's not Catholic, of course, and I know from other things you've said that you're not one of those people who thinks that non-Catholics like my sister Beth or even non-Christians like Jamie are going to hell, but do you think homosexuals are?"

To her surprise, Father Shea chuckled a little. "Celia, Celia, you keep me on my toes," he said. "No conversation with you is ever dull." He took a deep breath and continued more soberly, "I'm not given to making sweeping generalizations about who is or is not going to hell. I'm not a theologian or a Church Doctor, I'm just a lowly worker in the vineyard trying to help where I can to bring in the harvest. I don't have much experience with homosexuals that I'm aware of."

He picked up a cookie and started absently crumbling it onto his saucer. "I will say that I've known a few such men who came into the priesthood in hopes of escaping their nature. In my opinion, they don't make very good priests. If they do manage to stifle temptation, their anger and frustration comes out in other ways. They haven't embraced celibacy as a loving sacrifice but out of fear."

"You know," Celia put in, "you talked about 'loving sacrifice' to me once before. It was about giving up things for Lent, do you remember? It was a few years ago; I'd had myself a hamburger on Holy Saturday and mentioned it in Confession. You said, in this puzzled kind of tone, 'If it's bothering you, don't do it.' I literally couldn't understand what you were talking about. Then you said that the Lenten sacrifice should be joyous. I was stunned; nobody'd ever suggested such a thing to me before. As I told you then, I'd always assumed it was like iodine: if it doesn't hurt, it's not working. I've never managed the state of mind you were talking about, but it's been an ideal I've worked toward."

"I'm touched," he said. "I hope I didn't give you an exaggerated idea of my own virtue there; I'm really a sinner like everyone else. That's what keeps me from passing judgment on people like your brother. I think that 'hell' is the state of rejecting God, of rejecting the good, and—though I don't know him very well—I get the impression that he is someone who tries very hard to hold to the ideals of his faith, and I trust the mercy of God to account it to him for righteousness."

Mrs. Sossdorf had come back into the room and was staring at the mess Father Shea had made with the cookie crumbs, an expression on her wrinkled face like the one Ruby wore when Celia tracked mud in the house: exasperated but fond. "Father, it's three o'clock," she said. "You told me to remind you that you have that meeting with the Intercultural Council at three-thirty." She gave Celia a regretful smile.

Celia hurriedly put down her cup and napkin and picked up her purse as she came to her feet. "I know you're busy, Father. I'm sorry to have taken up so much of your time."

Father Shea stood as well. "Not at all, Celia. It's been a pleasure to see what a fine, thoughtful young woman you're becoming. I'm sorry to cut this short; I wanted to ask you how Laurie's doing in Nashville."

"That's all right; I have to get home and pack. I'm going back to New York tomorrow."

"On Holy Thursday?" Mrs. Sossdorf said in surprise. "You'll miss Easter with your family?"

"I know," Celia said. "I'm not happy about it myself. But I promised my roommate I'd spend Easter with her and her family. They live in New York, and Christine and I will be going with a group to Washington next week to protest the loyalty oath requirement for students who apply for federal loans. Anyway, it wouldn't be the same at home without Ruby. She and Laurie are both fine, by the way, though my brother Jamie had a horrible nightmare about Laurie last night."

"Perhaps he needs a 'funnel' as well."

"Maybe you're right. I'll write to him about it." Impulsively, she leaned across the coffee table and gave the priest a brief hug. "Thank you for listening. And thanks for the coffee and cookies, Mrs. S."

"Any time, dear," they said in chorus.

CHAPTER 57.

MONDAY, JULY 4, 1960

C elia sighed as she daubed camphor onto the mosquito bites dotting her ankles and the parts of her feet her sandals hadn't covered. "You and Steve had the right idea," she said as Joy came out of the bathroom, "watching the fireworks from the window of his room."

"Mmm," Joy said noncommittally, climbing into her bed.

"On the other hand, you missed an interesting conversation. Linda came over—it was kind of funny, come to think of it: Laurie's ex along with his current girlfriend, and Jamie's former girlfriend along with his current roommate. I wonder whether Joel's more than a roommate, though? He and Jamie have been joined at the hip since he got here, and Rima made some sly cracks that made it clear she thinks there's something there, too. What do you think?"

Joy shrugged. "Okay if I turn out the light?"

"Sure," Celia said, tossing her camphor-soaked cotton balls into the wastebasket between their desks. *Funny, Joy's usually game for a little late-night gossip.* "Something bothering you, Jo-Jo?"

But the girl didn't even rise to Celia's deliberate poke with the despised nickname. She clicked off the lamp by her bed and Celia followed suit on her side of the room. Silently, Celia said her nightly prayers; she knew Joy would be doing the same.

The moon was almost at the full, sinking now toward the roof of the Johnstons' house across the way. On this cloudless night, it filled the room with an effulgent silver glow, lending an aura of mystery to the familiar objects that surrounded them.

After few minutes Joy said, "So what was so great about this conversation?"

Ok, don't tell me what's up. "Julia mentioned this new group, the Student Nonviolent Coordinating Committee—'Snick' is how they say it. I mentioned that Rick had been at one of their organizing meetings at Shaw. So then Julia said—you know how snarky she can be—'You had a boyfriend who goes to a black school? But I guess you got rid of him, right?' So I said, 'No, he goes to Duke, but he's interested in civil rights and has been working to get the university to integrate. That's why he went to the meeting; he wasn't a delegate, he just wanted to pick up any tips, but they were mostly talking about sit-ins, so it wasn't too relevant to the Duke situation.' From there we got into what Julia and Laurie went through, sitting-in at lunch counters in Nashville."

Joy was lying flat on her back with her eyes open. "So far, not all that interesting," she sniped. "We've talked about that integration stuff a million times since Laurie and Ruby got back."

"Hey, who put the ants in your Japants? I'm getting to it. After a while Rima pipes up, 'Joel, tell them what you were talking about before.' Naturally, Joel clammed up altogether with everybody's attention on him, so Rima ended up telling us he'd been saying maybe someday there'd be, like, a civil rights movement for people like him and Jamie. That seemed pretty far-fetched to me, and Ruby suddenly said she was tired and needed to go to bed, but the other young people all liked the idea."

Joy's profile disappeared as she turned her head toward Celia. "Really? How would that work?"

Celia shrugged. "Start with those stupid laws, I guess. The idea that somebody could go to jail because of who they want to sleep with seems completely nuts to me. And there could be laws preventing employers, say, from firing people just because they're queer like the laws they're working on to prevent them from refusing to hire people just because of the color of their skin."

"That makes sense."

"So then I had a really far-out idea. Why not something like that for women?"

Now Joy had propped herself up on one elbow. "What kind of women?"

"Any women. A couple of things that happened this past semester got me thinking. There was this big flap because the president of Columbia said he didn't want Barnard girls coming to their classes wearing what he called 'inappropriate clothing.' The student council actually went along with it, and passed a dress code that said we could wear slacks or Bermuda shorts only at Barnard, and even then they have to be not tight or too short; if we cross the street to Columbia and don't have skirts on, we at least have to wear long coats to cover up our dirty, sinful nether parts."

Joy giggled. "That's the stupidest thing I've ever heard."

"Yeah, Coach Vaughan and President Kirk would get along just fine. Anyway, half the student body had signed a protest petition within the week. Kirk and our president, Dr. McIntosh, seemed surprised we got so het up about it.

"But that got me thinking about Mrs. Mac, as we call her: she's a wife and mother and has had this brilliant career as a college and university administrator. I'd think she'd be more understanding about girls wanting to be as comfortable as the boys are moving around campus. I guess she's had to stay pretty strictly inside the boundary of what people think is correct behavior to get where she has, though.

"Then I put that together with a talk I'd heard the week before. This couple, both of them academic professionals, spoke on the 'Role of the Educated Wife.' Even though they obviously both had careers, they were saying intellectual girls should be careful about getting married too soon because they'll be bored at home."

Now Joy seemed fully engaged in the topic, peering at Celia in the ghostly half-light. "And you think they won't be bored?"

"No, that's not it. It's that it suddenly struck me that they both assumed the wife would be stuck at home."

"But most people don't have somebody like Ruby to take care of the house and stuff."

"I know. I've talked to Mom about that. Live-in domestic help is going the way of the dodo. But why should the woman always be the one to stay in? That friend of Mom's from Smith, that Betty whosis, who sent out those questionnaires to her classmates, has written a couple of articles about it, about frustrated women who can't pursue their professions. Why can't they?"

Joy pondered, then said uncertainly, "Because they have the babies, I guess."

"I suppose," Celia said, and fell asleep in the silence that followed.

Some time later, the moon long gone, Celia opened her eyes to the sound of rushing water from the bathroom. *Is she taking a shower? In the middle of the night?*

The sound ceased; after a few minutes she felt the current of air as Joy passed on her way back to bed.

"Are you sick or something?" Celia whispered.

"No, I'm not sick, I'm fine. Go back to sleep, Celia."

Groggily, Celia did.

Chapter 58.

Most of the volunteers in the new Candy Striper program at the hospital were high school girls. That didn't bother Celia; taking part was her chance to observe real medical care, to give flesh to some of the theory she was learning in her pre-med courses at Barnard. Besides, Mom's friend Dr. Susan Matthiesson had taken Celia under her wing. Instead of reading to patients or filling water pitchers, she was getting to fetch supplies and hand them to the doctor, to follow her on rounds and listen to the diagnoses, to bring her coffee in the physicians' lounge and listen to her reminiscences.

Tonight was a slow night. Dr. Matthiesson was the on-call attending physician, reviewing some patient folders in the alcove that served as her office. Celia filed them as she finished with them, impatiently flicking aside the ruffles on her uniform, a silly pink-and-white striped pinafore.

They'd been talking about how difficult it was to get most physicians to take the relationship between mental and physical health seriously. "It's a crime," said the woman Celia was starting to think of as a friend and mentor, "that a psychologist like your mother isn't recognized as having professional standing here."

Celia's mind went back to that horrible night three years ago when she'd brought Carol in and Mom had come to the rescue. She told the story, then said, "But Mom claimed she had privileges here."

"She was lying," the doctor said with an indulgent smile. "Who'd she tell it to?"

"Some intern. Name that started with 'E' I think…Evans, that was it."

"I remember him. Self-important young jackanapes, always condescended to me because I was a woman, though I had twenty years' experience on him. I breathed a sigh of relief when his internship ended and he decided to go to Harrisburg. There've been plenty just like him to take his place, though."

Celia started to ask for advice on how to deal with the condescension and prejudice of male doctors, but was interrupted when a resident, a new-minted MD whose name Celia couldn't remember, showed up in the alcove entrance.

"I've just received a radio transmission from the ambulance service," he said. "An emergent case coming in. I think it would be best if you handled it, Doctor." His tone was respectful, but his face was sour.

"And why would that be, Doctor? Something beyond your expertise?" Dr. Matthiesson asked briskly.

The resident looked at Celia meaningfully. Celia kept all expression from her face. "Doctor?" Dr. Matthiesson repeated.

He turned his shoulder to Celia and spoke in an undertone, as though he could prevent her from hearing. "It's a botched abortion, evidently. Looks like she did it herself. They found her in a bathroom at the Harvon Motel, with a coat hanger." His voice, low as it was, was heavy with disgust.

Dr. Matthiesson got up. "Come along, Celia. This is something that, unfortunately, you'll need to see sooner or later."

"I have some patients to check on," the resident said.

"Your patients are all asleep, Doctor Radabaugh. You will accompany me and observe, so that you will be able to treat the next patient who presents with this problem."

Celia heard Radabaugh mutter, "'Problem,' huh," under his breath, but if Dr. Matthiesson heard him she gave no sign.

They got to the receiving area just as the gurney was being wheeled in.

Remember the boxes; remember the funnel, Celia told herself. *Let this flow through, don't be caught up in your emotions. Keep calm so you can help her.*

Still, she could hardly hear Dr. Matthiesson's directions over the blood thrumming in her ears, and she had to fight to get breath into her lungs.

She did hear the nurse who'd hurried up, a middle-aged woman whose starched white cap was still crisp in spite of the late hour, say, "This child shouldn't be here, Doctor."

"Neither child should be here, Nurse. But Miss McAlister is studying medicine. She'll need to know how to deal with cases like this. And she can ponder the public policy implications, as well."

"Public policy?" Radabaugh put in as they moved the limp body from the gurney to an examining table.

"What conditions drive a young woman to such desperate straits, and how to prevent this kind of thing from happening." She pulled away the blood-soaked blanket as the ambulance attendant rattled off vital statistics: blood pressure, temperature, what they'd done for her on the way in.

"What would prevent this kind of thing from happening," the nurse sniffed, "is if these girls learned to keep their legs together."

Radabaugh nodded at her approvingly but Dr. Matthiesson said, "That attitude is not helpful. You would both do well to remember that our job is to treat patients, not judge them. Miss McAlister, help Nurse Murdoch cut the rest of the patient's clothes off, please."

"Yes, Doctor," Celia managed to respond.

The next few minutes passed in a blur for Celia. Numbly, she fetched packets of plasma for transfusions, rolls of gauze for packing, syringes for injections. Her silly pink and white pinafore was streaked with blood, her cheeks with helpless tears.

Dr. Matthiesson worked doggedly, but they all knew it was useless, had been useless from the start. There was no response from the still figure on the table. Finally, she put her instruments down with a sigh. Her voice flat and emotionless, she said, "That's it. Call it, Radabaugh."

Looking pale and shaken, the resident glanced at the clock. "Time of death: twenty-three fifteen."

The nurse made a notation on the patient chart and began straightening and covering the body. Radabaugh went over to confer with the ambulance attendant.

Dr. Matthiesson looked at Celia. "Child, you look a wreck. Perhaps I shouldn't have subjected you to this after all. Go clean up, then if you would you can set out the death certificate form on my desk and then you should go home for the night." She turned to the ambulance attendant, who was filling out his own form in the corner of the room. "Do we need to fill out a police report? Where are her possessions? Do we have an ID?"

"No, the police were on the scene; the motel called them first. But she had nothing on her," he answered. "We took her as a Jane Doe."

Gathering all her resolve, Celia pulled herself together. "She's not a Jane Doe, Doctor," she said. "Her name is—was—Carol Prosky."

Chapter 59.

Saturday, August 5, 1960

The sun beat down on Celia's head as she stood by Carol's gravesite. The new cemetery outside of Carlisle was a flat, vast expanse of grass; there were no trees, and the gravestones were plaques set into the ground. Carol's gleaming white coffin with shiny brass fittings was almost too bright to look at, poised above the ground on metal rollers. Around it, the excavated earth had been covered with green tarps. *As though if we don't see the dirt it won't exist.*

Celia looked across at the canopy Hoffman's Funeral Home had set up. Beneath it, on folding chairs askew on the lumpy ground, sat Mr. and Mrs. Prosky. He was grim-faced and sour, she looked spacy and vague. *They've doped her up. God knows what's keeping him going.* Theirs were the only chairs; no other family sat with them.

Mom and Dad had gone over to Proskys' first thing in the morning after Celia'd come home from the hospital that horrible night. They returned fifteen minutes later; Mom said that Lulabelle, the Proskys' help, eyes red from weeping, had firmly turned them away, stating that Carol's parents wanted to grieve in privacy.

"I tried to talk her into letting me in to see Muriel," Mom had said. "But it was no go. They're saying Carol had mono and went horseback riding against their advice, so her spleen ruptured and she hemorrhaged to death."

"That's not even possible, is it?" Celia had asked, lifting her head from Ruby's breast, where it had lain ever since Mom and Dad had left.

"No, it isn't," Ruby had answered.

Another cover-up, Celia mused now. *Mononucleosis, the fad disease. Any unexplained absence or mysterious illness these days, they blame mono. Only they're not only blaming the disease, they're blaming Carol. "She went riding." Hah.*

Celia and her parents had agreed not to tell the rest of the family what had really happened, though. Mom felt that Celia was under the constraint of doctor-patient confidentiality. Celia, for her part, was sure Carol wouldn't want the others to know. The horror of what Carol had done to herself would never leave her; she didn't want that image in her sisters' minds.

Carol was alone, in that seedy motel, though her parents were a few miles away. She was scared, she was desperate, she had no place to go. I should have been there for her. But I didn't even know she was in town, and she didn't let me know. Could I have found her a doctor somewhere willing to brave the law to help her? Could Mom have? But she didn't call us, she attacked herself with a coat hanger instead. God, she must have been so frightened. Celia shivered in the heat and brought her mind back to the scene before her.

The minister or whatever he was—the Proskys were some sort of Protestant; Celia couldn't remember the denomination, but she didn't think this man represented it—had finished his few generic words and turned away to shake hands with Mr. Prosky. He offered a hand to Mrs. Prosky but, when she didn't respond, he simply walked off toward the parked cars on the cemetery drive.

There weren't many. The Proskys hadn't announced the funeral time in the paper. Mom had only found it out by calling all the mortuaries in town; Hoffman's had been the third one she'd tried. She stood beside Celia now, sweating heavily in the black faille silk suit she'd worn to bury Laurie's mother and then David in, back in Carlisle in the Colored Cemetery. Dad, roasting in his dress blues, held Celia's elbow on her other side.

Mr. Prosky was standing up now, helping his wife to her feet, propping her up with the crutches strapped to her forearms. She hobbled off with him behind her, neither of them speaking to or looking at the small group gathered on the other side of their only child's grave. Lulabelle was nowhere in evidence.

Celia had been expecting workmen to come and start cranking the mechanism to lower the casket into the ground, but evidently that process was also going to be sanitized and kept out of sight.

"I don't think the Proskys want the customary visit at their house," Mom was saying to someone. "Would you girls like to come back to our house?"

Celia turned to see Barb and Patty standing there like ghosts out of her past. They looked at each other, communicating silently, then Barb said, "Sure, Dr. Mac. That would be good. I've got the car; we'll see you over there. Ok, Celia?"

"Ok," Celia said.

Celia lingered by the grave a little till it became obvious that the workmen were impatiently waiting for them to leave so they could get on with their job. As they pulled away in Mom's new green Olds, Celia looked back at Carol's coffin, now the highest object in the cemetery, shining in the sun.

So the girls were actually already in the house when Celia and her parents arrived, sitting on the screened porch with iced tea and a plate of sugar cookies.

Ruby pushed the cookies toward Celia as she sat down with them. "Get some sugar in you, child," she said, "and some liquid."

Celia obediently nibbled and sipped, focusing in on her former friends' conversation. "...didn't even know she was in town," Barb was saying.

"None of us did," Patty agreed. Then she sniggered. "She should have gone to Puerto Rico, like Sally Grayson. She supposedly comes back from Florida as pale as when she left. The Anti-Tan Vacation, the new white girls' fun time after the real fun is over."

Barb frowned. "Really, Pats, it's not funny."

"Well, who do they think they're kidding? Mono. I mean, Carol was my friend, but give me a break. Everybody knew she was round-heeled. Bound to happen, sooner or later."

"Patty!" Barb scolded. "Don't you know better than to speak ill of the dead? And a friend, at that?"

Celia pushed away from the table so hard she knocked over her tea. Ice cubes and liquid streamed across; some dripped onto Patty's lap. The girl squealed and jumped up, dabbing at her pink cotton sundress with a napkin.

Pink. She couldn't even be bothered to wear a decent dress. "You don't know what friendship is," she snarled. "Either of you."

"Oh, yeah?" Barb snapped, getting to her feet as well. "You're such a hotshot friend, why weren't you there for her? Too busy with your fancy college friends, I guess. How long is it since you even talked to her?"

Celia stumbled into the kitchen, evaded Ruby's outstretched hand, and fled through the dining and living rooms into the hall bathroom. She locked herself in and stood there, shivering and weeping, listening to the distant sound of Patty and Barb's voices swelling and receding as they moved along the back walk and around the garage. Then she heard Barb's car leaving.

But you're the driver, she told herself. *You've driven them away. You'll never see them again, and you'll never see Carol or hear that little-girl voice of hers again, ever, ever.*

She came back out into the hall and dialed the phone with shaking fingers.

"Hello?"

"Judy—"

"Oh, Celia, how was your friend's funeral? Are you all right? Do you want me to come over?"

Celia started to cry in earnest. "They erased her, Judy," she whispered. "I left her behind and now she's gone, and they've erased her."

Chapter 60.

"Celia? Celia, what's wrong?" Her roommate's worried voice seemed to be coming to Celia from the far end of a tunnel. Her fingers felt numb and her head was spinning.

Suddenly she felt pressure on the back of her neck; Christine was pushing her head down. *She thinks I'm going to faint,* she vaguely realized. *Maybe she's right.* Obediently, Celia put her head between her knees and stayed that way until the discomfort of the position outweighed the disorientation of the dizziness. She sat up and took several deep cleansing breaths, the kind they'd taught Steve to do when he was in danger of going into one of his dissociative fugue states. *Steve. Oh, God. And Joy.*

Her breath started to hitch. She clenched her fists to get a grip on herself and realized the letter was still clutched in her hand. She stared at it, wondering whether it would say something else if she read it again; what it actually said was just too impossible. *And I'd been feeling so good today in the science lab, finally feeling competent in there. But how competent could I be, if I could miss something like this?*

Christine's voice interrupted her ruminations. "Celia, do you need me to call someone? I gather you got bad news—is anyone hurt in your family?"

The open concern on the face of her ordinarily reserved roommate grounded Celia enough to enable her to speak. "It's my little sister, Joy," she croaked. "And my brother Steve. She's... she's pregnant."

Christine gasped. "But she's only, what, sixteen? And what does your brother have to do with—oh, no. Oh, Celia, he's the father?"

As the full magnitude of the disaster bore in upon Celia, the tears finally came. Christine wasn't the hugging type, but she came to sit next to Celia on her lower bunk and pressed a hand on her knee. After a minute she leaned forward to pluck a box of tissues off Celia's desk and put it in Celia's lap, but her other hand never left that knee.

Celia focused on that spot of warmth and constant pressure till the storm of weeping passed and she was able to mop her face one last time—*for this time; there'll be more*—and pat Christine's hand gratefully.

Christine withdrew it and pulled away a little, but stayed sitting next to Celia. "Tell me what you're thinking," she said.

How Christine-ish, Celia thought with distant amusement. *Most girls would ask me how I felt. Too bad Jamie's gay, they'd be perfect for each other.* She mentally shook herself out of her meanderings and considered the answer to Christine's question. "They're not related by blood, you know," she said. "And they didn't even grow up together; Steve just came to us three years ago. But that's the thing: he's so frail, so... so breakable, still. I don't know what this will do to him. And her, oh, poor Joy, she takes everything so much to heart—well, anyone would, something like this, but I mean she's going to try to take all the burden on herself, and the blame... Mom says Joy told them it was her initiative."

"What are they going to do?" Christine said in a tentative tone Celia didn't understand at first, then a whole new set of emotions swamped her.

"She's going to have the baby, I can gather that much from what else Mom says in the letter. No abortion." The image of Carol's bleeding, ravaged body filled her mind's eye. "They'd help her if she wanted one, they'd get her to where she could have it done safely," she said, reassuring herself as much as Christine.

She smoothed out the letter and read it through again. "Mom seems to think maybe she and Dad could raise the baby, but I'd bet anything Joy wouldn't sit still for that. She'll insist on doing it herself."

"But they'll still help her, your parents?"

"Sure. But… Christine, she's so smart and she has so many plans and ambitions. What's her life going to be like now? And Steve: Mom says he's still going on this tour his and Rob's manager has set up. He's supposed to be launching a singing career. If I know Joy, she's got some romantic notion of what it's going to be like for them, but they're both just babies themselves, really. And there'll be so much gossip and nastiness, the downside of living in a small town."

Christine was watching Celia carefully. "That's all going to be difficult. I can see that. But that's not what has you most upset, is it?"

"No," Celia admitted. The question brought its own answer to her. "I'm most upset about myself. Why didn't I see this coming? She sleeps in the same room with me, for God's sake. How did I not know?" She thought back on the summer. "I was always either focusing on my own problems, talking about things I saw at the hospital…" *Though I never told her what really happened to Carol,* she thought. *Mom said I shouldn't but maybe… I don't know.* "…or nattering on about—Christ—about feminism and women being stuck at home to be wives and mothers. If I'd paid more attention, maybe I could have stopped this from happening. I failed her. I'm her big sister; I should have been there for her!" She started to cry again.

Christine pounded lightly on Celia's knee with her fist a couple of times. "Stop that," she said firmly. "She didn't confide in you; you're not a mind reader. Even psychiatrists need for their patients to actually tell them what's wrong before they can do anything about it."

"That's not exactly true. I mean yes, it's true in general, but there are things a trained professional can deduce from body language and affect and some external cues like that…"

"But you're not a trained professional yet, are you? And even if you were, you wouldn't be expected to be objective about a family member, or allowed to treat her."

"True," Celia said grudgingly. "But still—"

"But nothing. Listen to me, Celia. In the time we've roomed together, especially last year, you've told me a lot about your family. I don't know whether you've thought about it this way or not, but they've given you some unique qualifications to help other people. Your Negro brother, your gay brother, your blind sister: you understand situations that most middleclass white kids only know from the outside. That's a strength, not a weakness. And now there's this situation."

"My sister and brother's problems aren't some theoretical learning experience for me," Celia said sharply.

Christine was unperturbed. "Of course they are. They're also a source of worry and pain and personal turmoil for you, naturally. I don't mean to minimize that. But you have a way of seeing the larger picture, the ramifications of people's individual problems, that makes you an ideal person to be of help: not just sympathy but knowledge, not just theory but experience. So maybe you missed some cues from your sister on this business—or maybe you didn't, maybe she was careful not to let any out; you won't know that till you get a chance to

301

talk to her. But you can't go blaming yourself for not being all-seeing and all-knowing." Christine was watching Celia's face as she spoke and seemed increasingly frustrated by the response, or lack of it, that she saw there.

She reached out and grasped both Celia's shoulders, turning her on the bed to face her and make eye contact. "Your mother actually is a professional, right? And she didn't see this coming. You're thinking about assigning blame here, about the past, and you're worrying about the future. You already have what it takes to be a source of strength for your sister—and for your brother, too—right now, in the minute."

"How?"

Christine gave her a little shake. "They're probably terrified about what you think, how you'll react. Write them each a letter."

Celia closed her eyes and nodded her head, reaching to press one of Christine's hands. She blew out a long breath. "Right," she said, "you're right. I can do this. I can help now."

"Of course you can," Christine said.

Chapter 61.

The cab turned down the familiar street: almost home.

"My Marie says to tell you they all miss you down at the restaurant," the driver, Mr. Andretti, said. "They're all real proud of you, though, going to college and all. And going to be a doctor, we hear?"

"That's right," Celia said, wondering—not for the first time—how news spread in a small town. *Joy*. "Uh, please say hi to Marie for me. I'll try to get around there this weekend to see her myself; I want to thank her."

"Yeah?"

"Yes, she's one of the influences in my life that made me feel I could do things like deciding to go to med school. She's such a strong woman."

"Huh," he said, pulling into the driveway. Celia started to open her purse but he said, "No, no, your folks already took care of that."

"Oh, ok. Well, thanks, Mr. Andretti, and Happy Thanksgiving."

"Same to you," he said.

Celia climbed out of the rusty black cab, hauling her weekend bag behind her, and pelted up to the familiar front door. Probably because the old car engine made so much noise, Ruby was already waiting in the hall.

She pulled Celia into her arms. "Welcome home, child," she said, patting Celia's back. "Your parents will be home in an hour or so." She pushed Celia to arm's length and looked her over critically. "Have you been eating all right?"

"Oh, Ruby, when do I ever not eat all right?" Celia said fondly. "I eat like a horse, as usual. Listen, let me just dump my stuff and change out of these shoes and I'll come and help you get ready for tomorrow."

She turned toward the stairs and stopped. Joy was coming down them, not in her old helter-skelter dash but slowly, one hand on the rail. Celia had written her several times and called her once but this was the first they were seeing each other since *it* happened. Celia couldn't help her eyes dropping to Joy's midsection, though of course nothing was showing yet. Then she looked up at her sister's face: that's where the change was. *She looks… not older, exactly, but more knowing. Huh, she is more knowing. She's had sex and I haven't. There's an odd thought.*

Dimly, she heard Ruby say, "Never mind helping out right now; you two can pitch in later. Spend some time together first."

Celia stepped forward as Joy reached the bottom of the stairs. Celia had meant to embrace her in some kind of profoundly meaningful way, but Joy clasped her briefly about the waist and then let go, so Celia followed suit.

Joy looked at her expectantly for a second, then said, "Didn't you just say you were going upstairs? Come on, I'll carry your bag."

"No, no, I'll take it. You don't have to go upstairs again, either, you just came down."

Joy barked a short laugh. "I'm not an invalid, Cissy. I'm pregnant, not sick." She slung the strap of Celia's weekend bag over her shoulder and marched back up the stairs.

Celia followed, feeling that this meeting had not gone the way she'd expected at all.

After supper—Ruby's special baked pumpkin stuffed with ground beef and rice—Ruby said that with only five of them at home, she could clean up on her own. Steve and Rob were still on tour and Jamie had stayed in Massachusetts with Beth, who'd started at Perkins School for the Blind, while Laurie was spending Thanksgiving with Julia's family. So it was just Celia, Joy, and Mom and Dad who gathered in the living room.

It had started drizzling outside; the fire Dad started felt good as Celia settled on the floor in front of it. Mom and Dad cuddled on one settee, Joy curled up on the one opposite them.

They'd already talked at the dinner table about Celia's semester, the Kennedy election, and Barnard's involvement in CURE, Colleges United for Racial Equality, that Columbia had founded to coordinate academic Civil Rights efforts in the New York area.

Now a silence fell that was not quite comfortable. Celia was about to suggest turning on some music when Mom said, "Susan Matthiesson says to contact her when you're ready to apply to medical schools; she'd like to write you a recommendation. And she's hoping you'll volunteer at the hospital again this summer, that you weren't too traumatized to keep on with it." Celia cast a meaningful glance toward Joy. Mom answered it with, "I've told Joy about Carol."

"Really?" Celia was taken aback. "But all that you said to me about confidentiality and it being too upsetting for her and…"

"'Too upsetting'?" Joy said wryly. "I think I know the facts of life, Cissy."

"As to confidentiality," Mom explained, "rumors have gotten around anyway, I suspect from that nurse."

"She was awful," Celia remembered. "She acted like what happened to Carol was all her own fault."

Dad shifted position, leaning forward with his elbows on his knees. He cleared his throat, then said, "Obviously, what happened to Carol was a tragedy. But it wasn't something that just 'happened'; she had some agency. She wasn't a helpless child, she made choices that brought her to that pass. I can't help but think that there's something going wrong in our society. First it was the Grayson girl, then Carol—girls didn't used to do things like this."

Mom rolled her eyes. "For heaven's sake, Sean, women and girls have been aborting unwanted pregnancies since the beginning of recorded time. They used to use herbal concoctions more, which were uncertain and dangerous, but if anything the need was even more desperate when an unmarried woman could be shunned by her community or even executed for becoming pregnant."

Dad looked unconvinced, so she went on, "In some times and places they'd have the babies and then abandon them. My point is that there have always been ways of disposing of children, and there have always been women who needed to do it."

"But the Church has always—"

"Actually, it hasn't. St. Augustine and St. Thomas Aquinas both taught that the fetus isn't yet human in its early stages, and that—"

"You know what?" Joy broke in. "This is all very fascinating but I don't think I really want to hear about it just now."

Mom and Dad both started apologizing for their thoughtlessness, but Celia was more interested in how firm and mature Joy had sounded.

So she hesitated later, when they were ready for bed, thinking Joy might have grown beyond what Celia wanted to do. *Still, no knowing till you ask,* she told herself.

She pulled back her covers and got into bed, but didn't pull them up again. "Joy? Do you want to…?"

"God, yes," Joy said, flipping off the overhead light.

She slid in beside Celia, who covered them both and spooned around her. Celia breathed in her sister's familiar scent and tightened her arm around her waist. *Is it a little thicker than usual? Who cares. We're going to be all right.*

CHAPTER 62.

WEDNESDAY, DECEMBER 21, 1960

*A*t least he's not hiding in that cabinet any more, Celia thought. *But he's hiding, nonetheless. Well, Christine thought I could manage with him all right,* she reminded herself. *Time to see if she was right.*

Laurie, Jamie and Beth wouldn't be home till tomorrow, but Rob and Joy had been on hand to greet Celia when she came in with Dad an hour ago. It was easier coming home this time than it had been at Thanksgiving. The confidence Celia'd seen in Joy last month was still there; she seemed quiet but not particularly anxious. Rob acted more on edge, nervous about how Celia would cope with her first meeting with Steve since she'd heard about the pregnancy. But Steve was missing. She'd come up to her bedroom and unpacked, giving him plenty of time to come to her, but he hadn't appeared.

Now she followed the sounds of his practicing up to the attic music room. His voice drifted down the stairway, plangent and mournful as a violin.

> "Does your memory stray
> To a bright sunny day
> When I kissed you and called you sweetheart?"

He stopped singing and started fussing with the strings of his beautiful Martin OM guitar, trying various chords with his head cocked toward the gleaming instrument, blond as his feathered hair, with the rosewood and mother-of-pearl pick guard inlaid by the sound hole. Joy had told her that guitar was the only material object he'd been concerned about when they'd told the folks she was pregnant and he'd been afraid they were going to eject him from the family.

Now he was adjusting the tuning, still with his head turned away from her, though he must have heard her on the steps. She cleared her throat; he still didn't face her.

"That new Elvis song, right? 'Are You Lonesome Tonight'? They've been playing it in the dorms."

He gave her a quick glance, then bent his head to the strings again. "Not new, really. It's almost forty years old and a lot of people have covered it. But the Elvis version is part of his comeback, now that he's out of the army and back from Germany. Wolfie thinks people will want to hear me do it."

"So your tour went well? I saw you on *Bandstand*; that was great. The whole dorm, practically, gathered in the common room to watch it. My roommate couldn't believe she was living with someone whose brother was on television. Some girls asked if I could get them your autograph—I lugged back some of their autograph books and a few of your 'Bright, Warm Home' record sleeves for you to sign."

His face flushed, with pleasure she hoped. "Sure," he said. "Maybe tonight after supper."

She came on into the room, thinking to hug him, but he was barricaded behind the guitar and didn't look as though he meant to come out from there, so she walked on past him to look out the window just as a blast of icy sleet hit it.

"Awful weather," she said. "I'm glad to be out of it. I guess no white Christmas again this year. We had a huge snow in New York a couple of weeks ago, kept people from classes and everything."

"I know," he said. "We were there. Had a gig at a place called the Gaslight Café, in the Village. The weather kept most people at home, but a few turned out. They passed a basket and people dumped in a fair amount of bread, so I guess they liked me."

"Why didn't you call me? I'd have brought some people to see you, we could have gotten together after for a drin—I mean for coffee, after."

He twisted his mouth wryly at her slip, then looked down at the guitar in his lap again. "I didn't know if you'd want to see me," he said softly.

"Oh, Stevie." She came forward to perch on the piano bench near his chair. "I wrote to you, you must have known I wasn't mad at you."

"You don't have to pretend," he burst out, setting the guitar in its case on the floor and turning toward her. His face was flushed now with anger, his old defense against fear. "I know you're all being nice to me because Joy wants me here, and that's great, and I'm really thankful you're not throwing me out or anything, but don't pretend you're not mad at me because I know you are."

Celia squelched her first impulse at denial and thought about what he'd said for a minute, rubbing her hands slowly up and down her thighs, staring down at the taupe box-pleated skirt of the suit she'd worn to travel in. Then she clasped her knees and answered him.

"I have been mad, off and on," she admitted. "But not just at you: at Joy, too." She held up a hand to stem his protest. "I know you both try to take the blame, but it's not about blame, really. It's about opportunities lost, troubles you've made for yourselves. It's as though—I don't know, like you'd gone out into the street without looking and landed yourselves in the hospital with a bunch of broken bones and maybe a concussion. It's not the end of the world, but it's going to make being in the world a lot harder for you. Mad isn't quite the right word: exasperated is more like it.

"That doesn't mean I don't still love you both, that I wouldn't want to see you. You're still my brother, Steve."

He ran a hand through his hair and sighed. "You all say that, but I know it isn't true." Now he held up a hand to keep her from responding. "I'm not saying anything bad here, I'm just trying to be real. She's your sister, your real sister. Of course you care more about her. It would be crazy if you didn't. In fact, I want you to, I'm glad you do. You'll take care of her no matter how you feel about what we did."

"Of course we will. But we'll take care of you, too. I don't feel the same way about you as I do about Joy, that much is true." His face took on a grim satisfaction, so she hurried on, "But that doesn't mean I feel less. Joy's been my sister forever; I remember her being born, how she was as a little girl, fighting with her over toys, helping her when she fell and skinned her knee, watching her at swim meets, listening to her poetry, holding her when she cried over boyfriends, her holding me when I cried over boyfriends, yelling at her for borrowing my clothes—a thousand things, forming a... I don't know, a giant house of memories I haven't had the chance to build up with you.

"But I can hardly remember a time when she wasn't around; you came fresh to us. Watching you start to trust us, seeing you open up and stop being afraid of everything, listening to the incredible music you make—those are all precious things. Going through that hearing with you, realizing what horrors you've lived through, made me realize how strong you are and how lucky we are that you made it, that you're here with us."

She shifted forward on the bench and reached for his hands, which he let lie limp in hers. But his eyes were fixed on her face, searching, and she tried to put the truth there for him to see. "I don't love you the same way I love Joy; how could I? Why should I? Do you love Joy the same way you love me, or Mom and Dad, or Robbie? There's a million kinds of love, Steve, and there's no point trying to measure whether one is bigger or more important than the other."

He screwed his eyes shut. "I was afraid we'd have to do it alone, that you'd all be too mad to help us."

"Never, never, never. That wouldn't be love at all."

He opened his eyes again. His lips firmed. "At least I didn't dump her, like your friend."

"My friend?"

"That Carol. She got left all alone, whatever guy did it. Do you know who it was?"

Celia's mouth fell open as she realized she'd never considered the question. Carol's predicament had seemed like some stroke of fate that had befallen her. Dad had pointed out that she "had some agency" in the matter, but none of them had seemed to put much weight on the fact that she hadn't gotten pregnant by herself.

"I don't know," she told Steve. "She talked about a lot of guys she met at that boarding school, but I didn't think there was any particular one."

Steve's face closed and turned away from her.

"What?" she demanded. "What are you thinking?" He shrugged, and she pulled at his arm. "Come on, Steve, tell me what's in your mind."

His mumble was so low she only caught the words, "her old man."

What old man? Celia thought, then the penny dropped. She gasped but held back the spate of denials that sprang to her lips. Instead, a flood of images filled her mind: Mr. Prosky's face, purple with rage; his obsession with Carol's weight; Carol's anger at her mother, her disabled, helpless mother... *But... but her own father, how could anyone even think that?*

Then she brought her attention back to Steve, huddling miserably beside her, flinching as though expecting a blow, and his fear brought another set of images and memories: Steve, the night he'd broken down and Dad had been so angry on his behalf; the day she'd blundered telling Steve about Jamie's homosexuality, and their long sequestering in their room afterwards; the manner Joy had around Steve, loving, yes, but with a fiercely protective streak... *especially since last summer.* Whatever had happened or hadn't happened between Carol and Mr. Prosky, Celia was suddenly sure of one thing: Steve had suffered sexual abuse from his cousin along with the physical torture. *And look at him. He thinks it was his fault, or at least that it means he's somehow tainted by it.*

She reached out and pulled him into her arms. He resisted, but she held firm till he stopped trying to get away. What Joy and he had done took on a whole new aspect in light of this revelation. She'd been thinking of it as a thoughtless indulgence taken without regard for the consequences. Now she realized it was something much more complex.

Joy did it at least partly to save him, to stop him thinking so badly of himself. She was trying to take care of him.

Steve was crying softly now. She kissed his temple and rocked him a little, stretched awkwardly between bench and chair. *So I'll need to take care of both of them.*

Chapter 63.

Sunday, April 2, 1961

Joy's moaning woke Celia out of an uneasy sleep. *Too much Easter candy, I bet,* she thought vaguely. Then her mind cleared and she sat bolt upright, flicking on her bedside lamp.

"Joy? What's wrong?"

"I don't know. Something bad." Her little sister's voice came in short gasps between moans. "I woke up all of a sudden, feeling this awful pain in my belly."

"Oh, God." Celia jumped up and stood over Joy.

"But it can't be the baby," Joy said plaintively. "This isn't how the books said it would feel. And it's too soon; I'm not due till next month."

Celia opened the bedroom door and rushed out into the hall toward her parents' room just as its door opened and Mom's pale face and bed-tousled hair appeared. "What is it?" she demanded. "Is it Joy?"

"Yes, she says she's in pain."

"Sean, get Ruby," Mom said over her shoulder, and joined Celia by Joy's bed. *She looks so tiny with that huge belly,* Celia thought. An image of Carol in the hospital came into her mind; she pushed it away impatiently. *This is where everything you've gone through pays off,* she told herself. *Get a grip and focus.*

Mom was asking Joy questions and getting muttered answers. Celia grabbed her robe, shoved her feet into slippers, and went into the bathroom to use the toilet, wash her face and hands, and comb her hair out of her face, so she'd be ready to help.

When she came back out, there was an acrid, meaty smell in the room. Ruby was there, asking more questions. She turned to Celia. "Her water just broke; this bed is soaked. I want to move her into the other room anyway, where I can get around both sides of the bed."

Mom came back into the room, having hurriedly dressed. The three women managed to get Joy onto her feet and half carried her down the strangely silent hall. No one else was home. Laurie was in Washington with Julia at a CORE organization meeting, discussing what to do in the wake of the Supreme Court decision declaring segregation on public transportation illegal. Jamie and Beth had stayed in Boston over the Easter break. Steve and Rob were on another tour. *Childhood's over. For all of us.*

The trek seemed endless, past the shadowy empty rooms to the larger guest room. It had already been set up for Joy to stay in once the baby was born, with a crib and a changing table and a little white-painted dresser with bunny decals on it. They sat Joy on one of the twin beds, where she hunched over, groaning, "It won't stop. Why won't it stop? The book said they'd last a few minutes, with a break in between. Why won't it stop?" She grunted loudly.

"Don't push," Ruby said sharply. "I know it feels like you want to, but it's too soon; you'll tear, and that will increase the chance of infection for you and the baby. The baby doesn't need you to push; it can come out all on its own when it's ready if you just relax."

Joy whimpered but seemed to obey. Under Ruby's direction, Mom and Celia stripped the covers off the other bed, pulled down the shower curtain from the guest bathroom and laid it over the mattress, then layered towels over that.

Just as Celia was wondering where Dad had gotten off to, he appeared in the doorway, hair sticking up, shirt buttoned askew. "I've called the ambulance," he said. "But they're having trouble. The roads are like glass, a lot of trees are down, and they're on another emergency call—somebody slipped and cracked his head open."

"What?" Mom exclaimed. "It was almost warm today!"

"The temperatures dropped and all that rain that's been falling all day has turned to ice. They estimate they'll be here in half an hour."

"This child doesn't have half an hour," Ruby said grimly. "Martha, fill that bathtub with warm water, please, and bring me a basin of it. Celia, I'll need a lot more towels; bring me whatever's in the linen closet. Sean, come over here and support your daughter's head and back—she'll be more comfortable half sitting up."

By the time Celia had made the trip back down the hall to the closet and then once more to the spare room, Dad had seated himself against the headboard with Joy in his arms in front of him. *He doesn't mind not being in charge here,* Celia realized. *But he's also not afraid to be here, with all this female stuff going on. Some day I'll find a man like that. Or maybe not. In any case, I won't settle for less.*

She rejoined the scene before her with renewed focus. Ruby had covered Joy's raised knees with a light blanket and was reaching in between them, a look of concentration on her face.

As Celia dumped the clean towels on the other bed, Ruby nodded at her. "Her cervix is almost fully dilated. I want you to feel this. You'll find a spare pair of rubber gloves in my bag. Wash your hands again, then put them on and come help me."

Mom, setting the basin of water Ruby'd asked for on the nightstand, opened her mouth as if to protest.

Ruby said firmly, "Celia will be learning this in medical school; she might as well have a taste of it now. Your job is to comfort your daughter, Martha."

Mom nodded and settled on the bed beside Joy and Dad, gripping Joy's hand. "Breathe, darling," she said softly. "Remember how to center yourself. I know it hurts, but try to be calm. Breathe in through your nose now, that's right, two, three, hold, now out through your mouth, that's right, good girl…"

Celia managed to wrestle the thin gloves onto her still-damp hands and stepped forward. *This is a patient,* she told herself. *Joy doesn't need you to be her sister now, she needs you to be strong for her. Put your feelings down the funnel.* She again excluded thoughts of Carol from her mind and reached between her patient's legs.

She couldn't maintain the mental distance at first. *I have my hand in my sister's body.* The notion seemed so outlandish; still, she struggled to keep her head and focus her concentration on shifting the impossibly large lump—the fetus's head—at Ruby's instruction. After ten minutes that seemed simultaneously to last an hour and to flash by, Ruby said, "Ok, push!"

Joy's heels drummed against the mattress, then dug in. She gave a low, guttural cry. A tide of blood and slime and shit gushed onto the bed. Celia sopped at it and covered the mess with towels as Ruby drew forth a shiny, slick little homunculus with a thick, rope-like cord connecting it to Joy. Suddenly, there was another person in the room.

"Get the scissors out of my bag," Ruby said, "and cut the cord, as close to his body as you can without cutting him."

Him. It's a boy, Celia vaguely thought. The cord was tough, still pulsing. She squeezed the surgical scissors with both hands till they pressed through, then clamped both cut ends as Ruby directed. Ruby, meanwhile, was clearing the tiny mouth and nose with a bulb syringe.

She'd laid the baby on Joy's stomach; Joy, still panting, was trying sit up, to see, hands reaching. "Just a minute, sweetheart," Mom said. "Let Ruby finish."

Dad, looking from his higher vantage point, said, "You have a son, my Joy."

"Rory," she said. "His name is Rory."

Little Rory started to cry in feeble pulses of sound. Ruby wiped him down quickly and wrapped him in a couple of receiving blankets from the changing table shelf, then handed him to Joy. "I know you want to look at him all over," she said, "but it's more important to keep him warm just now."

The doorbell rang; Dad slipped out from behind Joy and went to let the ambulance guys in.

"They'll get the afterbirth at the hospital," Ruby said. "And make sure you and Rory are ok. He's little, but not as little as I was afraid he'd be; I think your due date must have been closer than we thought."

The men came in with a stretcher; Celia stepped back to give them room.

"I'll get my coat," Mom said.

"Mine, too, please," Celia said.

"You can't go now, child," Ruby said. "Neither of us can."

"Why not?"

Ruby spread her arms wordlessly and Celia looked at her: she was smeared with blood and other substances. She was also still in her nightclothes. *So am I. And if anything, even bloodier.*

Celia shook her head, laughing slightly at herself. She leaned forward and kissed Ruby as the others disappeared down the stairs. She paused a moment to let in what had just happened.

I did it. She's ok; I was here for her. And for little Rory, and for Steve— Steve! We should call him; the folks must know where he is right now. And the others, they'll all want to know. But I was the one who was here, was able to help.

She went back down the hall, to the room she used to share with Joy, without thinking any more about the past, the childhood that was over now for both Joy and herself. She stripped off her bloody nightgown, letting it fall to the bathroom floor.

Joy's going to be fine. I'm fine, she thought as she stepped into the tub shower and let the water sluice the rest of the blood away. *It's all right to be smart, it's all right to be strong; it's not bossiness to be competent. What I can do is what I am—here, at Barnard, wherever I go in the future. I'm going to be just fine. There's nothing wrong with me at all.*